ALSO BY PAIGE BADGETT

Novel
Against Every Expectation

Anthology
An Inducement Into Matrimony

The MAKING of LADY CATHERINE DE BOURGH

A Pride and Prejudice NOVEL

PAIGE BADGETT

Paperback: 979-8-9916152-0-4
E-Book: 979-8-9916152-1-1

Edited by Jennifer Altman and Holly Kuck
Cover designed by Evelyne Labelle of Carpe Librum Book Design

For John,
for believing in me and my dreams, no matter how big or small

"*The engagement between them is of a peculiar kind. From their infancy, they have been intended for each other. It was the favourite wish of his mother, as well as of her's. While in their cradles, we planned the union: and now, at the moment when the wishes of both sisters would be accomplished in their marriage, to be prevented by a young woman of inferior birth, of no importance in the world, and wholly unallied to the family! Do you pay no regard to the wishes of his friends? To his tacit engagement with Miss De Bourgh? Are you lost to every feeling of propriety and delicacy? Have you not heard me say that from his earliest hours he was destined for his cousin?*"

- Lady Catherine de Bourgh
Pride and Prejudice

The MAKING of LADY CATHERINE DE BOURGH

CHAPTER ONE

JANUARY 1782

B eing perfect is not as effortless as it appears. It begs decorum—nay, it requires control, above all. Control that Lady Catherine Fitzwilliam's younger sister Anne could never understand nor endure.

Catherine had no patience for her sister's selfishness and indifference. Nothing disturbed Catherine's equilibrium quite so much as her sister's belief that fate was in command of her life.

If Anne were a season, she would be autumn—raining dirty leaves onto the neatly kept paths and shaking the vibrant blooms from expertly cultivated shrubs. Catherine took little pleasure in spending time out of doors, but especially not after Michaelmas. Watching the colour drain away from the ornate gardens at Oakley was unfortunate, and above all, she abhorred sneezing. It was very unladylike.

A quick glance to her sister confirmed all her worst fears. Wild curls had abandoned their required placement, the sleeves of Anne's gown were pushed up to display her freckled arm, and the ribbon around her waist hung loosely on her slim hips.

Her chest tightened, and a wash of mortification poured through her.

"Heaven and earth! Of what are you thinking?" Catherine scolded her younger sister.

Catherine straightened her sister's sleeves and tied the ribbon around her waist in a more pleasing manner. Anne's coiffure was beyond help. Their mother, the countess, would have to speak to Anne's maid. Propriety demanded her sister be kept under greater regulation.

"I should think the Darcys care little for the state of my gown or hair," her sister answered flippantly.

She appeared bored, and that irritated Catherine even more. Could not Anne conduct herself in a manner befitting their position in the world just this once?

"Today is a most auspicious day, Anne. Our family—all of us—are under much scrutiny!"

"Would it not be the Darcys whose burden it is to be anxious?" Anne asked. "They shall benefit most from this partnership. Our noble blood absolves us from such examination. Your fortune alone should ensure Mr Darcy proposes."

"Of course, he shall propose. It is not a question of *if* he proposes, but when," Catherine hissed back to her sister. "And our mother would like to expedite the timeline so that you may make your curtsey and have your first Season in town."

And if the countess wanted the marriage expedited, swift it would be.

While Catherine put on a brave and stalwart face for her sister, she was anxious to see the ceremony long behind her—for she was the second of the Fitzwilliam daughters with whom Mr George Darcy had been promised to. Before Catherine, her elder sister, Eloise, had spent most of her life planning to become

Mrs Darcy. Eloise had been Catherine's beautiful and flawless sister, who had been ripped from the bosom of her family by a fever that moved to her lungs. Her death had seized not only Catherine's beloved sister but also Mr George Darcy's future bride.

And now their families expected Mr Darcy to marry Catherine in Eloise's stead. The idea that Catherine could live up to her parents' expectations as his intended was at first objectionable. She could never be Eloise—lovely, entertaining, and talented Eloise—but her mother had rationalized at length that those concerns were unfounded. The countess had explained that Catherine was just as she should be—exactly what a young gentleman of means would require. And marrying him would please her family. Her mother also reminded her that this method of marrying would remove all burden of "catching" a gentleman in town. This, in particular, boded well for her. Appealing to gentlemen did not come easily to Catherine. For one, she was much taller than the average man. And for the second, she was not Eloise—and never would be. And while the countess had lauded these concerns for the last two years, claiming loudly and often that Catherine would end up a spinster, she had to agree that if her mother now found these concerns surmountable, then they must be.

This demand that she marry Mr Darcy became as simple as her answer to all other pronouncements from her parents. She would do as told. Being practical was easy for Catherine.

Lady Anne blew a misbehaving curl off her face, and Catherine reached out to secure it for her, looking down into her sister's light blue eyes. "Please, I beg of you. Be on your best behaviour."

A nod sufficed as a response, and Catherine squeezed her sister's hand before turning back to the drive. A carriage and four carried the Darcys—and her future—closer and closer to the front steps.

Mr George Darcy's father, the Mr Phillip Darcy, exited the carriage first, followed by his wife, and finally the son. The younger Mr Darcy was even more handsome than Catherine remembered—rather intimidatingly so. It was strange to imagine that she would spend the remainder of her life with this compelling creature—so noble in his bearing, even if his blood lacked proof of such. His family was an old and respected one, and her fortune would secure the future of his estate, Pemberley. It was a fine match her parents had made for Eloise; and one Catherine was only happy to submit to in her stead.

Because of Eloise, Catherine's first London Season had caused her little concern. Second daughters did not seek husbands before their elder sisters were married. It had mattered not whether she impressed the gentlemen she met there or their eager mothers. And the next Season had been spent at Oakley in mourning. She was not accustomed to putting herself on display as she would on this day.

"Darcy! Mrs Darcy," Catherine's father, the Earl of Barringer, cried once the guests had ascended the front steps. "You are most welcome at Oakley!" The gentlemen shook hands, and their wives greeted each other in a warm embrace.

"And you, young man," Catherine's father turned to her future husband. "Mr Darcy, you are welcome as well. You know my wife, Lady Barringer; as well as Ashby and Lady Ashby—" Her father trailed off as Mr George Darcy stopped to say a few words to her elder brother, the viscount, and his wife.

Her father stepped in front of her, his eyes locked on hers, and a silent agreement passed between them. Lord Barringer expected her to be impeccable, as always. And her mother would never be satisfied with anything less than perfection. In accord with her parents, she straightened her posture and nodded her compliance.

"—and my daughter, Lady Catherine," her father continued as the Darcys made their way down the line with the younger Mr Darcy at their side. The young man bowed to Catherine, bringing to mind the importance of this visit. She tried to suppress a blush but was not certain of her success. Catherine had been in company with Mr George Darcy in London during her Season in town, and yet she had been merely on the periphery—the younger sister to his expected bride. He had little acknowledged her presence in their past dealings.

"My lady," he said, as his pale blue eyes met hers.

His soft smile put her at ease. The kindness in his gaze reminded Catherine that Eloise would never have agreed to marry a gentleman who was unpleasant. It was not clear to Catherine why her sister and Mr George Darcy had not married sooner. Any delay of the happy event had been simply a postponement of the inevitable. At six and twenty years old, the younger Mr Darcy was the same age her brother, Viscount Ashby, had been when he chose to marry.

After curtseying and welcoming the family to Oakley, her father continued past her with their guests. "Please allow me to introduce you to my youngest, Lady Anne," the earl said to the younger Mr Darcy.

Mr George Darcy stepped in front of Catherine's sister. Anne was not yet eighteen years old and was infrequently around those who were not family members. While she had become acquainted with the Darcys as a child, more than a decade had passed since she was in the company of the younger Mr Darcy.

"I have not had the pleasure in many years," Mr George Darcy said, smiling warmly at Anne.

The tightness in Catherine's chest eased as she watched her sister perform a perfect curtsey. She had not expected Anne to swoon or take a tumble, but even so, it was a relief. She was not surprised to see Anne's cheeks tinted pink when she rose to gaze at Catherine's future husband. It was not often her sister was in company with fine-looking, eligible gentlemen.

Their own brother was not borne of the same splendour. Lord Ashby was, in great opposition, a man whose character and noble blood had aided him in securing his highly sought-after wife. Of course, being a viscountess, and later the Countess of Barringer, was equally appealing to Catherine's sister by marriage. Elinor St. John, as was her name before her marriage, had been highly desirable to many of the eligible gentlemen of the peerage during her first Season.

Catherine continued to study her younger sister. Though Anne's greeting had been sufficient, she was now gazing upon their guest rather too long. Catherine looped her arm through her sister's to gain her attention and, hopefully, retain the respect of her suitor. Had not Mrs McKenna, their governess, taught Anne not to stare so?

"You must join us in the drawing room, sir. Perhaps you would like some tea?" Anne ventured to their guest.

How neglectful had Anne's education been?

The countess stepped in, as was her place. As mistress of Oakley and host to their guests, she sent a knowing smile to Mr Darcy and turned to speak to her youngest daughter. "Anne, dear, I am sure our guests would like to see their rooms and refresh themselves after their journey."

Hopefully, he understood that Anne's age had not permitted her to be much in society, especially having been in mourning for half of the last year.

"On the contrary, I would very much like to join you," Mr George Darcy replied with a warm smile.

"Darcy," her brother addressed his friend jovially. "There is no need to stand on ceremony while you are a guest here. We are nearly family, are we not? Forget the tea and join me in my study."

"I am sure he only means to greet Lady Catherine properly. It has been some time since they have been in company," Lady Ashby remarked at her husband's side. She sent an encouraging smile Catherine's way.

"And so, he has greeted her." Amusement saturated her brother's tone. "What say you, Darcy?"

Catherine turned to her suitor, finding no trace of his true feelings upon his face.

"If you will excuse me," he said to the ladies, with a small smile.

Catherine was happy to see Mr George Darcy follow her brother into the house. Her nerves had nearly gotten the best of her, and she was relieved to see the gentleman go before she said the wrong thing. Luckily now, she would have until dinner to think of some thoughtful conversation topics.

As the rest of the party moved inside and gathered in the entrance hall, Mr Phillip Darcy and his wife spoke quietly with her parents until they were taken to their guest chambers.

Finding themselves very much alone after the front hall cleared, she shared an expression of satisfaction with her mother who nodded her approval from the doorway.

Lady Barringer took hold of Catherine's stays and shooed away her daughter's personal maid, Jones. It was a rare occasion indeed when the countess joined her to prepare for dinner. Her mother pulled tightly, disavowing Catherine of any previous expectation she may have had of taking a deep breath for the remainder of the evening.

"Doing your duty shall be accomplished easily, my darling. Mr Darcy looks not for fault, for his promise to our family is already secured. But I do warn you, gentlemen can be fickle creatures. You must remind him tonight of his commitment to our family and ease any doubts he may have."

Her mother's contradictory statements did not increase Catherine's confidence. Was the marriage secure or was Mr George Darcy to decide this very evening if she was worthy?

Regardless of her questions, a rebuttal would not do. "Yes, mother," Catherine replied.

"Remember to soften your voice."

She pulled tightly once more. Catherine gasped and answered more quietly. "I always do."

"Remember to flatter him but not overtly. Let him take the lead. If you have an opportunity to gently guide the conversation, find a way to encourage him to speak more about himself. It is not polite to speak of yourself, and gentlemen like to speak of their own preferences. You could ask him about his properties, for example. If he makes a joke, respond with good cheer, but do not laugh loudly. Remember that curiosity is not becoming, merely a sign of stupidity. He will not thank you for endless questions about the running of his estate. You must curb your appetite to host an inquisition about your future life. If you must ask about Pemberley, ask of the gardens or the neighbours. You shall learn more in due time."

Catherine nodded.

"Keep your opinions to yourself. They are insignificant," Lady Barringer warned.

"Of course."

Lady Barringer took a step back, apprising herself of Catherine's looks. She nodded in approval, which was a blessing, as Catherine's broad shoulders and curves differed from both of her sisters. While Eloise and Anne were built soft and petite, Catherine was often told she had strongly-marked features. She was also the only Fitzwilliam child to inherit her father's formidable height.

"Thank goodness your Mr Darcy is tall. I did not have to worry about such things with Eloise." Lady Barringer released a sigh.

The mention of Eloise turned Catherine's stomach. And not for the first time that night, she felt a flutter of fear telling her to *run, run, run*.

"The outcome shall be as we expect," her mother continued. "Your excellent brother has already spoken to Mr Darcy. He understands why he is here and why we can no longer delay."

Her mother cupped Catherine's face in her hands, and she was warmed by this uncommon sign of affection. The countess's teased and powdered hair soared behind her like a beacon signalling her importance. It was no wonder that St Paul's Cathedral in London had to be raised four feet to accommodate the latest mode of hairstyling. The thought almost made Catherine chuckle, but she kept it to herself, as usual.

"You shall be betrothed by tomorrow, and we shall celebrate the joining of our families before your Mr Darcy's parents depart on Monday. I am sure your intended will stay on for at least a fortnight after his parents set off. You may use the remainder of his stay to come to know one another better."

A quiet knock on the door interrupted her mother's speech.

Lady Ashby joined the fray, observing Catherine's appearance and smiling.

Lady Barringer nodded at Catherine encouragingly and departed.

"Your mother has imparted some wisdom, I presume?"

Catherine smiled at her sister by marriage. "I must endeavour to perfection this evening, it appears."

"Gentlemen do not desire perfection, my dear. Do not forgo your mother's guidance, but also do not sit mutely or fawn over the man. Gentlemen desire obedience as much as they enjoy a challenge."

"A challenge?" The advice was not clear to Catherine.

Lady Ashby shifted Catherine aside to confirm her own advantageous looks in the mirror. "I know they do not teach such things in seminary, but it would do you some good to ensure Darcy has some interest in you. He must likewise exert himself. And for a gentleman as dashing as your Mr Darcy, it may take a little effort to see him come to the point. Let him see how lovely you are tonight—how impeccably dressed and proper and correct you are—but also make him perform for your attention somewhat. Make sure he knows he must not only propose but win your interest. You have far more choices than he, of course."

"Choices? You know I have no say in this. My future has been decided—"

"Yes, but he has not asked, and you are not yet his. A promise from his parents to yours does not a marriage make. Let him desire you—*compel* him to want to know more. Instead of listing out your many accomplishments, perhaps mention one. This will entice him to ask more about you."

"Mother says to guide the conversation so we might speak about him. I should rather not speak of my accomplishments. They are lacking, as you well know."

Lady Ashby turned Catherine by the shoulders to face her. "What of your talent with water colours, my dear? Besides, I cannot boast of knowing more than half a dozen, in the whole range of my acquaintances, who are truly accomplished. Gentlemen need not know the specifics, only that you are just as you *should* be—a proper young lady with the correct education. He cares not if you can net a purse or cover a screen, but he might enjoy trying to identify which pursuits you prefer."

"I do enjoy dancing," Catherine offered.

"A wonderful example. Instead of saying 'Mr Darcy, I do so enjoy dancing,' bring up the subject of music and nothing more. Leave the subject vague, available for the taking, you see. This may persuade him to ask if you play the pianoforte."

"I do not."

"And then he might ask if you enjoy attending music performances."

"I do."

"And... perchance next he shall ask if you enjoy dancing. You see? Let him believe it is he who is in control of the conversation."

"I see."

"I am sure you do." Lady Ashby reached up, patted Catherine's shoulder, and then excused herself.

Except Catherine did not see—not truly. Why should one not simply say what they mean? Exact instructions were much more to her liking. Why must she concern herself overmuch? Their family's understanding was as longstanding as it was inevitable.

Catherine had already failed in one aspect—she had nearly reached her majority, and she was not married, while Lady Ashby had accomplished all that was expected of her at a much younger age. She had married well at eighteen and birthed the heir to the Barringer earldom before she was twenty.

The viscountess had been even more efficient than Lady Barringer, for she produced a spare merely two years later. Master Luke Edward Graham Fitzwilliam, the heir to the earldom, was not three years old, and baby Richard had been born just after Michaelmas. While Lady Ashby's efforts had been exceedingly successful, the countess had spent nearly a decade attempting to be delivered of a second son, only to have three consecutive daughters.

Jones returned to put the finishing touches on Catherine's hair, including the addition of a few delicate diamond hairpins. Catherine could admit she was in advantageous looks that night. The cut of the *robe à l'Anglaise* reduced the appearance of her wide shoulders and, in her opinion, bound her waist in a most flattering way. The elegant, sapphire-coloured silk lay beautifully—cinching her waist and pouring out into a fashionable, pleated skirt, splitting in the front to reveal a striped blue and ivory petticoat. The effect made Catherine feel feminine and mature. She was no longer a girl in the nursery. She was a woman grown—and a woman who would find her fate this very night.

Jones took her by the hands and told her affectionately, "My lady, you look lovely. I shall wish you very happy tomorrow morning."

Before Jones became a complete watering pot, Catherine excused her favourite servant and took herself downstairs for dinner.

CHAPTER TWO

The entire party was gathered in the West Drawing Room when Catherine appeared. She had expected a reaction from the younger Mr Darcy, but he was busy in conversation.

She hoped Anne was not blathering on about some dull subject only she could care about. It was a great kindness to permit her to join them for dinner that night. As Anne was not yet out, it was rare indeed that she was allowed to dine with guests, but just so, this friendly party was nearly family, so it appeared all was done correctly.

Catherine approached her suitor and Anne quietly.

"I take Artemis to the folly each morning," Anne was saying.

Heavens above, she was speaking of her horse.

"I should like to see the folly. Does not this January weather often deter you from your outdoor pursuits?" Mr Darcy gave the impression that he was rather intrigued to hear Anne's answer.

"No, not often. I should ride in any season, so long as my mother does not restrict me to the house." An indifferent confidence concealed her obstinance. Catherine knew full well that Anne would do as she liked, regardless of the countess. All the stable boys bent to her whims, and the servants kept her secrets well.

"Is the folly especially far from the house?"

"No, sir," Anne replied. "I would be happy to show you."

It was so good of him to make Anne feel comfortable. They might invite Anne to stay with them at Pemberley after their marriage. Perhaps not in the first months, but a long visit in the summertime would suit. Mr George Darcy's gentle nature could offer Anne some brotherly affection as she began to navigate these important years of entering society.

Catherine internally beamed—this match, which she had been uneasy about for many months, was very suitable. The younger Mr Darcy had a serene assurance about him that would naturally complement her careful, particular nature. It was a comfort to know that he would be the one to advise her once she had left her mother.

The idea of leaving home made her heart beat more quickly, but she kept a polite smile on her face just as she had always been taught. It was best to ignore such thoughts.

No doubt, Anne would continue to bore him with details of her newest mare in their stables, so it was important that Catherine join the conversation. His cool, blue eyes and small smile were inviting. He must make friends easily.

Travelling into the peaks in January was not unfamiliar to the Darcys, who also resided in Derbyshire, but she should inquire about the state of the roads and the weather.

"Mr Darcy—" she began, rather too loudly.

"Do you ride, Lady Catherine?" Mr Darcy's mother had joined them. It was a kindness that his mother would help Catherine join the conversation, however little she relished speaking of horse flesh. She had hoped to turn the conversation elsewhere.

"A little," Catherine responded. It was the answer her mother had advised using when she was questioned about interests she knew little of or cared little for.

Catherine would rather talk about the grounds at Oakley since he showed interest in riding to the folly.

"The grounds are not unlike the scenery you are familiar with at Pemberley. On a cloudless day, one can view the Kinder Scout from the folly. Our steward would be happy to show you. I believe he is currently overseeing the removal of some woodland near there for some additional sheep he means to take on. It is a much more enjoyable excursion in the summer when you might view some of the nearby natural springs. However, many like to climb the plateau at this time of year because the cloughs are dry."

"The young people should make an outing of it," Mrs Darcy interjected, gaining the attention of her son. "I am sure Lady Catherine would be happy to join you."

"It is not accessible by carriage, but Artemis knows the way by heart." Excitement pervaded Anne's tone.

Mrs Darcy smiled and nodded at Catherine in an encouraging manner, but it was no use. Catherine had naught to add to a conversation about horses. She could converse all day about the peaks, but not livestock. She had hoped to speak about music, as Lady Ashby had suggested, or to learn more about Pemberley.

Until such a time as Mr Darcy better understood her preferences, she could not very well tell the man that she disliked horses.

"Do you have a folly at Pemberley?" Catherine asked at same time as Anne said, "Let us ride there tomorrow morning."

Mr Darcy turned away from Anne and opened his mouth to answer, but he appeared confused about which lady to respond to. Perhaps he too was just as nervous as Catherine. She ought to say something soothing to reassure him that she would welcome his addresses at any convenient time.

"Have you seen the gallery, Mr Darcy?" Catherine asked him. "I would be happy to show you our collection after dinner."

Speaking of art was a matter of course for Catherine.

Anne's murmur about stuffy old landscapes was not overlooked by their mother.

"Anne, dear," the countess spoke up. "Join me please."

When dinner was ready, the earl took Lady Anne's arm, leading her and his wife into the dining room, followed by Ashby and Lady Ashby.

Mr Darcy's parents stood back to allow Catherine to precede them. It was left to Mr George Darcy to lead Catherine into the dining room, which was just as it should be. He took up her left arm and mumbled something quietly to her, which she was unable to comprehend. Rather than ask him to repeat himself, she simply smiled in his direction.

A childhood illness had deprived Lady Catherine of proper hearing on the left, so she was at greater advantage when people were sat to her right.

Surely her mother would inform the younger Mr Darcy of her condition at a later time. It was certainly not appropriate dinner conversation. Until he was advised, she would continue her attempt to moderate her volume. Once he knew, Mr George Darcy would understand her tendency towards speaking more loudly and hopefully would not ask her to regulate her tone as often as her mother did.

Mr George Darcy was given the honour of sitting to her mother's right, and Catherine was seated to her father's left.

Unable to hear the conversation the younger Mr Darcy had with her sister was just as well; all she needed to know could be witnessed in her mother's expression of approval.

He was sure to propose.

Once the gentlemen joined the ladies in the West Drawing Room after dinner, Catherine was pleased that the younger Mr Darcy immediately sought her out.

Mr George Darcy chose a chair facing the pair Catherine and her sister had selected near the fire.

Unfortunately, the gentleman appeared to want to continue his equine conversation with Lady Anne. Hoping to change the subject and utilize Lady Ashby's advice, Catherine took her first opportunity during a lull in the conversation.

"What think you of music, Mr Darcy?"

She must have spoken quite loudly, for both her sister and the younger Mr Darcy turned their heads in her direction far too quickly.

"I enjoy music. Do you play, Lady Catherine?" he asked.

"A little." She held her chin high.

She would rather not do anything unless she could do it exceptionally, so 'a little' was quite the farce. Appearances were important.

"And you, Lady Anne?" The younger Mr Darcy angled his body towards Anne.

Her sister preened. "I love to play. Mother has engaged a music master for me when we arrive in London."

He was supposed to ask Catherine more about herself, was he not?

Their mothers approached the group.

"George enjoys the theatre. Do you also enjoy such performances, Lady Catherine?" Mrs Darcy was once again bringing her into the fold of conversation.

Once Catherine ascertained that she had Mr George Darcy's attention, she responded. "Yes, I do."

She smiled gently at the younger Mr Darcy. Perhaps now he would ask more about her preferences.

"And do you enjoy the theatre also?" Mr George Darcy turned the question on Anne.

"I do, but I much prefer dancing. I am looking forward to my first Season in town."

He smiled widely but did not ask Catherine if she too liked to dance or who her favourite composer was. Mayhap she was wrong to take Lady Ashby's advice.

"Tell me more about Pemberley, sir." Catherine was desperate to take hold of the conversation. Her mother had said he would enjoy speaking of himself.

Her suitor's depiction left much to be desired. The natural gardens and rough paths through Pemberley Wood he described were of no interest to her. She smiled and thanked him for the description. All great homes in the Peak District were one and the same.

When she was mistress, she would take the garden in hand. It had been many years since she had visited, but she did remember a smallish formal garden. She would look forward to expanding it, planning clean, neat walkways—near to the house, of course—with very carefully pruned and cultivated plants. Nothing so wild as the current Mrs Darcy preferred. If one must be outside, it was best that the conditions were neat and tidy.

In the breakfast parlour the next morning, Catherine found the Ashbys and the younger Mr Darcy missing. Her sister was also absent, but Anne rarely joined the family for the morning meal. It could be that the gentlemen got off to an early start. Men in the country did enjoy spending time out of doors, of course. Perhaps they were making plans to go shoot something.

Catherine lifted a porcelain plate and carefully selected the exact foods her mother advised for this portion of the visit—one roll, one egg, and a cup of tea.

As it stood, Mr George Darcy had not proposed to her the night before, and that left Catherine feeling the weight of the day. It was nearly a certain thing that she would be a lady planning her wedding by the time she retired for sleep.

Catherine sought her reflection in the window overlooking the rear gardens and silently congratulated herself for choosing her newest *redingote* to wear that morning. The deep rose hue looked lovely against her fair skin. Not one freckle to be seen. If the gentleman of the hour would seek a private audience with her this morning out of doors, she might have a chance to wear her matching hat as well. It was a fetching combination.

Lost in her own thoughts, she added butter and preserves to her plate until some motion outside caught her attention. There amongst the trees that framed the stables stood her brother and the younger Mr Darcy—and Anne. She would know that riding habit anywhere. Anne strolled between the two gentlemen, walking arm-in-arm with Ashby. Her sister's deep indigo gown stood out amongst the trees, with the fashionable train carried over her free arm. She appeared as she always did—relaxed and invigorated by sport.

If only one need not ride a horse to own such a gown.

The wind whipped Anne's curly hair around her smiling face. Her lady's maid ought to have used more hair pins, Catherine thought. Anne looked positively wild.

It was pleasing to see her future husband with her brother and sister. It would be satisfying if they might all be friends one day. It would be better than the impersonal and formal relationship she witnessed between her parents and their families.

A very dainty shoulder nudged Catherine away from her thoughts, and she greeted her sister by marriage who had entered the breakfast parlour. Lady Ashby had a sly look about her. "How was your ride, my dear? Shall I wish you joy?"

"My ride?"

"Yes, Darcy came looking for Ashby quite early this morning seeking to take you riding," Lady Ashby whispered enthusiastically.

No one had visited her room that morning, besides Jones.

"As you see, that is not the case." Catherine gestured to her modish jacket and skirt. "I was in my apartment all morning."

Catherine indicated for Lady Ashby to look beyond the windowpane. "See for yourself. It is your husband and Anne who have gone riding with Mr Darcy."

"I see." Uncertainty pervaded Lady Ashby's tone.

"Do not make me guess your thoughts, my lady," Catherine whispered quickly.

"Oh, it is nothing," she answered hastily and waved her arm in agreement. "I must have misheard."

Who would want to be out of doors this time of year anyway? Not Catherine. A warm fireplace would suit very well for their private audience, or perhaps she might still find an opportunity to show him the gallery.

Once the gentlemen and Anne joined them at the table, the morning meal confounded Catherine as much as the dinner the night before. Each time she offered a piece of interesting conversation to the table, Mr George Darcy grunted with agreement or disagreement, but offered no details that might help her better understand his character. She was quickly ascertaining that she would need to better learn what type of encouragement would help him be more verbose—he would have to participate more. Did not a tutor or nanny provide the same guidance she had received as a girl? His quiet nature forgotten, the man only seemed interested in the absurd dribble that came from Anne. It was one thing to court Catherine's family to ensure their support for their marriage, and it was quite another to overlook her entirely.

Catherine prepared for dinner with as much attention as she had the previous night. She received no special visits from the countess or the viscountess, which relieved some of her nerves. She trusted that their inaction meant that they were confident in her abilities to secure this match tonight and had no additional words of wisdom to provide.

Catherine felt no apprehension about leaving her family to start her own. She had been raised for this. Fitzwilliams were always looking to the future.

Jones swiped a tear from her eye as she beheld Catherine's lovely gown and hair. It had long been decided that when Catherine married, Jones would move home to Buxton to care for her family. They both knew the end was nearing, and it warmed Catherine's heart to see that the affection she felt for her lady's maid was indeed shared. Whomever was chosen as her next personal maid would never match up.

When Catherine arrived in the West Drawing Room, she was surprised to find only the younger Mr Darcy present. He stood at her entrance and welcomed her with a slight bow.

"How do you do, my lady?"

Catherine's stomach turned. It was bewildering that her body rejected this important moment when it was the culmination of a lifetime of preparation. It must be nerves. One only receives a proposal from a gentleman once.

It was gratifying to see that he had negotiated to have a private moment with her.

They were on the precipice of their new life, and it invigorated her to know that she had succeeded in securing the match.

"I am well, sir. Thank you," she responded.

Approaching her suitor with the gentility that had been so engrained in her that she wore it like a second skin, she smiled softly when she arrived in front of him.

Mr George Darcy appeared to be having an uneasy moment of his own, for he looked around the room for many seconds before coming to the point.

"Did I have the wrong time for dinner?" he asked.

Catherine smiled. He was extremely nervous, it seemed. "The dinner gong sounded. Everything is as it should be."

He walked to the clock on the mantle above the roaring fireplace and viewed the time.

"Punctuality is a lovely characteristic," Catherine softly encouraged him with her words.

He grunted an agreement and cleared his throat.

"My apologies," he hurriedly replied. "I have forgotten something in my chambers. Please tell your mother that I shall return directly."

He could not leave the room fast enough. He left not out of the double doors that led to the main corridor in the front of the house but through a back door that would take him nearer to the library than the main staircase. He was clearly edgy. Did he have a gift for her that he had forgotten in his chambers? It was not unnatural to give a bride a gift at the time of one's engagement.

After many minutes of waiting, her father entered the room. His raised eyebrows and searching gaze betrayed his confusion at finding Catherine there alone.

Catherine curtseyed to her father, who acknowledged her with a small smile.

"I thought to find Mr Darcy with you," the earl said.

"He was here when I arrived but excused himself some minutes ago."

"Shall I wish you joy?"

"Not as of yet." Catherine laughed lightly. "He has not come to the point."

Her father was unable to hide his beleaguered expression. It was a comfort to see that she was not alone in her impatience.

"I see. Pray, excuse me for one moment." Her father went back out into the main corridor and returned with Mr Phillip Darcy and Mrs Darcy, the Ashbys, the countess, and Anne. Now that everyone else in the party was present, it appeared that the time for a private audience had passed.

Breaking her fast the next morning was just the same as the previous day. The younger Mr Darcy arrived late, red-faced, and wind-blown from a ride and added little to the conversation.

Lady Barringer left the young man little time to attend to his plate before she gave Catherine a pointed look and nodded subtly at their guest.

"Mr Darcy," Catherine ventured, "do your neighbours near Pemberley host many parties?"

Mr George Darcy lifted his napkin to his lips and dabbed each side of his mouth before answering. "They do. The Wilsons live not ten miles from Pemberley and enjoy hosting musicians, and Lord and Lady Haythorne throw a ball each autumn."

Anne's face lit with excitement. "Miss Margaret Haythorne and I were at school together."

The younger Mr Darcy responded, "Yes, I am acquainted with Miss Margaret."

Catherine joined the conversation. "Have you known the Haythorne family long, sir?"

Anne laughed openly, rather too brazenly, Catherine thought. "Of course, he must. The Haythornes have lived in that part of Derbyshire for hundreds of years. They host a hunt each spring and autumn. I should like to attend—I have written Miss Margaret to say as much."

"I see," Catherine answered.

"They are known for their lavish, week-long fox hunts," Mr Phillip Darcy offered quietly to Catherine.

Lady Barringer intruded, "I am sure Miss Margaret does not join the hunts, Anne."

"Of course, she does, Mother," Anne replied. "All of Lord Haythorne's daughters join the fray."

Mr George Darcy smiled over his teacup. "Trackers, the lot of them."

The countess pursed her lips.

"And would you join a hunt, Lady Anne?" Mr George Darcy asked.

"Am I so very obvious?" Anne tittered.

"It is quite fashionable these days," Lady Ashby offered.

Catherine would like to hear more about the hunt, but it was clear the conversation was upsetting her mother.

"Mr Darcy," Catherine attempted to engage her suitor in another topic, "what think you of recent news emerging from the American colonies?"

Lady Barringer coughed into her napkin and shook her head at Catherine.

"I have seen the broadsheets, my lady," Mr George Darcy responded. "It appears our men have had significant setbacks."

Lady Barringer's wide-eyed gaze stifled any interest she had in continuing that line of questioning.

Catherine shifted the topic with great aplomb. "Our weather has been woefully inconsistent, has it not?"

The younger Mr Darcy seemed confused by the quick change of subject, but he had not seen the look on her mother's face.

"That it has."

Catherine attempted to engage him in additional topics—livestock, travel to the continent, the state of the roads—and was impatient and irritated to find naught that interested him. He was certainly kind but rarely charmed, it would seem.

Ashby kept Mr George Darcy holed up in his study the rest of the day doing whatever it was that important gentlemen did in their personal domain.

Before dinner that evening, the younger Mr Darcy approached Catherine and apologized for abandoning her the previous evening. A ray of hope shone brightly as Catherine comprehended that he was reinstating his intentions, but it was quickly and awkwardly dashed when he mentioned that he had merely realized his valet had chosen the wrong cufflinks. "My mother would never permit me to sit at the dinner table without being properly dressed."

Catherine cared not if he was properly dressed, only that he was supremely stupid for not having proposed to her by now. Taking him in hand would be the work of her lifetime, it appeared. His wavy brown hair and crooked smile endeared him to her, but she was growing impatient.

Catherine noticed there were chairs missing from the table when she entered the dining room. Their party finally had an even number of people. It pleased her to see the structure—gentleman, lady, gentleman, lady—with perfect symmetry. Something about the rightness of it warmed in her veins. Everything was just as it should be, however bad she felt that Anne was feeling poorly and was unable to attend.

When the ladies left the gentlemen behind after dinner, Catherine was surprised to see her younger sister meet the ladies in the drawing room. She was exchanging heated words with their mother. Their whispers, while quiet, were clearly spirited. Catherine did not need perfect hearing to comprehend the expression on their mother's face. She was incensed.

The assumed quarrel thankfully ended abruptly when the gentlemen joined the ladies. The elder Mr Darcy smiled and nodded at Catherine while the younger Mr Darcy went immediately to the countess and Anne, likely inquiring about Lady Anne's health.

Mr Phillip Darcy approached Catherine and offered his arm. He led her to two chairs near the warm fireplace. After complimenting the meal and seeing to her comfort, he called over his son.

"George, please sit," his father said, gesturing for him to take the chair next to Catherine's. "Tell Lady Catherine about Michaelmas at Pemberley."

The younger Mr Darcy sent a pointed look to his father, before a polite smile settled on his features.

"There is quite a feast, my lady. We welcome many of our neighbours to join in the celebration."

Mr Phillip Darcy sent a kind smile to Catherine. "The ladies often pick blackberries in the afternoon, and then cook prepares a plump goose for dinner. When I was younger, there would be dancing and singing."

"It sounds a lovely tradition," Catherine offered.

Mr Darcy seemed a bit distracted, clearing his throat and looking to his father.

"I am sure Lady Catherine is familiar with such traditions, Father."

A jolt of discomfort unsettled Catherine. She looked back and forth between father and son, sensing a silent conversation was being had without her input.

"We do, certainly," Catherine said softly to the younger Mr Darcy. "But it does not follow that I do not find pleasure in learning more about your family and your estate."

The elder Mr Darcy excused himself, patting his son on the shoulder before leaving the two to conversation.

Mr George Darcy glanced at the clock on the mantel and straightened his cuffs. He was a man of few words.

Mrs Darcy approached and said to her son, "I have been asked to play. Come turn the pages for me."

Mr George Darcy stood, excused himself and thanked Catherine for the conversation, while following his mother to the instrument.

While Mrs Darcy played, her son obediently turned the pages for her and eventually joined his mother in song when she played a familiar tune. It was heartening to see their closeness, but she could not deny the doubt that was beginning to creep into her once hopeful attitude about their future attachment.

CHAPTER THREE

M r George Darcy abandoned the morning meal quickly
the next day and had been shut away with his parents in
the salon for more than an hour. Catherine would have to forgo
seeing him until dinner if he followed the same schedule as the
day before.

The weather was very fine that day, and so the ladies expected
a few morning callers; however, the room and its inhabitants had
lost their warmth—especially Mrs Darcy who was subdued and
less encouraging to Catherine than she had been throughout the
visit. She and the countess held a quiet conversation through
most of the morning, sharing varying levels of pitying expressions. Twice Mrs Darcy's lady's maid entered to whisper to the
gentlewoman. Each time, the lady simply nodded in response.
The gentlemen were nowhere to be seen.

Her mother eyed her from head to toe more than once. Eventually, she felt so on display that she could hardly keep her own
expressions under regulation. *What was amiss?* She mulled over
the events of the previous day but could not find it in her to ask
the countess about her sour expressions in company.

Naught but kindness could be found in Mrs Darcy's countenance, but Catherine's uncertainty continued to grow. As the minutes went on, the flinty looks from the countess and the pitying glances from Mrs Darcy became almost too much to bear.

When Mrs Darcy departed early, Catherine feigned a reason to excuse herself as well and decided to spend some time alone in her chambers.

The potent mix of anticipation and concern was finally fraying Catherine's even temper. She knew her mother would have words with her about leaving before the afternoon was complete, but she could not find it in herself to care.

To escape the notice of anyone else, she slipped quietly down a few of the servants' passageways to arrive at the back staircase more quickly. After returning to the primary corridor, she heard what might have been voices coming from the library and stopped to test her accuracy. Oftentimes, her hearing was untrustworthy.

She was pleased to see that she was correct. Mr George Darcy and Lady Anne were in the library. Curiouser and curiouser—she had not realized the gentleman enjoyed reading. That could be a lovely addition to their conversation that evening, for she was exceedingly well read.

Not wanting to be seen, she continued quickly to the private rear staircase that would bring her directly to the family wing on the upper floors. Finding her lady's maid in her chambers, Catherine released a sigh to finally be away from all the tension.

Catherine's personal chambers were her favourite rooms at Oakley. While the rest of the estate was comfortable and stately, her rooms were simply divine. Decorated in sumptuous fabrics and beautifully ornamented with items to her specific taste, they were a haven for her peace of mind. She ran her fingers across the new shelving recently added to feature her most beloved books and small embroidered pieces gifted to her from friends at school.

She may not have the talent to thread a needle into charming patterns like many of her acquaintances, but she congratulated herself on identifying the aptitude in others. She encouraged all her friends to do their best work and was often the recipient of their finest efforts.

One's chambers should express their personal preferences, she thought. Alterations were necessary to remain fashionable and current. Her parents were kind enough to allow renovations at her leisure. She also saved all her pin money for such necessities.

One summer, the housekeeper assisted as she perused the attics for articles of past inhabitants of Oakley. It was there that she had found tapestries, small sculptures, and an elegant bronze candelabra. Some of the items in her rooms were far superior to those gracing the shelves and tables around the estate. Catherine had a keen eye for style, indeed. The rest of the house was relatively modest, representing without ostentation or extravagance, their importance and position in the world.

Just as she was directing Jones to swap a vase for a lovely painting she had recently found in Derby, her mother appeared.

Jones must have also noticed the irritation in the countess's expression, for she bowed and departed quickly without a word.

Based on her mother's pursed lips, this morning's performance had been a disappointment as she had expected—even though she had followed her mother's directions impeccably.

It was not until attending seminary that Catherine had begun longing for a closer relationship with her mother. Most of the other girls at school knew their mothers well. Lady Barringer, on the other hand, had been away from home more than she had been present for most of Catherine's childhood. All she had ever wanted was to feel some little affection or approval from the countess.

"Mother," Lady Catherine acknowledged Lady Barringer with a nod of her head and stood from the deep violet, over-stuffed chair in the corner of her room.

"Catherine." Lady Barringer was a woman of few words today, it seemed.

The countess rubbed her gloved fingers across the mantlepiece that hung over the warm, stocked fire burning brightly in her daughter's room. "Mrs Darcy has expressed her continued approval of your marriage to her son."

Catherine's cheeks heated. When had that been in question?

"However, I do think the boy requires additional attention from you. He is showing too much interest in your sister. *Anne* has found no trouble displaying her good qualities and seeking to find commonality with your suitor. Gentlemen like to feel wanted. He must not leave Oakley without comprehending that *you* desire him to be your husband."

Feeling disgracefully vain, Catherine could not even bear to imagine that her sister had made a better impression upon her suitor. Nor could she fathom that Mr George Darcy could possibly prefer Anne's particular flavour of casual defiance. It was unpardonable.

"Have I not agreed to the arrangement? I have shown interest in his conversational topics." Navigating her mother's sentiments was not always easy for Catherine.

"Men expect more than a simple inquiry, my dear. You were educated by the best tutors and then attended the most excellent seminary in all of England. You are a Fitzwilliam. You are the daughter of the Earl of Barringer."

"Yes, your ladyship."

Her flinty expression lingered a little too long on Catherine's waist. She turned her daughter towards the mirror set in the corner of the room and stood beside her. The countess's hair was teased to unhuman proportions, lightened with white powder, and bolstered by large, rolled pieces of wool padding to create the illusion of curls stacked upon her head. She was the height of fashion—and of cruelty, if she so desired.

She was angry, and Catherine felt her stomach drop at the expression on her mother's face. She had disappointed her somehow, and yet, she had no idea what she had done wrong. Was it not Anne who was behaving inappropriately if it was her attentiveness that was swaying Mr. Darcy's attentions? She was not even out—she was not an option for him.

Lady Barringer continued, "Young Darcy has been taking the time to show you that he will be an affectionate and attentive brother to Anne and Ashby, and you should be thankful for his kindness, but we must ensure that while we acknowledge that goodwill, we do not forget the purpose of this visit. He is here for you, and you must remind him of that."

"Yes, of course."

"A good marriage is owed to one's family."

"Yes, it is."

"Good breeding and excellent connections are imperative."

Catherine nodded.

"You are the prime example of a true English rose. Your skin is flawless, your dress impeccable. Mr Darcy is a lucky man."

It was not clear whether her mother was trying to convince herself or Catherine, but she nodded along with her mother's diatribe.

"Mr Darcy and Anne have similar temperaments. You can use that to your advantage. You understand how to speak to your sister."

Catherine nodded once again. That was not necessarily true. Anne was a puzzling creature. And yet, Catherine had no desire to answer in anything but the affirmative.

"Good." Lady Barringer seemed quite finished but then began again. "I will leave you to reflect on the morning and think of engaging topics of conversation you might leverage in your next encounter with Mr Darcy."

Parroting her mother's behaviour had not succeeded in finding Catherine engaged—and now she had been reprimanded, no less! Were not her manners impeccable? Did she not ask questions of her suitor as suggested? Did not she lower herself to speak of pursuits that mattered woefully little to her?

A soft knock at the door interrupted Catherine's line of thought. Lady Barringer admitted the viscountess into the room and excused herself.

Lady Ashby's cold acknowledgement of the countess fell away as soon as Lady Barringer disappeared out into the corridor. The viscountess displayed warmth to few people, and her immediate sympathetic expression once they were alone confirmed that Catherine should be worried. Catherine surely did have something to atone for.

"Your mother thought it best that I come speak to you."

Lady Ashby rarely did as she was told unless a directive came from her mother by marriage.

"Your mother is concerned that Darcy has not yet proposed. I do not see what all the fuss is about. It is Darcy who will benefit from a marriage into this family, and it is his wandering eyes that are currently standing in the way of your future happiness. While I do believe that Darcy will come to the point, I will caution you to beware your sister's intentions during Mr Darcy's visit."

Warmth poured through Catherine's cheeks. Elinor's mention of wandering eyes felt like a blow to her spirit. So, Anne was not the only one showing interest.

"I do not mean to injure you in any way—nor do I wish to speak ill of your sister," Lady Ashby continued. "You know I have a penchant towards telling the truth, and I want to ensure you have all the information necessary. If your sister continues to pursue Mr Darcy—"

"Pursue?" Catherine cried out in disbelief. It was one thing to hear of her sister having some infatuation but completely another to imagine she should try to take Catherine's place. "Lady Ashby, surely you do not suggest that Anne is trying to usurp my role as the future Mrs Darcy!"

"I do not blame your sister for her interest. Mr Darcy is a kind and handsome man. His family has the means to give her a comfortable life."

"A life! What life?" Catherine was exasperated. "You mean the one that is intended for me?"

"And it shall be yours. I only mean to caution you."

"I am sure you are wrong!"

Lady Ashby's pitying look was enough to compel a shine to Catherine's eyes. "No. Surely not." She repeated, more for herself than the viscountess.

"I only mean to protect you. You have little experience with gentlemen."

"Little experience? I have had a Season in town. Albeit some time has passed since then. But Anne has no experience at all! I am sure you are wrong. She is only happy to have guests at Oakley. I am certain that is all. Perchance Mr Darcy is only making my way easier. He is making my sister comfortable as she will likely play a large role in our lives. Until such a time as he is more comfortable with my manner, he is simply gravitating to those in our family with whom he shares particular inclinations."

She began parroting her mother's impression, "Mr Darcy and Anne are both early risers who enjoy outdoor pursuits. They are both soft spoken. He is merely attempting to impress our family through brotherly affection to our rather quiet sister."

The more she spoke, the less she believed it. Catherine felt overcome with concern. It was all too much. She covered her face in embarrassment. She would surely drown in self-deprecation when this interview ended.

Lady Ashby removed Catherine's hands from her face. Her stern but confident expression stared back at Catherine. "You are a Fitzwilliam. We do not cower behind our hands. And no matter what your mother has instructed you to do, we certainly do not beg gentlemen to marry us."

Catherine sighed and moved across the room to look out the window. She had not been directed to beg the younger Mr Darcy to marry her, but if that is what Lady Ashby perceived, then there was clearly an awful lot of talk happening at Oakley that she was not yet privy to.

Across the field, Catherine could see her brother, the earl, and both Mr Darcys riding in from some time in the hills. He did ride quite a lot.

"I certainly did not have to force your brother into marriage," Lady Ashby continued. "He saw an alliance with me as advantageous. It was favoured by both families. And I gave him some reason to expect I would be a dutiful wife."

At that, she laughed—a sly smile on her face.

Catherine beamed at her sister by marriage. It was not often that she shed light into the history of her marriage.

Lady Ashby continued, "No one would be demanding Eloise drop to her knees and beg Mr Darcy to marry her!"

At that, Catherine shuddered. Was everyone truly so worried? Why had she twice alluded to begging? Everyone had expected he would have proposed by now, but there had been no promise of *when* only that he *would*. And he would, Catherine was certain of that. Why else would he travel to Oakley with his parents?

And Lady Ashby was correct. No one would ask Eloise to beseech a man to take her as a bride. It was more likely that the younger Mr Darcy would have come pleading on his knees to have even the slightest bit of attention from Eloise. Catherine knew this to be true, for she had watched gentlemen flock to Eloise during her first Season.

But no man had ever sincerely courted Eloise's attention because her understanding with Mr George Darcy had been long-standing. And the *ton* knew it.

Catherine had been happy to simply watch from the sidelines. She had had no interest in gentlemen or marriage arrangements—she simply loved to dance and socialize and sup at the best tables in Mayfair. She ought to have made some attempts to befriend a few young gentlemen, for now she found herself very much in over her head. The prospect of ensuring her suitor proposed now loomed over her like a guillotine.

She was terrified.

Desperate to avoid humiliation in front of Lady Ashby, Catherine crossed the room to discreetly wipe a lone tear from her eye. She had never had such pressure on her. Her mother had promised the engagement was settled. What more did this gentleman need to know about her to be sure of this alliance between their families? Was not their mothers' close friendship proof enough of her worthiness?

Considerate and sensible, Lady Ashby turned Catherine to look in her eyes.

"Darcy will come to his senses. Everyone who is *anyone* knows that he is promised to you. Your mother is instigating dramatics for no reason. If she is concerned for his interest in *Anne*, the countess should have instructed me to speak to Anne and not you. If he is as sensible as I believe him to be, he will not want to court judgment from society by walking out of Oakley without proposing. It is in his best interest to continue with the scheme as planned and come to the point. He could not walk into London this Season unattached and not garner questions from the rest of the *ton*—I assure you."

"What is he waiting for? Have I not shown myself to be a capable bride? I have done all that my mother has asked."

"Of course you have, my dear."

"Eloise would not be blundering this as I am. She was so elegant and accomplished."

Lady Ashby smiled warmly. "Yes, Eloise was lovely. And so, too, are you. And yet, that is beside the point," she said with a chuckle. "Marriage is not about who is lovely and who is not—it is about securing a future for yourself and your children. Darcy perceives this as do his parents. There is no room for personal feelings when it comes to marriage. You shall soon be Lady Catherine Darcy, and that is all there is to it. Be sensible, my dear, as you always are."

It would be easy to talk of loveliness being unimportant if you were Lady Ashby. She was just as stunning and elegant now as she was during her first Season. During the viscountess's first and only Season, she was the talk of the *ton*. Even now, after giving birth to her second son less than three months prior, she was as captivating in her looks as always. Her hair was always woven into the perfect design. She had no need for wires and wool padding to add to its height like the countess. A halo of auburn curls surrounded her face, with one small hank of longer hair curled into a smooth ringlet that hung low on her back or over her shoulder, flirting with the bodice of her gown.

Lady Ashby interrupted her thoughts. "And perhaps take less of your mother's excellent advice. I do believe that it is time Mr Darcy began to worry about his *own* standings in this arrangement." Her sly gaze emboldened Catherine to laughter.

"Worry! I shall not make that gentleman anxious. The matter is settled, and so you know it."

"Of course I do," Lady Ashby said with a clever smile, "but Darcy does not. Make him work for it, just as I advised before. It should be his turn to be overlooked, and then he shall finally come to the point. It is impolite to make a lady uneasy in this way."

A very unladylike snort erupted from Catherine that surprised even her, and she immediately looked away from Lady Ashby in shock. This entire marriage business was putting the worst of her manners on display! Eloise would never do such a thing as snort.

And in that moment, Lady Catherine wondered if it could be that the younger Mr Darcy was missing Eloise as much as she. That thought garnered some sympathy from her, knowing how dear her elder sister had been to all who loved her.

"Could it be that Mr Darcy was in love with Eloise?"

As soon as the question left her mouth, Catherine knew deep down that she did not really want to hear the answer. If she were to spend the rest of her life worrying that her husband loved only Eloise, it would cause great discomfort.

"No, my dear. Were you not in London just as I was for Eloise's second Season? There is no need to be apprehensive about an undisclosed romance between your sister and your future husband, for that is fiction. They were not in love. If they had been, I am sure one of them would have insisted on marrying sooner. You and I both know a date was never set. It was imminent, but it was never settled."

The answer calmed Catherine more than she would care to admit. To compare herself to Eloise for the rest of her days would be torture.

Timely as always, Jones entered the room quietly and acknowledged the two ladies with a quick nod.

"Yes, Jones?"

"You mother requires your presence downstairs to help see off Mr and Mrs Darcy."

"Is all well?" Catherine inquired, confused by the request.

"They are for Pemberley, my lady." Jones looked apologetic.

They were leaving. As planned. Before their son proposed.

Lady Catherine felt a sudden shudder of anxiety thrum through her body. She nearly reached for the back of the nearby settee to steady her fast-beating heart.

"And the younger Mr Darcy?" She held her breath, waiting for Jones's response.

"Remaining at Oakley, my lady."

The breath released, but not her trepidation.

Shortly thereafter, Catherine found herself side by side with her family to say goodbye to the elder Mr Darcy and Mrs Darcy. She observed her mother's gentle hug to one of her dearest friends and watched them share a private, sad smile. Could it be that Mrs Darcy was as confused by the delay as Catherine?

When Mrs Darcy reached out and squeezed Catherine's shoulder in goodbye, she felt a sense of disappointment—not in Mr George Darcy, but in herself. She must have done wrong.

Her mother and Lady Ashby's persistence that she make herself more desirable to the younger Mr Darcy was confounding. Why must she convince him to follow through with a settled agreement? She had been raised to meet this moment with compliance, and her future husband's indifference was the puzzling aspect.

Perhaps she should overlook him so *he* might know the insidious stab of anxiousness that had been wounding her since his arrival.

Or perhaps not. Maybe it was just as Lady Ashby had said—all was well and as it should be. Could it be that they were departing because it *was* all settled? The younger Mr Darcy must have told his parents that the deal was done—the alliance was set. Catherine would only permit that unwavering confidence she was often praised for to carry her through the rest of her evening.

CHAPTER FOUR

Problem solving came easily to Lady Catherine. She was always determined to find solutions to difficulties. Once, while attending seminary, the Amtower sisters were in an uproar over who was the most talented player of the pianoforte. Admittedly, they were both very skilled and need not have argued over who performed more beautifully, but Catherine was determined to assist, as always. Lady Barringer made sure she had the skills to achieve any goal. Catherine resolved then that both sisters should choose another instrument to study so they might find better harmony with one another. Rebekah played the harp beautifully now, and Araminta may not excel at the lyre, but the sisters rarely quarrelled over musicality any longer. Though both, admittedly, did miss the pianoforte.

It was her own strength of forthrightness and courage to do what was best that led Catherine to believe that ignoring Mr Darcy was the next step to ensuring an engagement by week's end.

Convicted she was—and convinced that Mr Darcy need only see what life without Lady Catherine would be like to ensure he proposed expediently.

Lady Barringer would likely champion Catherine as her best pupil in the ways of moving through society once this was all settled. At least, that was her dearest wish. Catherine was nothing if not a great student of manners and expectations.

It was not difficult to ignore Mr Darcy at breakfast because the gentleman had forgone the meal for a gallop through the countryside. Better yet! Catherine thought this information unsettling at first, that the gentleman rode in all weather, but of course, that would mean Catherine would find more time to herself in her married life. A quiet breakfast would be just the thing to set her days on the right path each morning. Time to clear her head and plan her day! No need to simper around a gentleman and bend her ear to his every thought throughout her morning meal.

She would have to speak to her sister, however. It was not ladylike for her to be galivanting around the grounds with her future brother by marriage, even if accompanied by a servant. How could Catherine compete for his attention or ignore him if he was never in her vicinity?

Lady Ashby joined Catherine by the large windows that looked over the estate from the breakfast parlour and gently began pulling the curtains shut.

"It is rather too sunny this morning, is it not?" Lady Ashby asked the room.

No one looked particularly keen on answering her. The room faced east, and as such, the morning sun poured into the room by design. Would she move the breakfast parlour to the west wing when she was one day countess? What a strange choice.

If anything, Catherine would remove the curtains entirely. All families of good breeding broke their fast in the east wing, did they not?

Lady Barringer interrupted her thoughts, "Lady Ashby. Please do not disturb the curtains."

"Yes," Catherine agreed. "It is such a lovely morning—"

Her mother interrupted, "No need to protect Lady Catherine. She is conscious that her suitor has gone for a ride this morning."

Catherine froze at that—even the footmen who were bringing out steaming plates of new food for the latecomers halted at her declaration. Catherine felt her face flush with embarrassment.

Lady Ashby, stern-faced and stubborn, grabbed Catherine's arm and began leading her out of the room. "Of course, Lady Barringer. I only thought—"

"You were not thinking. Were you, Elinor?"

Lady Ashby froze at the use of her Christian name. Though Catherine had heard her brother use it in personal interludes with the viscountess, it was never used in front of the servants. The countess was drawing a line in the sand. She was displaying her position as lady of the house.

"It seems I was not," Lady Ashby purred—her voice laden with resentment.

The two strongest willed women Catherine knew faced off in a silent battle. But of course, the countess won out—as always.

Catherine hoped to dull the tension between the ladies. "I have taken the time to learn of Mr Darcy's preference for riding in the mornings. His pastimes are important to him, and as such, they are of value to me."

It sounded like the right answer. Lady Barringer had asked her to examine the preferences of her future husband since he arrived, and scrutinize him, she had. He was a quiet, unassuming man—quite dashing as well—and it appeared that cold, winter mornings were refreshing to him. She could see him crossing the garden from the stables now, running his hand through his dark, curly hair and smiling.

Glances around the room reiterated everyone's concern for Catherine's chance at success with the man. Expressions of distaste and pity sunk Catherine's futile hope.

Catherine, no longer feeling a desire to eat, quietly dismissed herself from the room. The tension in the breakfast parlour was enough to send her in the direction of the last person in the world with whom she would want to confide—but the person she trusted the most to tell her the truth.

She gathered her skirts and took the stairs two at a time to her brother's study.

Lord Ashby was found where he always was—lighting a cigar behind his large mahogany desk on the third floor. His study used to be a small, private library for the family before his marriage. Once Lady Ashby had joined the family, it was decided that they both needed rooms to address their personal affairs until such a time as they would themselves inherit the estate. Catherine often regretted that her favourite room in the house, which used to contain the family's most favoured tomes, now held ledgers and cigar boxes and various male-leaning items she could not name.

"Ashby," Catherine announced to the room when her brother did not acknowledge her entrance.

"Sister," he responded around the cigar in his mouth. "To what do I owe the pleasure of your company this morning?" Boredom suffused his words.

Ashby was a gentleman of power and wealth but a man who never appeared too eager for anything at all. Nothing excited him. Naught lit his eyes with joy—perhaps apart from solitude.

"Brother, I must speak to you at once."

A deep breath expressed his disinterest, but Catherine forged on.

"Mother feels I must show more attention to Mr Darcy," Catherine said.

"No one can tell our mother that she is wrong in her schemes."

"I would not dare. The countess accomplishes anything she sets her mind to," Catherine continued. "And I feel—I feel I have made some headway in getting to know the gentleman during his visit."

His blank, bored response did not increase her confidence.

"And so, I was feeling certain—fine—comfortable—until yesterday. And again, this morning."

He raised his eyebrows in question, puffing out slow circles of smoke into the room. The smoke encircled his face, the same colour as the curled wig he wore on top of his head. Though she felt it aged him far beyond his three decades, it gave him a fashionable distinction that he had lacked in his earlier adult years.

"Mother and Lady Ashby have shared some concerns." Catherine finally came to the point.

"Out with it, Kitty. What is it you want to know?"

She loathed being called Kitty. "They are worried that our sister, Anne, is attempting to gain Mr Darcy's attention."

There. She had said it. And soon, he would rebuke it, and she would go on as she had before.

"And?"

"And—and I hope you have spoken to your friend and explained that our younger sister is not yet out. She has been little in society—little even welcomed to our own dining table! Mother says I simply must work harder to gain his attention. But your wife has implied that Anne is going out of her way to seek him out and show interest. But Anne would never do such a thing, would she? She is simply intent in getting to know someone new—a guest in our home who will soon be her new brother."

His apparent disbelief at her speech made her feel unwell.

He finally responded, "I wish you would listen to mother less and attend to your own mind more often. Surely you have seen his fascination with Anne and hers with him."

No response was coming, even though she willed her mouth to argue against his supposition. She had hoped to hear him disabuse her of her worst fears—that her own sister would attempt to court scandal and steal away her future husband.

He continued, "Lady Ashby is nothing if not observant. You may take her opinion as truth. She is only looking out for your position in this family."

"Is—are we worried about my position in this *family*?"

"Of course not," he bit back. He set his cigar down on a bronze dish. Leaning forward, he placed his elbows on his desk and folded his hands under his chin, staring into her eyes. "They do appear to be getting on, but that will not change our plans. We agree that younger sisters do not marry until their elder sisters are settled. I will speak to our sister. I had hoped our mother would handle Anne, but apparently she is shirking her duties. Do not fret. Darcy will not be making a mockery of the house of Barringer, I can tell you that much! He would not dare cross our family. Even for their rumoured 8,000 pounds per annum, they cannot hold a candle to the earldom."

Menacing, his words may have been, but Catherine released the breath she had been holding. "Thank you, brother."

"And what's more—I will not allow it. If he wants to remain in my good graces, he will go along with the arrangement as planned. Anne will have her debut next month, and your wedding will follow shortly thereafter. Mother is already preparing a come-out ball for Anne and your engagement ball—quietly of course—but we must not get in the way of mother's arrangements, must we?"

Catherine nodded.

Her brother picked up his cigar and leaned back into his plush, brown leather chair. The conversation was clearly over, and so Catherine excused herself.

Catherine pretended a headache for the afternoon. She had no interest in seeking out Mr Darcy, nor any other company, to be frank. In her chambers, she could be herself—read books to her own liking, daydream about topics that would concern no one else, and peruse letters from her friends.

She could not, however, continue her ruse for the entirety of the day. Her family and their guest were promised to visit Eastwick Manor for a card party. Just days ago, Catherine had looked to the evening with excitement, but now she was feeling the crush of defeat. The Baron of Eastwick was a close friend of her father's and likely knew why the Darcys were visiting. If the baron's youngest daughter knew about the non-existent proposal, then so too shall every nitwitted young lady in England soon enough. The Honourable Matilda Wright did not know how to keep her mouth shut—nor her pen from writing slander across all the counties in the country. Avoiding the lady would be Catherine's chief object that evening.

Their party took two carriages. The viscount joined her parents in the first carriage, while she and Lady Ashby rode with Mr Darcy. Conveniently, Anne was not present, as she was not yet invited to such events.

Mr Darcy took the rear-facing seat and Lady Ashby sat close to Catherine on the forward-facing bench. The viscountess encouraged many topics throughout the ride—woefully few in which Mr Darcy attempted to join.

Catherine fought against her best nature to lure Mr Darcy into conversation as she had been taught by her mother. Lady Ashby clearly understood gentlemen of this generation, and perhaps her mother's views were rather dated. If she must force the man to pursue her instead, then she would. Or, at the very least, she would try.

"It has been a very long time since you have been to Eastwick, has it not?" Lady Ashby looked to Catherine for a response.

"Yes, I believe it was around Michaelmas, when our parents came out of mourning," Catherine replied.

"Mr Darcy," Lady Ashby tried again, "did you know that Lady Catherine and the baron's daughter attended seminary together?"

"No, my lady," he responded quietly in the darkness.

"Yes, his youngest, Miss Matilda. Are you familiar with the family?"

"Only the eldest son, Benjamin. We were at Oxford together."

Lady Ashby nudged Catherine with her elbow. Catherine had no reason to wish to speak about Benjamin Wright, nor any of his sisters. Harridans, the lot of them. She only attended parties at Eastwick because she was expected to.

Rather than immediately turning a question to Mr Darcy, Catherine searched through the vault of her mind for something more appealing to say about a family she did not care for. Catherine turned to Lady Ashby and looked her in the face, "I have heard it said that Miss Matilda swooned when she performed her curtsey."

The sharp intake of breath from Mr Darcy amused Catherine. Finally, a reaction!

The viscountess coughed to hide a laugh.

Catherine continued, "The baroness was so distraught that she bought out half of London for Miss Matilda's come-out ball. Though Queen Charlotte did not attend to see her triumph, many believe she was attempting to provide a better impression of her daughter to the *ton*."

Even in the dark, Catherine could see Lady Ashby's wide-eyed gaze. Catherine had certainly surprised herself. Mayhap she had more of a bite to her than she had even herself imagined.

She could see some amusement on the gentleman's face and felt it a particular triumph.

She would no longer fall over Mr Darcy's every word—not that the gentleman ever had much to say.

It went against her nature to not address a person sitting so close to her directly. He must have been just as responsive to their proximity, for he kept adjusting his long legs to ensure they did not brush up against her gown. It was the only thing that endeared her to him. And it was such a lovely gown. She would rather not have any stray horse hairs falling upon her new *robe à l'Anglaise* from all the time he spent in a saddle.

The gown was divine. A light blue creation that met at her waist with concealed lacing and light boning to ensure a smooth line. The deep "v" at the centre of her spine accentuated her curves, making her feel quite ladylike. No padding at the waist was necessary because of Catherine's natural curves. The petticoat underneath was a simple pattern of flowers that reminded her of the primrose that grew wild on the grounds at Oakley. She had longed to wear the ensemble ever since she was measured for it in London many months ago.

The party began like many others, with a receiving line of the estate's family and guests, and a drawing room full of young ladies, their families, and a smattering of eligible gentlemen. These smaller parties in the country were an opportunity for ladies and gentlemen to meet each other before the Season in London began in earnest. While many of their fathers were required to travel to open parliament soon, the Season would not start for many weeks.

At the strong encouragement of her mother, Catherine asked politely if Mr Darcy would like to make up her pool of Quadrille. His game play was amateurish, and their interactions bored her. Even when she played cards of lesser importance to allow Mr Darcy an opportunity to win a hand, he showed no interest in winning—the same quiet politeness surrounded his manner no matter the outcome of each round.

It was helpful that some of her friends from seminary were in attendance, for they always knew to stand to Catherine's right when they whispered the best *on dit* from the *ton*. The ladies were very *un*helpful, however, in that they did not stop Catherine's glass of punch from being filled too many times. She should blame the villainous Miss Matilda, who kept directing the footmen to fill up her glass. Either way, her discomfort decreased as the party waned on.

Lady Barringer had to pull her aside and tell her to eat something before the entire room began commenting on the volume of her voice. "Ladies speak in soft tones and never over imbibe. Go ask Mr Darcy if he is enjoying the party."

Catherine did not, in fact, want to follow her mother's advice. It was clearly better to draw him in by showing more of herself, as Lady Ashby had prescribed. He should ask *her* whether *she* was enjoying the party.

When next Catherine approached Mr Darcy, she stood quietly waiting for him to speak. She coughed, to ensure he knew she was there and smiled good naturedly when he looked her way. When it was clear he would not ask, she simply said, "Why yes, I am enjoying the party."

At least her mother would be satisfied that she had approached the gentleman.

She must have spoken far too quietly because the gentleman asked her, "Pardon me? I cannot hear you when you whisper in that manner."

He also must have felt she was standing much too close, for he backed away from her as well and looked around the room seemingly to confirm they were not being watched.

Lady Ashby approached her next when she was filling a plate of food as her mother had suggested. "Ladies should not be seen eating so much at a party," she scolded. She removed the plate from Catherine's hands and set it down on the banquet table. "You should go tell Mr Darcy that you long to see Pemberley once again."

When she found the gentleman, she approached with caution. Ladies do not speak too loudly, and as she had just learned, they also do not whisper too closely to a gentleman. So much time was spent reminding herself how to regulate her speech that the alcohol content in her blood obstructed the memory of what she was supposed to say. Her last thread of sobriety was used to moderate her volume. "Let us go to Pemberley."

Wide eyed and startled, the gentleman did not even respond. He sighed with displeasure and excused himself.

The countess approached her daughter with a slice of cake and demanded she "eat at once" before she "fell into the nearest piece of furniture."

Catherine took her mother's advice and ate the slice in two bites. When Mr Darcy came and offered his arm to her at the time of their departure, she felt triumphant. She was doing all that was asked of her. Even in the haze of her inebriation, she felt happy for the first time in many days. She even waved and smiled at Miss Matilda when she saw her staring from across the room. Perhaps Mr Darcy would ask for a private meeting this very night!

CHAPTER FIVE

The new plan was working. Not only had Mr Darcy forgone a morning ride and joined them for the morning meal, but Anne had taken a tray in her room. Even with a pounding headache reminding her of the many glasses of punch from the night before, Catherine felt nearly giddy with her prowess in acquiring a husband. It appeared that Lady Ashby had been right all along—it was better to find ways to make the gentleman desire to know her more.

"What think you of an outing to better enjoy the peaks?" Lady Barringer asked and took a sip of her tea, her question addressed to Mr Darcy.

Mr Darcy nodded and wiped his mouth with a napkin. "That sounds lovely, your ladyship."

"You cannot visit Oakley without a picnic in the hills. We could stop in Hayfield for some shopping and make a day of it."

"It has been many years since I visited the village," Mr Darcy replied.

"I am certain not much has changed, but it is good for the villagers to see a great gentleman now and again." Lady Barringer nodded along with her own suppositions. "My daughter would enjoy some time out of doors."

Catherine would rather drown in the River Sett than go on a picnic in January.

Before she could respond to her mother in the affirmative, Mr Darcy replied, "Yes, Lady Anne does seem to be something of a nature enthusiast."

Her mother seemed stricken at that comment—left unusually mute.

It was up to Ashby to save the conversation. "Lady Anne has a very busy schedule, what with her *London debut* approaching."

"I would enjoy a picnic," Lady Catherine spoke into the tense void. She would not, in fact, enjoy a picnic. Nay—a picnic sounded like torture.

"Yes, as I said, Lady *Catherine* would appreciate some time out of doors, much like yourself, sir." Lady Barringer smiled at Mr Darcy. Her mother had drawn her name out, spoken with a reverence and gentleness that was foreign to Catherine's ears.

Catherine glanced at Mr Darcy to see what his answer would be and found a nod from him was considered a sufficient response.

Luckily for their entire party, a gentle rain covered Oakley by the middle of that morning and continued laying a light, icy glaze over the entire estate and the peaks that watched over their property in the distance. Alas, the picnic would not be.

Peppered with information about Catherine's many interests and preferences, Mr Darcy seemed less and less attentive as the day waned on. Whether it was the countess, Ashby, or Catherine herself, the gentleman was merely polite in his short responses. Efforts to ask about his interests or share her own were both failures. No matter how hopeful she had felt that morning, all of the actions she took seemed to falter no matter her level of exertion.

She rose the next morning with a new plan in place—she would simply ignore him. If she sought to have him become the pursuer, then she would give her suitor nothing. She did not look in his direction nor inquire after his health for two full days.

She triumphed over her ability to fashion an air of mystery with respect to her person. *He* should feel the weight of his inaction and labour for *her* notice.

While Catherine was floating on the high of her success, it appeared that Lady Anne was not experiencing any pleasure of her own.

Without knowing any of the details, Catherine came upon a scene of Lady Anne exploding in a unique brand of anger she had never seen from her sister before—and with their mother as the recipient, no less! It horrified Catherine to see her sister abuse their mother in such a way.

When Catherine entered the library with a plan to help them find a way to harmony, Anne immediately pretended an ennui that was very fashionable indeed. Catherine had studied the emotion at length but could never quite perfect the art of caring little. If anything, she spent most of her time quieting all her strong feelings, as she had long been taught.

Shove would be too strong of a word for how Lady Barringer forced a fur-lined wool cloak into her hands and physically moved Lady Catherine out the terrace doors the next morning. Appalled by her mother's lack of manners, Catherine glanced back at her, saw her immovable expression, and huffed in private annoyance.

It was frigid—January in the peaks was not a time to be taking a *stroll* anywhere. Thankfully, the snow and frost had melted under the sun all morning, and while she would have to deal with her skirt being muddied, at least she would not be sliding down the terrace steps today. It was regretful that she did not have time to retrieve her newest muff. Mothers were always forgetful of these types of details—Jones would not have overlooked the opportunity to have Catherine looking her finest.

Adjusting her cloak and holding her chin high, Lady Catherine marched towards the stables. She need not even open her eyes, because the odour of the animals would have guided her steps on their own. This was not a place she enjoyed spending time—it had been years since she had visited the horses in this manner.

But her future husband was forever visiting the stables in the mornings, and according to the countess, ignoring one's suitor was not in their best interest.

"If he must spend time in the stables, so must you," Lady Barringer had told her before scooting her out onto the terrace.

A sennight had passed since the Darcys first arrived, and her mother was becoming impatient. Surprisingly, Catherine was caring less and less whether she had Mr Darcy's good opinion.

It was not difficult to find Darcy, but her shock was physical when she saw Anne in the stables as well. No servants were present—only her sister, dressed in her newest, deep violet riding habit, backed up against the door to a horse stall.

Artemis reached her long nose over the stall door and nudged her sister's wild, chestnut hair. Anne reached back over her shoulder to rub the horse's nose, never taking her eyes off Mr Darcy.

Catherine knew she must think of some reason for visiting the stables and announce her presence. And yet, she had not selected an appropriate excuse. It was why she had not yet called out to the gentleman and her sister upon entering. The absurdity of it was that her quick mind could think of no reason a sane person would be out of doors, breath hanging in the air in front of their faces, in this weather.

Mr Darcy reached out and brushed her sister's wind-swept hair off her face and tucked it behind her ear. Catherine's own face heated in response, but not Anne's. Anne held his gaze with a courage Catherine could not know—seemingly daring him to stop touching her. And he did not. His fingers ran gently across her cheek and traced the length of her chin. Anne reached her hand up to grasp his arm—but not to stop him, as she should. Instead, she squeezed his forearm and smiled gently at him. Hers were the batting eyelashes the ladies in seminary had all longed to achieve. Her long, dark lashes fluttered closed, and Catherine watched as Darcy leaned forward to kiss her sister's freckled forehead.

The affection was startling. Catherine had never witnessed anything like it. Her own stomach had dropped in a foul sensation that had her desiring to run for a chamber pot at once.

As startling as the behaviour was, Catherine was worldly enough to comprehend what had transpired—betrayal.

Duplicity—and from her only living sister! Catherine's hands shook as she hurried back to the main house and in through the servants' doors at the lowest level. There was no sense in going to her mother, she would simply see this as another failure on Catherine's part.

All this time, Catherine had worried she would not be as perfect a bride as Eloise. Now there was something to finally laugh about! She felt near to hysterics at the thought—a maniacal laughter bubbled in her breast, though she did not let it out.

She had imagined that Mr Darcy had wanted the poised and polite Eloise, when it appeared he wanted to burn within the fire that was Lady Anne Fitzwilliam. Anne was the embodiment of young joy and a flippant disregard for society. Never one to care for rules or limits, Anne crossed as many as she could each day. And, she had finally crossed right over a boundary that would shake the entire house of Fitzwilliam—the very earldom of Barringer could come toppling down because of one careless moment in a stable. Damn Anne. She was always up to no good.

Could not Anne fathom what her actions would render? What disharmony would soon come over their family? Did her selfishness know no bounds?

Catherine was not quite certain where she was headed until she stood before the door of one of Oakley's principal rooms—her father's study. A rare guest in his domain, she felt the nerves overtake her as she knocked on his door.

Her father appeared to be as surprised to see her as she was to be entering. She would not call her father unkind, but he was a private man. The earl was very busy, and as such, Catherine saw very little of him.

"Please close the door," was his only instruction, as he gestured to a sturdy chair that sat before his desk. She imagined he might speak to her much like her brother had done from behind his desk. Alternatively, her father stood, abandoning his well-used chair that held his imprint from many years of use.

He moved around his desk and sat in the chair accompanying her own.

Once settled, he gave her his full attention—and it was so unique and so long missing that Catherine's heart twinged at the consideration.

"What can I do for you, my dear?"

Unsure how to begin, Catherine froze. Her upbringing had been very specific about how to handle most situations, but she was uncertain even about the words necessary to explain what she had witnessed.

A gentle hand met her knee, encouraging her to speak and melting away some of the fear in her heart. "I believe Mr Darcy would prefer to marry Anne."

"Oh posh! Has your mother been in your ear?"

"Well, of course, I have spoken at length to my mother on this subject. But that is not why I have come."

"Hmm?" His raised eyebrows prompted her on.

"I have just come from the stables."

"In this weather?" The earl looked out his window to confirm the frigid day.

"Yes, sir."

"And?"

Catherine swallowed past the catch in her throat. "And I came across Mr Darcy and my sister."

Now that got his attention. He sat farther upright in his chair.

"They were—I mean, as I understood it—the situation was—" Catherine's face reddened with embarrassment. She could not stop her hands from shaking nor bring her gaze up from her lap.

The gentle father was gone. The tall, strong earl in his place—fearsome in his visage.

"Are you trying to tell me that your sister was compromised by Mr Darcy in our stables today?" The earl inquired, completely still.

She nodded in response. She did not know whether to cry or run from his study. This was all her fault.

The earl stood and opened the door, speaking quietly to the footman in the hall.

"Your mother will join us."

Catherine could not look at her father as he took his rightful place behind his large mahogany desk, and they awaited the countess.

"We shall send Anne to my sister in Kent," her father said.

"What of her come out?" Lady Barringer argued. "The entire *ton* will be in an uproar to find out we are no longer going to town for the Season! What shall I tell my friends? The last I spoke to many ladies of the *ton*, I had informed them that in due time Catherine would be well disposed of in marriage."

Catherine continued to sit in her father's study, but she had not been invited to participate in the conversation.

"If only Catherine had taken greater advantage of her first Season, there would be another gentleman to consider—"

"Pray, let us be clear!" The earl bellowed. "I will not be made a mockery of. I was wrong to leave this in the hands of you and Mrs Darcy. I should have forced the young man into a written contract long ago."

"But, sir, I wanted to allow Mr. Darcy some time—do you not see how tall she is? Her square shoulders? Did you see how she ignored him for days? Heaven and earth, what of the loudness of her voice?"

Catherine wanted to hike into the peaks and never return.

"The boy has known our family for his entire life! What was there to learn about Catherine in the past sennight that could not have been known before? He knows all that he must—she is a young lady of distinction, marked as such since her birth!"

"Well, she is certainly not Eloise," the countess murmured.

And with that, all hope and courage dissolved from Catherine. She resigned all ambition and let herself wallow in fear.

"What if we increased her dowry?" Lady Barringer asked, unexpectedly hopeful.

"Madam, do you hear yourself?" The earl yelled and slammed his fist down. "I trust that you comprehend that Catherine is a perfectly lovely girl, and her 40,000 pounds is quite enough for any young gentleman. It is the other daughter of yours I am concerned over."

"Anne?"

"I am sending her to Kent before she ruins us all. I will send an express to my sister tonight. She mentioned in her last letter that her neighbours were visiting the peaks soon. She might join their party to travel here."

"What will we say?" Lady Barringer, who always knew what to say and how to act, looked stricken with uncertainty.

"Until Rosamund arrives, we have time to make plans. We shall take Catherine to town as soon as Anne is gone to Kent, and we shall secure a husband for her as quickly as possible. And this time, you will not mistake me when I say I expect a gentleman who will follow through—someone whom we can trust."

"Yes, sir," her mother responded through gritted teeth.

"No more of your friends and their empty promises," the earl commanded.

Lady Barringer did not reply.

In the privacy of her bedchamber, Catherine finally shed the tears she had been holding back in her father's study. She had been raised to have great ambition and had failed miserably. Would she ever know acceptance from her parents?

Jones entered quietly, joined her on the bed, and ran a hand down Catherine's cheek. The only woman who had ever shown any affection to Catherine held her while she poured out all of her emotions.

"My lady, all will be well," she crooned.

"How can it be now? I have disappointed my mother, and every expectation for my future prospects is now beyond my grasp."

"Your path may not be that which your mother laid out for you, but it does not mean there is no way forward. Set your own course."

"I would not know how. If only Eloise were here."

Catherine mourned her sister once again—privately, as she had for the past fourteen months. Emotions were not welcome at Oakley. Fitzwilliams did not bother with tears and passion. They were built more strongly than that.

"I fear I have some news that may add to your distress, my lady," Jones mentioned quietly.

Catherine turned her eyes to the dearest servant in all of England.

"As you know, my mother is ailing. My brother has written to call me home. I have just received word that the countess has approved an extended absence. I came to take my leave of you."

Heart already breaking, Catherine felt it crumble into nothing. Without Jones, she would lack the support and encouragement she had become accustomed to for many years. She had heard Jones speak of her mother with such kindness, and it made her heart ache for the same. Her mother had not even shed a tear over the death of Eloise. Catherine would have to be made of sterner stuff to endure a Season in town without Jones.

Hoping to keep a shred of dignity intact, Catherine told Jones to travel safely. She could not live with herself if she begged a servant to stay at her side rather than travel to care for a dying mother—even if she felt the sting of jealousy.

Catherine took a tray in her chambers that evening. She was too mortified to dine with the family.

She had been unworthy of this marriage arrangement from the start and would now live with the consequences.

Anne's lady's maid, Reynolds, joined her later that night to prepare for sleep. Reynolds was young for an upstairs maid and far more like Anne than she—flighty and too quick to speak her mind; however, that tendency was beneficial when Catherine was looking for information.

"How is my sister?" she asked while Reynolds brushed the knots from her hair.

"Lady Anne is overwhelmed with sentiment, my lady. Her feelings for the younger Mr Darcy were strong, I suspect."

Catherine pursed her lips. So, everyone had known what was going on except for her. The servants must have been laughing at her foolish efforts to secure the match.

"The countess is rightly angry with her, my lady, but none so angry as the earl. He called her wanton and threatened to keep her at home until she was a spinster, he did! Lucky for Lady Anne, Lady Rosamund will come and take her to Kent. Maybe she will meet a nice gentleman in the countryside."

Catherine rolled her eyes at this. Reynolds and all the servants were empathetic to Anne's plight, hoping she would still make a fine match, when she was not the one whose reputation was now damaged. Anne had nearly set the entire Fitzwilliam family into a true scandal—who was to say she had not already done so! If word got out, both ladies could be ruined forever. And then who would marry them?

CHAPTER SIX

The next morning found Catherine splashing as much cool water on her face as was possible. Her tear-soaked pillow was flipped upside down to preserve what little dignity remained when Reynolds joined her. She almost inquired whether Reynolds might go fetch some snow from a nearby peak to reduce the red, puffy appearance of her face.

Alas, forgoing another meal would not be tolerated, and so she lifted her heavy skirt and made her way down to breakfast.

"Catherine, please come here."

Her father's booming voice escaped his study and caught up with her as she was passing by. She sighed with defeat as she turned to join her father. Unfortunately, her mother was also present.

"Good morning," her father welcomed her and waved a hand towards a chair.

She took a seat quickly and squared her shoulders for their worst.

"Mr Darcy's valet is packing his things now, but the gentleman can be found in the breakfast parlour."

"Oh," Catherine answered, startled. She had imagined him travelling at first light to escape Oakley.

Her mother chimed in, "We would like you to speak with him."

Catherine's revulsion at that suggestion must have been evident in her expression because her mother narrowed her eyes. "You will speak with him, young lady. And you will convince him to give you another chance. It is the only method we can comprehend to see our way through this situation without landing ourselves in the middle of a scandal! Do you want to be known as the lady who was jilted by a simple farmer?"

Her father chuckled at that. "A simple farmer? Is that what we are calling gentlemen who own half of Derbyshire these days?"

He turned a warmer expression on Catherine and steepled his hands under his chin. "My darling girl, I know this is difficult, but we have spoken at length. We do believe the best way forward is for you to apologize for your neglect and the behaviour of your sister and ask him if he is willing to start anew."

"My neglect?"

He raised his eyebrows at her in question. "If you think we missed the way you ignored the man for two full days, you must think us all simple minded. I trust that you understand what must be done."

Catherine huffed with annoyance. She had only resorted to that once all else had been attempted!

"What am I to say about my sister exactly?"

"You need to remind him that Lady Anne is not yet out and that she is too young to understand her appeal to gentlemen. Tell him you forgive him his part and remind Mr Darcy that it would not look good if society knew he was preying on young ladies still in the nursery."

The nursery! Heavens above, that was an exaggeration. They had planned for Lady Anne to be out on the marriage mart in a few short weeks.

"I would hate for Mr Darcy to consider that a threat," Catherine responded gingerly. The entire recommendation made her stomach turn with worry. *Run, run, run.* That bothersome voice inside roared once again. Detest him, she might, but she would not accuse the man of preying on young, innocent ladies.

"Then call it a promise," her mother answered. "Tell yourself whatever you must to be easy. But we are decided that this will be better accepted coming from his bride than from the earl."

Catherine's head moved back and forth between her parents in confusion. They wanted her to threaten Mr Darcy with scandal. What level of absurdity must her life plunge to next! She had to remind herself to close her mouth, such was her alarm.

Catherine entered the breakfast room to find Mr Darcy alone—truly alone. Not a footman nor the butler remained. Steaming hot dishes sat out on the banquet table untouched, except for the small amount that the gentleman had chosen for his own plate.

Her entrance must have surprised him, for he looked startled from being deep in thought. Why he did not scurry off in the early morning hours, she would never know. If she were a man in his situation, she would have called for a servant to wake her before sunrise and would have been climbing into a carriage just as the sun cleared the horizon. Oakley would have been far behind. But this man stayed—how unusual.

"Good morning, sir." Catherine curtseyed upon capturing his attention.

"My lady," he responded in kind, standing to greet her.

Instead of filling a breakfast plate, Catherine stood tall and approached the table. Mr Darcy pulled out the chair she stood behind for her and asked her to join him.

Under the table, Catherine's hands were gathered in her skirts with anxiousness; however, she sat still and courageously where Mr Darcy could see her. Strength of character had been engrained into her since her first breath. Fitzwilliams never stand down.

"I understand you are leaving for Pemberley this morning."

"Yes, I am."

"I owe you an apology." The words left her lips, but her heart was not in it. Her very being quaked at being forced into this conversation.

"I beg your pardon?"

"I have no need to pardon you, sir," she ground out. "It is I who should apologize for not allowing us more time to get to know one another. We should start anew. I will spend more time with you, and we can continue the path our parents have set for us."

Mr Darcy looked suspicious and confused. "I fear there is no path forward for the two of us. I must apologize for my part in all of this business—" He waved his hand in the air as if to brush away the hurt and betrayal of his kissing her younger sister when he should have been proposing to her. If only it were that easy.

This was not going the way her parents requested, and Catherine interrupted him to continue on her mission. "I must also apologize for my sister."

"Your sister?" His brow furrowed; his blue eyes injured.

The hurt in his eyes brought a pang of sympathy and completely confused Catherine about the next bit. "You should not prey on young girls." That was not quite right.

"Pray, tell me what that is supposed to mean."

"And young girls should apologize for—for—" Damn it all. "Well, I must apologize for my sister's intolerable behaviour. She is not even out, sir. She does not know what it is like to be around eligible gentlemen just yet. You, see? I am sure you have been flattered by her attentions, but we must put that aside and move forward."

"Lady Catherine." Darcy stood from the table looking quite affronted, and Catherine panicked.

"Do not leave just yet, sir," she said in desperation, staring at the door and praying no one would enter and that he would decide to stay rather than bolting at this very moment. "It is only that my father would like you to consider how this will look to society. You see—"

"I do not see! And I refuse to hear this any longer." He began stepping towards the door. "If the earl would like to paint me as a man who—who—I cannot even repeat it, my lady."

Catherine grabbed his arm in desperation, "Please, sir. We can continue a courtship. I forgive you. All is not forsaken—"

"There is nothing to continue! There was naught ever begun!"

Mr Darcy must have seen something in Catherine that created some sympathy, for he stopped his forward motion and gentled his tone. "My lady, please tell the earl I am at his disposal should he like to speak before I depart within the hour."

His look of pity as he exited the room was mortifying. Catherine was ready to fling herself into the fireplace without delay. That would solve this problem! If she were dead too, Anne would be next in line to have him. And have him she may! Catherine did not care a whit for Mr Darcy.

Catherine waited some minutes before she too exited the breakfast room. She had no interest in seeing Mr George Darcy ever again.

As she was leaving the breakfast room in shame, her brother, Ashby, grabbed her by the arm in the corridor and pulled her into a quiet alcove.

"You must go to my study at once and calm your sister who will not stop caterwauling about her broken heart."

Her brother's indolence knew no bounds.

Patience running thin, Catherine took a deep breath before responding. "And how do you propose that I—the woman whom Mr Darcy was supposed to marry—am going to calm the woman who was cuckolding her future groom? Hmm?"

Catherine pinched the bridge of her nose. It was the first time in her life that she had spoken in such a way to her brother, but she had no patience left. Every thread of who she was seemed to be fraying this very day.

Lord Ashby continued, "How should I know what to say to the girl? You are her sister. You know her best. I cannot possibly demand that my wife handle this. She is far too important to waste her time with such passionate antics. It is beneath her!"

But not beneath Catherine. Message received.

It was strange to be named the person in this house who knew her sister best, when she understood her motives little.

They were nearer to strangers than friends.

"How should I know how to pacify Anne?" Catherine cried out.

"Are you not a female? Go reason with the girl. She is beset by personal grievances, and I have no temper to resolve them. Tell her to go speak to Darcy."

"I certainly will not." Why did everyone expect Catherine to fix this problem? Had not she displayed her incompetency adequately?

"She needs to tell Darcy that she has no fondness for him and that he should propose to you."

"This family has gone mad! I shall go and do as I am told, but then I am done. Done with Mr Darcy and done taking advice from any of you."

Mortified or not, Catherine removed her arm from her brother's grip and moved towards the stairs. She ought to get this interesting conversation over with.

It was possible she might feel even more foolish after this next interview, which would offer some nauseating continuity.

Catherine did not address her sister upon entering the room. The surprise and hurt on Anne's face was enough to make her second guess her abysmal choice to attend to her sister, but go forward she must.

Taking her brother's place behind his desk, she placed both hands on the smooth wood and gathered some courage. "You must go to Darcy at once." A ray of hope shot through her sister's shiny, blue eyes. "And you must tell him you do not care for him—that it is *I* he must marry. Do it now. We have no more time to waste. He is departing within the hour."

"I could never!" Anne wailed.

"Just as I suspected."

Catherine stood immediately and departed. She had no time for her sister's fervour and heartbreak either. Let the viscount handle it.

"All the kitchen girls were crying over the departure of Mr Darcy's valet," Reynolds gossiped while preparing Catherine for bed.

"Mmm." Reynolds had a knack for overstepping, and Catherine was almost at her limit. Tears threatened to escape, but she held them back. She would not put on such an undignified performance as her sister had.

"But do not feel bad, my lady. They shall get over it soon enough. They are not angry with you. They understand these sorts of things."

Catherine was not sure what "sort of thing" this was. Was it Anne's betrayal? Was it a gentleman who turned out to be a coward? Was it meddling parents who forced two people together who were never going to marry?

Or was it simply the loss of the best sister in the world and the life a gentleman had dreamed of having with her? It was unlike Catherine to be so sentimental, but the shock waves of Eloise's death continued to reverberate through her life, and she suspected they would for the remainder of her days.

CHAPTER SEVEN

Before the sun could stretch its arms and cover the hills in light, Catherine was wide awake. She pulled her quilt up around her chin to stave off the chill. The servants had not yet visited her chambers to stir her fireplace to life, and yet, and she was already melancholy. It had been nearly a fortnight since Mr Darcy's departure, and the family avoided her still.

Tears ran down her face, a physical reaction to the yearning she felt for Eloise. In her dream, her elder sister had readied Catherine for her wedding day, advising her along the way. Eloise's gentle demeanour and handsome face had bolstered her faith—and yet it was all wrong.

It was not real. The wedding she had prepared herself for her entire life had slipped through her fingers, and her sister too was gone. What more could she do? She was nothing if not prepared for marriage. Fitzwilliams were always ready. But it was out of her control now.

Hope tugged at her heart knowing her aunt, Lady Rosamund, would arrive that day. Perhaps all was not lost.

A winter storm settled into the hills and peaks in the late morning that had the entire house on edge. For the most part, the winter season had been irregularly dry, and while those who cultivated the ground may be happy for some rain and snow, Catherine could not but worry for her aunt making her final push towards Oakley.

Lady Rosamund Raleigh had sent a note the night before to tell the family of her intention to stop in Buxton and arrive at Oakley by the following afternoon. But with the state of the roads and the elevation, it would be a difficult day to travel. They all hoped Lady Rosamund might have remained in Buxton until the weather cleared, but they could not know.

Once the family sat down for dinner, everyone was quiet. Country hours or not, Lady Rosamund had still not arrived, and conversation was stilted with everyone's shared distress. The sun would set soon, and if her aunt did not arrive by then, Oakley's servants would likely gather to travel into the night to attempt to recover the travel party.

Just when the soup course was being removed, the butler entered the dining room and bowed to her father's ear to share a message. The entire room held their breath as they awaited news.

"She is arrived," the earl declared, loosing a sigh of relief. "Please, all, let us go greet her immediately." He turned to the butler and murmured that a tray should be prepared and sent ahead to his sister's rooms. "She will be fatigued and hungry."

Lord and Lady Ashby were slow to rise from their seats, but Catherine's anticipation was much like her father's. She was eager to see her aunt after many years apart.

Lady Rosamund was nearly a decade younger than the earl, closer in age to Lady Barringer. A thrice-widowed lady of some property in Kent, she was a pure delight.

After greeting the earl and countess, as well as Lord and Lady Ashby, Lady Rosamund approached Catherine with a warmth in her eyes that immediately settled Catherine's spirits. She felt she could take a deep breath for the first time in weeks.

She put her hands on Catherine's shoulders and pulled her close, kissing her on the cheek and murmuring, "I have worried over you for days, my dear. Please tell me you are well."

Lady Rosamund eagerly looked into Catherine's eyes for a signal of fortitude, it seemed. And while rapidly feeling she might lose her composure and fall into her aunt's arms, Catherine nodded. Abruptly, she was overwrought with feeling. Her emotions were on the precipice of pouring out of her.

A light squeeze to her shoulders told Catherine that all would be well.

"I must immediately attend to a warm bath and refresh myself, dearest," Lady Rosamund said to her. "But when I am through, I will send my lady for you. I wish to speak at the earliest opportunity."

"Yes, ma'am."

One final squeeze on her upper arm, and her aunt was taking the stairs up to the family wing of the house.

Catherine stood alone in the front hall and glanced outside through the front doors that had been unintentionally left open to the frigid elements.

The snow had changed over to a driving rain that had turned the lane that led to Oakley into a treacherous mud pit, with deep ruts in the drive where the carriages had pulled in front of the house. The harried, muddied servants moved quickly through the muck and rain, hurrying to do their duties so they too might sup and find warmth by a fire inside the house.

Rather than return to the dining room, Catherine stepped out onto the front terrace. Under the awning, she tipped her face to the sky to give thanks for the safe arrival of Lady Rosamund. She felt a twinge of confidence that this was just what she needed to feel courageous once again. The steady pounding of the rain and cool breeze seemed to energize Catherine. That is, until the wind pushed the rain sideways for a moment, drenching the front of her gown and drowning her newly found peace of mind.

A deep chuckle caught her attention across the yard, where a tall muscular man was barking orders to all the servants. Her eyes met his, and he turned his attention to the remaining servants.

The man was covered in mud from head to toe, his wool riding coat soaked through. His once cream breeches were splattered by the road, making Catherine pull back in horror. Poor Lady Rosamund! The storm must have given her such a fright.

Her aunt's man continued pointing to various servants, directing their movements as they attempted to push one of the carriages out of a deep rut in the drive. When they were unable to budge the conveyance, the man joined the other men at the back of the carriage to help. Digging his tall boots into the slush and muck, they finally pushed the carriage out of the rut.

With that momentum, the horses were finally able to move. At length, the two carriages were directed around to the back of the house, along with a party of cold, grimy servants who walked alongside them.

Soaked from head to toe now, Catherine knew she should return inside, but she was mesmerized by the sheer will it had taken to free the carriage and horses.

Her aunt's man watched the carriages disappear around the back of the house and turned to smile at Catherine. How proud he must be to have finally released the carriage from its hold in the ground. Catherine nodded in acknowledgement. What did she know about his type of work?

The man began approaching, climbing the steps to the terrace at the front of the house.

Catherine took a few steps back in confusion and looked around for the housekeeper to direct the man, but she was entirely alone.

"My lady, I presume?" he smiled as he reached the top of the steps. His mahogany brown hair was dishevelled, and she guessed that the abomination in his hands was a tricorn hat that was well past its time. Catherine almost laughed at his audacity, climbing the front steps of the house like he lived there.

"Have you lost your way, sir?" She finally found her voice.

His eyebrows pinched in confusion. "Pardon?"

"I am not certain what you are accustomed to, but at Oakley, the servants do not carry their mud into the house through the front doors."

This seemed to amuse him and irritated her more.

"The servants' entrance is around back, as you very well know," Catherine declared.

Understanding dawned on his face. He was well and truly caught.

The unknown man smirked and tipped his head in a mock bow, chuckling as he turned back into the rain to return down the steps. No matter how much she respected her aunt for her liberality, Oakley was grounded in tradition. And as such, their servants were not welcome to enter through the front door—no matter the heroics this man might have performed to ensure Lady Rosamund arrived safely that night.

She did not like his manner, nor the way he turned back to stare at her before reaching the ground. The attention was peculiar and unwanted, certainly.

"Tell me your name. I shall have a word with your mistress." She smirked right back. Two could play these games, and Lady Catherine dearly loved to win.

"*You* may call me Lewis."

He smiled, grinning ear to ear in an absurd manner while the rain picked up speed and drenched him right there at the bottom of the terrace.

"*I* shall call you nothing," Catherine chided back.

The nerve of that man!

Catherine moved quickly through the entryway and up the staircase to her bedchamber. She would have to change clothes. She was soaked.

Upon arriving, she saw her reflection in the mirror and thanked the heavens that no one of importance had seen her make such a scene. It was a rare moment when Catherine was not perfectly in control, and the unknown servant had caught her completely unawares with his conduct.

After changing and then finishing a dinner that seemed to drag on for far too long, Catherine was able to excuse herself from joining the ladies in the drawing room and instead visit Lady Rosamund in her chambers. The Sapphire Apartment in the family wing was aptly named, designed to include some of Lady Rosamund's favourite combinations of sumptuous, rich blue fabrics chosen at a warehouse in London.

When Eloise had been taken to bed ill, Lady Barringer had rightly found tasks for Lady Catherine to keep her busy. And as such, Catherine had led the redecoration efforts of the guest room two summers prior.

The renovation had been a labour of love. Catherine always found pleasure in pleasing her aunt and felt a strong pull of connection to her. Lady Rosamund liked to tease that they were close because Lady Catherine now lived in the same apartments that she had also spent her girlhood in. Fate may be a fickle thing, but Catherine always loved that anecdote and imagined the full circle connection they felt was not simply surface level. It was deeper. And Lady Rosamund's reaction at her arrival earlier that night had solidified Catherine's faith in that feeling.

Looking refreshed and very fine, Catherine joined her aunt by the fire to talk.

"How terrible the roads must have been!" Catherine said.

"We had no expectation of rain until we had travelled more than halfway to Oakley. Our drivers argued over a course of ac-tion—one wanting to turn back and the other anxious to move on. In the end, we decided to keep to our plan so we might not cause you all distress."

"Indeed, we were worried!"

"I am certain you were, but as you see, I am well. No harm is done," Lady Rosamund replied kindly.

"I am relieved to hear it. You cannot imagine how much I have anticipated your arrival."

"I am sure I can guess at it. Your father's note left much to be desired in the way of details, my dear. Of course, I understood his urgency, that you are not engaged as we anticipated and that I must take Lady Anne back to Kent. But please, I beg you—tell me what has happened, and do not leave out any particulars."

Catherine explained the events of the last month—from the Darcys' arrival and exit to the younger Mr Darcy's departure as well. She felt her face burn with humiliation when she described the event that took place in the stable. And Lady Rosamund looked equally ill when Catherine described her family's efforts to entice Mr Darcy to remain and propose as planned. The weeks that had passed had not eased any of her discomfort.

"Oh, my darling girl." Lady Rosamund pulled Catherine into a warm hug, and Catherine felt the tension in her shoulders ease at her touch.

"I see why your father wants Anne banned to Kent, but I would rather hear what you want."

"What I want?" No one ever asked Catherine that. "My parents plan to take me to London with great haste and secure a speedy marriage so that my reputation remains intact."

"I imagine that means you will have even less say in the matter. Surely you know the risk of securing a gentleman who is overly eager to find a bride."

The thought had not crossed her mind. She trusted her parents implicitly.

"My father and mother will make the right choice for me. They understand the importance of a marriage partner."

Lady Rosamund looked less than convinced but quickly changed the subject to that of recent happenings in her corner of the world. Catherine had not visited Kent since she was a girl—and only once. Her parents rarely allowed the children to accompany them on their travels. However, one summer when she was a young girl, she and her sisters were taken along and spent a month full in Kent with Lady Rosamund and her second husband, a Mr John Harrowby. Since that time, Lady Rosamund's second husband had died, and she had married and widowed once more. Catherine had never visited Whitmore, the estate her aunt currently owned, that was left to Lady Rosamund by her third husband, Jasper Raleigh.

The stories of her aunt's neighbourhood amused Catherine. It sounded very different from Derbyshire society.

"Thus, when my neighbour learned I had been summoned to Oakley, I was asked to join their travel party. They were already travelling in this direction and had sent ahead for fresh horses and rooms the entire way. And so, it only made good sense that I accompanied my friend north. Now that I have been safely delivered to my family, they shall go on to Manchester for some business dealings there."

"Business dealings! How scandalous." Fitzwilliams did not socialize with the working class.

"Not all landowners rely on only their property for income. It may be hidden from much of good society, but many know the secret to success in England is having your hand in many purses."

Catherine had to wonder about what types of people her aunt called friends, but it would mean nothing to her what strangers in Kent got around to.

CHAPTER EIGHT

After taking her morning meal on a tray in her room, Catherine was very pleased indeed to join the ladies in the drawing room for morning callers. It should not have surprised her that the rain from the day before precluded anyone from visiting, but she still cherished the conversation she had with her aunt.

Unfortunately, the day did not continue on in such an easy fashion. It all began with Reynolds, who was late to prepare her for dinner because "Lady Anne was in such a state" that Reynolds was unable to leave her side.

Catherine came rushing down the staircase at half past five to find that no one remained waiting for her in the drawing room. She supposed that Reynolds's message to the housekeeper to hold dinner had been lost in the business of preparing the meal. Her mother would have her head for her tardiness.

Catherine tried to make herself as small as possible as she entered the dining room. She took her regular seat, across from Ashby, and realized they had company.

Her face reddened with shame.

Luckily, her father had a plan to smooth her way by making introductions.

"Please allow me introduce my daughter, Lady Catherine Fitzwilliam—"

Before her father could continue the introduction, providing Catherine with the name of her father's acquaintance, the guest interrupted the earl.

"We have already had the pleasure of meeting last night upon my arrival to Oakley," he responded kindly.

Catherine turned slowly to the gentleman on her right.

He was smiling at her—all friendliness and a little bit of mischief.

Catherine stared at the stranger and was perplexed.

She regarded his short and wavy brown hair, sharp jaw, and strong shoulders. He wore a dark blue frock coat with a high turned-down collar and wide lapels. A less than fashionable beard was lightly tinged with an auburn hue. His grey eyes danced with mirth.

And then it dawned on her. The man from last night. The man she had assumed was a *servant*. How did he come to be at their dinner table?

She looked frantically to her father for direction, and he looked at her with a question, too, in his own eyes.

She cleared her throat as the recollection of her behaviour the night before unsettled her.

"Erm, Mr Lewis, was it?" she asked desperately.

A gasp from her mother caught her attention, and then she was conscious of being the object of the entire family's notice. Everyone was staring at her.

"Sir Lewis de Bourgh, at your service, my lady." He broke the tension before anyone else could.

The self-same smirk adorned his face—the one from last night. A smile that revealed that he was full of obstinance and recklessness.

But she saw it in a new light now. This man was taunting her! He had had the nerve to ask her to call him *Lewis*. And now he was laughing at her!

Oh, but her blunder was much worse—astronomical! She had accused him of being a servant, sent him back out into the rain, and had watched as he made his way in the direction the carriages had gone.

She stared back at him in horror. What if he told her parents what she had done?

He must have seen the fear in her eyes, for his smile softened and he murmured kindly, "It is lovely to see you again, Lady Catherine."

It felt as if he was throwing her a lifeline.

"And you as well, Sir Lewis." She could not take her eyes from him. His light eyes were in such contrast to his rough exterior.

Lady Rosamund cut the tension with a well-natured explanation that Sir Lewis was her neighbour in Kent. The one Catherine had inferred the night before was a tradesman until her aunt told her that landowners often dabble in other money-making schemes.

A full picture of this gentleman was converging in her mind while her aunt engaged the rest of the table in tales of their travels north. He was addressed as *Sir*, making him a knight or a baronet, and her aunt also mentioned he was a landowner. He looked of an age with her brother, though he did not wear a wig as Ashby did. His hair was unpowdered, a sign of the changing times. And the oiled beard, which was in better shape than the night before, gave him an edge of mystery and cunning.

Catherine quickly observed the table and noted that a wife had not accompanied him. Had he left his family at home? He looked of an age to be married. Most men his age were—or were making attempts to be so.

The earl and countess seemed taken with his easy manner, especially her father. The viscount seemed less intrigued, but then again, he was impressed by few.

Catherine offered very little to the conversation. She was not worthy of it after her performance the night before. And he showed her a kindness by not sharing the truth. Even if he appeared somewhat coarse, he had saved her from additional scrutiny that her fragile heart could not bear.

Catherine awoke early the following morning—a surge of energy pulsing through her knowing she would gather with her family in her mother's private sitting room during the breakfast hour for a "chat."

Fielding questions about the prospects of her future without giving vent to her emotions would be a trial. She had rather find something to distract her until then. Pulling on a simple dress and wrapping her plaited hair into a simple bun at the nape of her neck, she slipped out of her chambers.

The library seemed the best location for a welcome retreat ahead of heavy conversations, and so she let her feet carry her to a room with no judgment and no rules. Reading could be a sanctuary as equally as it could be a diversion—and that was necessary to keep her nerves settled and still.

As her slippered feet arrived at the bottom of the staircase, the front doors opened at the end of the front hall.

Sir Lewis and an unknown man entered while in deep conversation. The gentleman handed off his gloves and hat to the man he entered with, stopping only when he discovered he was not alone.

"Lady Catherine," he said, bowing in an overly exaggerated way, each flourish of his hands displaying his distaste for her haughty behaviour two nights prior.

Should she admonish him for the exaggerated greeting—one fit only for the queen and clearly putting her in her place? Or should she thank him for not telling her father of her ill behaviour?

Sir Lewis dragged his eyes from the gleaming marble floors up to meet Catherine's gaze.

"Good morning, Sir Lewis."

The gentleman crossed the room and stood before her.

"An early riser, are you? I had thought the entire family was still abed."

Catherine could think of nothing to say to that, and the silence between them was heavy. He, with a questionable gleam in his eye, and her, wary of what the gentleman would do next.

"Well, I must take my leave of you, my lady. Please thank the earl and countess for their hospitality. I am off within the hour."

Catherine curtseyed with practiced precision. "Thank you. I shall pass on your kind words."

Imagining the conversation was quite through, Catherine was surprised when he took a few small steps closer to her, leaning in close to her left ear to whisper something she could not hear well enough. He pulled back to meet her gaze with a chuckle—surprised, it seemed, to receive no response from her.

"I cannot hear well on the left, Sir Lewis. Perhaps you might speak more loudly so that all may hear you," Lady Catherine responded tartly, eyeing his servant who awaited Sir Lewis by the doors.

His presumption irritated her. She was not accustomed to telling the truth about her trouble with hearing, but she had no need to protect her reputation with him. He could assume her deaf and blind, and she would be relieved to no longer be forced to communicate with the confounding man.

He smiled softly at her and this time said at a regular volume, "My apologies, my lady. I was saying how gladdened I was to be allowed use of the front door."

Catherine's embarrassment was physical—she felt her cheeks heat, her skin dampen with sweat, and her hands shake. Her ill choices from two nights prior would never be forgotten—by him nor her, it seemed. A resentment unlike she had ever known burned in her, in complete opposition to the smug smile on Sir Lewis's face.

"I wish you safe travels," she responded with gritted teeth and a forced smile, turning to return immediately to her chambers rather than seeking refuge in the library. She wanted to be as far away from Sir Lewis as possible.

She called for her morning meal and continued hiding from their guest until she was certain he had taken his leave.

Later that morning, she joined her family in her mother's private sitting room to finalize details for Anne's removal to Kent and Catherine's precarious trip to London. Why could her mother not just say it—they were gathering to decide the fate of her and Lady Anne.

It became very clear upon entering the room that no one wanted to have the first word. There were uncomfortable, stilted greetings among the family as everyone took a seat.

Lady Ashby and Anne were not present. Strange to think that Lady Anne's future was the object of the discussion, and she was the lone person not allowed to participate.

Lady Barringer was the first to speak. "Anne will go with Rosamund to Kent at the earliest possible date, and I will spend the coming weeks preparing Catherine for her second Season in London. I should like to see if Mr Darcy has had a change of heart once we arrive. With Anne out of the way, hopefully the boy will see reason and propose. That will be much simpler than finding a new groom altogether."

The earl looked less convinced. "I know that you and Mrs Darcy have plans of your own, but you cannot coerce the boy into marriage."

"If the children would only spend additional time together, I am certain all will be well. Mrs Darcy is as committed as I to seeing her son do his duty."

"His duty!" The earl finally erupted. "If the young man knew anything of duty, we would be planning a wedding just now."

"Darcy is an imbecile," Lord Ashby drawled from his comfortable chair in the corner, looking bored as ever. "I cannot imagine why we are still considering this match. I, for one, have lost all respect for the man."

Her brother's opinions were as capricious as ever. Did he not tell Catherine he would ensure that his friend proposed? Why then did he suddenly seem disinterested in her reputation?

"What about Lady Anne? Does not the boy feel more for her? Why are we not considering the match?" Lady Rosamund appeared confounded.

Catherine's mother looked stricken by the comment. "Because she is not yet *out*—our neighbours, society, the greater part of *England* knows of our intentions! What are we to say? That we changed our mind? That we allowed Darcy to select whichever daughter he preferred? That we set Catherine aside? I will not forsake the reputation of one daughter to secure a marriage for the other. It is insupportable."

The earl broke in. "I did not believe we were still contemplating a marriage between Mr Darcy and Catherine. Let us take her to London and find an alternative option. I know many gentlemen of good breeding and status who desire a wife and many others who have sons seeking one. Do you not have any other gentlemen in mind?

Lady Barringer sighed. "I cannot simply write letters to the mothers of the *ton* asking about quality suitors. They will all know something is amiss. The tittle tattle will begin before we even arrive in town. If we are to find a new suitor, we shall have to go about this very carefully and discreetly. It will take much time for me to inquire cautiously, and without rumours beginning, once I am in London. Is it not easier to attempt to change Mr Darcy's mind?"

"Your plans shall make Lady Catherine a spinster before long, mother. This is tedious, indeed. Tell me why you are still putting any faith in Darcy." Irritation pervaded Lord Ashby's voice.

Catherine winced at the mention of her becoming a spinster and brought her eyes to her lap. The cruelty of it!

"Why do I not take Lady Catherine with me to Kent?" Lady Rosamund asked. "Take Lady Anne to London. Host her first Season as planned. Advise the *ton* that Catherine was always to go to Kent for the Season. Host Anne's ball, have her make her curtsey, and tell Darcy to propose after a short but appropriate amount of time. When they remark that they thought it was Lady Catherine who was promised to Mr Darcy, you shall laugh and titter at the absurdity. Ensure they feel it was *they* who remember wrong. Once she is married, I shall bring Lady Catherine home, and you can plan her second Season for next year."

The room was contemplative. A quiet roar of excitement pulsed through Catherine. It was an interesting point. And one that brought her some hope. But it did not resolve the state of her reputation. Society would *know*. Their memories were long, and the whispers of why Mr Darcy married Anne instead of her would haunt Catherine for many years—perhaps even impede her own chances of a good marriage.

"And how do you propose we sustain Lady Catherine's reputation through this ruse of yours?" Lady Barringer asked sharply.

"Ruse of *mine*?" Lady Rosamund's tone was laced with disbelief. "Your suggestion that removing Anne will increase Mr Darcy's affection for Catherine is just as false—and nearly as harmful as rushing her to London for a hasty marriage."

Lady Barringer huffed in frustration.

Lady Rosamund continued, "Perhaps first you require the engagement to Lady Anne. Immediately. Send the earl to Pemberley now and obtain Mr Darcy's agreement. Allow Mr Darcy and Lady Anne a quiet, secret engagement—one that is supported by documentation. This would sustain Anne's reputation, because we all know that servants talk. Ensure they dance together at every ball. He shall make morning calls at Barringer House and send flowers. The *ton* will begin talking of his interest in her on their own. Tell them Lady Catherine is visiting her aunt; or say I am ailing, and she is caring for me—I care not which narrative you share. And then, once Anne has had four weeks in town, you announce the engagement formally."

"It will send Catherine directly into spinsterhood . . . they will still question it. Everyone knows what it means when you send away an eligible daughter for an abbreviated time. It spells scandal," Lady Barringer mumbled. "Not that I ever had great ambitions for the girl."

The comment stung.

Her mother continued. "Even with her large dowry, there will be some who consider her jilted."

"Not if you control the narrative, my dear," her father cut in. He was obviously considering this ruse.

Ashby rose from his seat and mentioned more important business he must attend to than "husband hunting." His disinterest in what became of her injured her pride further.

"We shall all think on this," the earl said. And then he walked over to Catherine and kneeled before her. "I want you to consider these paths—for they are exceptionally different and very significantly affect *your* life. I shall speak to you in my study early tomorrow morning. I will want to hear what you have to say after a good night's rest."

"I am certain Catherine shall do what we think is best. She knows what is owed to her family," Lady Barringer chimed in. And know this, Catherine did.

The earl looked up at his wife, "Nevertheless, I shall hear what her thoughts are on the morrow. And I wish for you to leave her to her own contemplation, wife." Lord Barringer gave the countess a pointed look.

Her mother's pursed lips were the last thing Catherine saw as she excused herself.

Sensing apprehension from the countess, Catherine knew not where to begin when sorting out how she felt about her options. It seemed clear, however, that the option to travel to Kent with Lady Rosamund was not her mother's wish. Likewise, it was not in Catherine's favour to upset the countess.

So, Catherine would be married as quickly as possible. She would go to London soon and continue to pursue Mr Darcy or an alternative precipitous marriage would be arranged by her parents. As Mr Darcy's dependability was imperative to the former scheme, it was easily deduced that the latter, finding a new suitor, would better befit the situation. Unpredictable or not, her brother's new distaste for Mr Darcy raised concerns—not to mention the uneasiness she felt in seeking to marry a gentleman who preferred both of her sisters to her.

She felt some relief that it would be decided in a few short months, perhaps even weeks. She would be a wife by summer and begin the life she had been trained for since her infancy. Who could object to their parents arranging their lives so well?

There had been trepidation, however. It was unlike Catherine to question her mother's abilities, but even the countess seemed to think they could not begin the search for a new suitor in earnest until they arrived in town. And could a man of good breeding and good family and wealth be found so quickly?

In Catherine's first Season, her mother had been so focused on ensuring Eloise welcomed Mr Darcy's advances that she gave no direction to her younger daughter. That liberty had been the envy of all of Catherine's friends. While her acquaintances laboured for gentlemen's attentions, she had paid little heed to her future matrimony.

And yet, not once had she wondered who the gentleman would be that her parents would arrange to marry her. She only knew that choose they would, and that she would be relieved when that decision was revealed.

If her own marriage had never been decided, and it appeared that it had not, Catherine wondered if her mother would indeed have enough time to seek a man as worthy as she had claimed Mr Darcy to be.

The idea that her mother still considered Mr Darcy the best candidate did not improve her faith in this plan. Ever the planner, though, Lady Barringer would make the right decision once they took their place in town.

Catherine wondered what Anne would think of this plan. Did her sister desire to go to Kent, or did she want to marry Mr Darcy? The idea made Catherine's stomach turn. Marrying a man who desired her sister, whose feelings were returned, did not sound pleasing. It felt dreadful. She did not want to be Mrs Darcy, and the realization broke her heart in a way she had never expected.

Could she tell her father that? She had never gone against her mother's wishes—in any aspect of her life.

Her mother's opposition to seeking a new suitor, though, confused her. Was it really that complicated? If the countess found the idea insupportable, it was likely not an excellent choice. The entire business was disorienting.

Lady Rosamund's suggestion that Catherine travel to Kent in Anne's place felt like an option in some obstinance. Would her mother ever forgive her if she voiced an interest in that path? She did not know. The earl paid Catherine quite the compliment in letting her decide—and yet all she found herself considering was how others should perceive her choice.

Was it possible to travel to Kent with Lady Rosamund and find a gentleman of her own choosing? That would impress the countess—overcoming this obstacle without her mother having to lift a finger. And Catherine dearly did love to solve a problem.

The freedom of it was strangely appealing! She let out an excited breath. It was the most daunting—and yet, thrilling—of the selections before her. To her dismay, it was unlikely that Catherine would consider going to Kent. Not really. Not when it could incite resentment from the countess. Could she really forge ahead on her own and choose her own groom? A moment of maniacal excitement flowed through her, and she released a foreign laugh—a brash and persistent cackle that surprised even her. Let Anne go to London and parade around on Mr Darcy's arm! What did she care?

Oh, but care she did. That was the problem.

Perhaps her forbearance would be rewarded. For her part, Catherine dearly hoped so—for whatever choice she made would be the making of her.

"Lady Rosamund said I could go to Kent in Anne's place . . ."

Catherine had asked Lady Ashby to join her while she dressed for dinner. She wanted the truth from her sister by marriage about what the best way forward was.

Catherine let the sentence drag out in the space between them before adding, "And I wonder if I might have a better chance of securing a husband on my own."

Catherine had dismissed Reynolds to avoid any additional gossip reaching the lower floors. In her place, Lady Ashby was putting the finishing touches on Catherine's hair and selecting jewellery.

"Do you?"

"Well, if Anne goes to London and has her come out . . . and if she and Mr Darcy become engaged . . . it was not my idea, it was our aunt's . . . she suggested that perhaps the earl and countess might convince the *ton* that it was Anne all along who was promised to Mr Darcy. And, if they went to London, I could have some time to—to sort through what has happened. A time to . . . explore my options?"

"There are not likely to be many eligible gentlemen in Kent," Lady Ashby said, but Catherine could tell she was considering it. "Most will be in London for the Season, but it might be good practice for you to enjoy some society on your own and converse with other gentlemen outside of the common way."

"Could it truly be a sound choice?"

"Perhaps. But I will remind you, your parents will only tolerate a marriage to someone of your sphere, so you are not to go traipsing about the countryside falling in love with the first farmer who smiles in your direction."

Catherine chuckled. "What a farce!" She batted Elinor's arm as the viscountess threw her hands up feigning innocence.

Lady Ashby whispered conspiratorially, "You know, they call your aunt the black widow of Kent. Thrice widowed, with no children of her own, and wealthier each time . . . No gentleman is safe! We might warn Sir Lewis, the poor man.

"Sir Lewis?"

"Why else would an eligible man chaperone a woman grown on her travels? They are both widowed. Why not? I wonder if it is already a torrid love affair . . ."

"You jest!"

Catherine was shocked by the accusation. Lady Rosamund was likely two decades older than Sir Lewis, but what would she know about what her aunt looked for in a gentleman?

"One would never know," Lady Ashby continued. "They have both been married. People look the other way when a person is widowed. Some of the happiest women I know are widows. No one worries about them going anywhere unchaperoned, and they run their own homes. They answer to no one. No one takes notice of them."

"How could you say such a thing! And who are you implying you answer to, *Viscountess*?"

Lady Ashby looked appalled at Catherine's reaction. "You think I answer to myself? I reside in your *mother's* homes, which I am allowed to remain in because they are my *husband's* parents. What power do you believe I have in the world?"

"But you are a member of the peerage!" It seemed like an empty sentiment when she considered the world the way the viscountess had just described.

"Yes, and I am happy to be a viscountess, and a wife to your brother, and especially delighted to be a sister to you, my dear."

Catherine had always looked up to Lady Ashby, but the past few months had certainly brought them closer together. She felt raw in the face of such affection.

"I too, Lady Ashby."

"Call me Elinor. I insist," she said. "And I know we Fitzwilliams rarely speak of such absurd philosophies like fate, but I feel as if you are on the precipice of something. Finding your voice, perhaps? Follow the path that feels the most correct. And I will ensure that at least your brother supports whatever decision you make."

This was certainly a new page in their friendship. *Elinor.* Could she make this selection for herself?

It was an idea that Catherine had rarely considered. She had never made a decision with such meaningful and possibly lasting consequences. What would it feel like to find one's voice? She would wonder about that comment for days, indeed.

And that little voice inside whispered once again, *run, run, run.* But run where? She would rather not run away from something, but the idea that lit some hope in her belly was that she might be running *to* something.

"First, I have some questions." Catherine sat opposite her father, each of them in a comfortable chair near the fireplace in his study.

"As I would hope you would," the earl responded.

"It has occurred to me in my contemplation that Eloise's partner was chosen for her at such an early age—nearly her infancy. Were there also young gentlemen chosen for Anne and myself?"

"Why do you ask?"

"If such gentlemen exist, why are we not considering them now?"

"Ah, I see—no, Catherine. We did not select husbands for you and Anne. And if we had, you would have known of them for many years. We would not keep that knowledge from you."

"I see," Catherine was disappointed by his answer. It was hard to keep her hands from fidgeting and giving away her anxiousness. "May I . . ." She was uncomfortable questioning her father's reasons.

"Do not be timid now. Ask me what you must know."

"May I know why? Why was a husband chosen for Eloise and not for your other daughters?"

The earl removed his spectacles and set them on a nearby table. He rubbed his furrowed brow. "Mr Darcy was chosen for Eloise because of the close relationship of your mother and Mrs Darcy. They have had it in their heads since they were girls that one day two of their children would marry. When Mr Darcy was born, your mother prayed she would soon birth a daughter. And it took five years from that time for her to have another child at all. When Eloise was born, the ladies were elated and began their plans immediately.

"It has not been a Fitzwilliam habit to make these choices for their children, only I did not see any harm in the scheme. It was a relief to know that one of my children would be taken care of so well. I only hoped we would find such fine matches for you and your sister."

"Oh." She had not realized.

"And of course, I am sure you have uncovered that I was not as motivated to renew the scheme in the wake of Eloise's death. But I could see that continuing the plan—for Mr Darcy to marry you—brought your mother joy after the loss."

"I see."

"You have always been such a devoted daughter, Catherine. Your mother knew you would go along, and when you seemed relieved and open to the idea, it felt as if once again the scheme removed the burden of seeking someone worthy of you."

"But I was not Eloise, was I." It hurt Catherine to admit it.

The earl took her hand in his. "No, you are not. But do not allow that knowledge to sink you. I am not disappointed in you, but with myself. I should never have gone along with this scheme without knowing Mr Darcy was as committed as your mother and her friend. Look at me. This does not define you. Mr Darcy has missed out on a life with a lovely, delightful young lady."

Catherine shrugged a very unladylike shrug. She felt fragile at his kind words.

"Now, are those your only questions?"

"Yes, sir," Lady Catherine responded.

"And what have you decided?"

Was this really happening? Was she truly being offered an opportunity to decide for herself? She took a deep breath and responded with as much confidence as she could pretend, "I should like to go to Kent with Lady Rosamund."

"Good girl."

Catherine gasped. "Was that what you hoped I would say?"

Her father patted her hand and chuckled softly before responding with great feeling, "I hoped you would choose for yourself."

"I think that's it for the morning gowns, my lady," Reynolds said as she closed the second trunk.

They had been packing all afternoon. Apparently, Lady Rosamund was eager to return to Kent. Catherine could not say the same for herself. While it had been her idea, she was not yet certain this was the wisest decision for her future.

"Well, then," Catherine said, "we shall move on to the hats now."

Catherine had a rather substantial collection of large hats, adorned with ribbons and feathers, made of straw and silk. As she began pulling out her favourites to take to Kent, they were interrupted by a soft knock on the servants' door.

A young lady, likely not much older than Catherine herself, entered the room with the housekeeper.

The housekeeper, Mrs Culpepper, explained that the maid was Martha, a servant from the upper floors who had been selected to accompany Catherine to Kent while Jones was away caring for her mother. "Martha has been working with Reynolds to learn more about dressing and hairstyling."

Lady Catherine asked Martha, "Are you packed and ready to depart on the morrow?"

"Yes, my lady."

Hopefully that time spent with Reynolds had been adequate for Martha. Catherine excused them both and returned quickly to the job at hand.

"I must return to Lady Anne shortly, my lady. She is also packing," Reynolds said.

"Is she? I had not heard."

"We are to leave for London in two days' time. She is overjoyed, and I have never been to town myself."

"Well then, it appears that our time to prepare for my travels is shorter, and as such, I require your assistance. You can help my sister tomorrow when I am gone."

It was difficult to hear about Anne's joy. She was angry with her sister. When she had lain awake the night before, considering her father's offer to choose her future, she had felt some guilt for potentially separating Anne from someone she cared about. But on this day, she would quiet that voice in favour of keeping the distance between them. Perhaps one day that would change. But it would not be any time soon.

Catherine took a dinner tray in her room. There was much to oversee before her departure.

It was a surprise, therefore, when she found her mother entering her chambers.

"You are not at dinner?" Catherine asked.

"No. I took a tray as well."

Her mother looked tired. Her sunken cheeks and sharp angles conveyed her distress very easily. Dark circles under her eyes told Catherine that she too had slept little the night before. Was her mother worried for her?

"The earl informed me that you will accompany your aunt to Kent."

"Yes, ma'am."

The hard expression on the countess's face revealed that she did not agree with the decision. And it reminded her of what Lady Ashby had said the night before—about women with true freedom. It appeared that even the Countess of Barringer had been overruled by her husband. Catherine felt guilty for her choice and worried it was the wrong one.

"I came to check that your trunks were ready and to wish you well."

"Thank you."

"And—and to tell you that I shall see you soon. When the Season is over, I expect you back at Oakley for the summer."

The countess looked about the room, nodded her approval that all was in order, and told her she would see her off in the morning.

Her mother had never been one to be emotional. Fitzwilliams never gave way to dramatics.

After she watched her mother go, Catherine sat down on the nearest trunk and beheld her room. She would miss Oakley, but most of all this perfect refuge she had created for herself.

The room felt a flawless reflection of her taste, and yet, she still was thinking about Lady Ashby's comment about finding her voice. Was that what was reflected before her? Was her purpose to discover more about her own style and taste?

If Lady Ashby was implying she needed to discover more about her own wants and desires, she was not certain that was possible. Her sense of self was nowhere to be found and apprehensive when it appeared. Her mother's opinions were buried so deep they had taken root—like the weeds that crawled up the beautiful roses in the gardens at Oakley—and she had no longer any room to thrive as her own person.

Her private self-deprecation only increased her nervousness. And yet, she was heartened by the little voice inside that screamed that she might be meant for more than this life had yet offered her. More than even her mother, perhaps.

Saying "yes" to the unknown—that was why she was going to Kent.

Maybe Elinor was right. Perhaps she was on the precipice of something truly splendid.

CHAPTER NINE

The drive to Kent was thankfully uneventful. Nearly all the innkeepers along the way commented on their great fortune in such decent weather.

On the fifth day of travel, they stopped to change horses at the Bell in a village called Bromley, and Lady Rosamund declared, "This is our last stop, my dear. There are not ten miles left in our journey."

Catherine was relieved. Though they travelled with as much speed and comfort as was possible, her back ached, and she longed to take a rest in her chambers at Whitmore, which surely would be an improvement to the beds she had slept in on the road.

Her aunt had, thankfully, talked little of Mr Darcy, Lady Anne, or the debacle that had led Catherine to this point in her life. They had conversed mostly of the fine weather conditions, the villages and counties they passed through, and of the society she would soon encounter in Kent.

Lady Rosamund had spoken favourably of the local vicar and was already planning a splendid friendship between Lady

Catherine and his daughter, a Miss Virginia Sedgwick. She promised they would take tea with the lady upon their arrival. It sounded as if Miss Sedgwick was crucial to making acquaintances in the area. She was described as a lively girl with many friends and the granddaughter of an earl. Lady Barringer would certainly approve of their acquaintance.

Of course, her aunt also mentioned Sir Lewis when she spoke of local society. Catherine was thankful that the gentleman would be many weeks behind them in returning to Kent. There was no appeal in resuming that acquaintance. The mortification of their first and last encounter would certainly be enough for her lifetime.

During the last few miles of their journey, Lady Rosamund indicated many points of interest along the way: "that lane would take you to the Hawkins estate," "the village of Westerham is where we might do some shopping," and "the village of Hunsford is within walking distance if you pass through Rosings Park." It would be some time, indeed, before she comprehended the neighbourhood.

Whitmore Manor was not precisely what Catherine had expected. A more modest house than the previous estate she had visited in Kent as a child, she thought the home stately in its own right. The property had a short drive, and just as they had turned from the lane, she could see the house appear behind a line of trees. A small garden was situated to the left and a modest stable and some outbuildings sat on the other side of the property.

Catherine espied a well-worn path through the trees that marked the edge of the lawn.

Some servants stepped out of the house as they heard the carriage approaching.

Catherine noticed the young Martha at once among her aunt's people. They had sent one of the carriages ahead to settle their trunks more expediently.

The guest chamber provided to Lady Catherine was well appointed. Not precisely in the same style as she would have chosen for herself, but the warm, cream-coloured paper on the walls and soft lavender fabrics on the bed were welcoming.

After refreshing herself and taking a luxurious and very necessary bath, Catherine joined her aunt in the front room for some tea and refreshments.

The black widow of Kent. This is what they called her. An amusing assertation if she ever heard one! Her aunt was all that was kind and lovely and her home, warm and welcoming.

After some time, Catherine did navigate the conversation to the manor house and her third husband's family. Catherine had not known Mr Raleigh, for the marriage had been a short one.

"Jasper's mother left him this manor. It had been in her family for nearly a century. And when he learned that his illness would not be overcome, he quickly ensured that I would assume ownership of this estate. His elder brothers might have sought to take it for a younger son, but Jasper had promised not to leave me to the earl's care."

"And will the property return to the family one day?"

Lady Rosamund chuckled, "Already wondering after my death, dearest?"

"No!" Catherine nearly choked on her tea. "Of course not. I only wondered if his family still seeks to retain possession of Whitmore."

"No, my dear. My husband ensured it would be wholly mine. He was not threatened as so many other gentlemen are about a woman managing her own property."

It sounded overwhelming. Catherine had never considered being solitary in such a way. She would never want to live alone. It would be much better if her aunt had a son to help carry the burden, would it not?

"Were you not disappointed to never have any children?" Catherine asked.

Lady Rosamund looked startled by the question.

"Pardon me," Catherine apologized. "I should not ask such a personal question of you. I do not know of what I was thinking."

Catherine was sensing she might be becoming much too comfortable around her aunt. She should not repay her aunt's kindness with such rudeness.

"I am not bothered by the question, only amazed that you had the courage to ask it. Good on you."

She laughed heartily when Catherine did not offer a response.

"Well, my first husband imagined we would have many children. It was expected of us. He was a very fine match indeed and required an heir to the Southcott earldom. Henry was disappointed that I was never delivered of a child. His younger brother went on to inherit the earldom. My second husband considered it something of a challenge." Her aunt smiled fondly. "He was a dear man. John and I might have had many children for all our efforts." She laughed at that. "And yet we came to the same results."

Catherine's felt a pang of loss for her aunt. "I remember Mr Harrowby from my visit to Kent as a child," Catherine said. "And your third husband?"

"My third husband was thrilled that I had no offspring and hoped it might remain as such. He was not overly fond of children."

Lady Catherine found her aunt's answers peculiar. Lady Rosamund only mentioned the aspirations of her husbands but never answered whether she had sought to be a mother herself. After all this time, perhaps she was simply resigned to her life as it was. Or perchance, the pain of the question was so significant, and their acquaintance too minor, that she did not feel comfortable divulging such personal thoughts.

Lady Rosamund made good on her promise to introduce Catherine to the parson's daughter on their first morning in Kent. It was a short drive from her aunt's home to the parsonage near Hunsford village. They passed a large, pleasing estate on the way that was surrounded by impressive formal gardens, which could be seen from the lane beyond a hedgerow.

They were directly welcomed into a small parlour in the parsonage by Mrs Sedgwick, who called instantly for her daughter to join them. The room was aptly named the Small Parlour, for it was a quaint space with declining fabrics. The tallow candles within sputtered and smoked, producing an unpleasant odour. Some little attempt at ornamentation had been accomplished, though Catherine had nobler ideas of how the space could be employed to ensure the comfort of company.

At length, Miss Sedgwick joined the ladies. Catherine was immediately impressed by the young lady's style and beauty. Beyond that, she was an entertaining conversationalist, listing out the many events she would accompany Catherine to in the coming months. An assembly was being held in three days' time, in which Miss Sedgwick would introduce Catherine to more of the local society, and once the weather improved, there were many plans for picnics, outings, and card parties hosted by local families. It seemed that while Lady Ashby had voiced a concern for there being very few people not in London this time of year, there would be much to do in this corner of Kent.

"Lady Rosamund told my mother before she travelled north that she planned to bring back her niece, and I was positively impatient to make your acquaintance straight away." Miss Sedgwick addressed Catherine privately once her aunt and Mrs Sedgwick had left the younger ladies to some conversation of their own. "I have travelled very little, and we do not often have newcomers in the neighbourhood. Tell me about Derbyshire. Have you ever been to town? My grandfather, the earl, had promised me a Season in town when I turned eighteen, but since his death, my uncle Robert sees no sense in bringing me out in London when my parents have already given their permission to a local viscount."

Though she asked many questions, Miss Sedgwick rarely left any space in the conversation for Catherine to answer. It was just a well, because she was not used to conversing with someone so new to her acquaintance who made so many personal inquires.

"So, you are engaged?" Catherine finally asked.

"Not as such. Lord Metcalfe has made his intentions clear to my parents and myself, but I told him I require some time to consider."

That was a shocking piece of information. Was the gentleman unsuitable? How fortunate she was to have it all settled! And yet she hesitated. It baffled Catherine.

"If your parents have given permission, he sounds a worthy gentleman."

"Oh, he is!" Miss Sedgwick replied. "Lord Metcalfe is everything a gentleman should be. He lives not five miles from here—he has a lovely property, called Persimmon Park, and it is a charming home. It is only . . . I have not yet experienced much in the world, you see. And so, I would like some time before I marry any gentleman—worthy or not. My father is not in favour of this delay, but Lord Metcalfe is very compassionate. He fancies that I should be happy. And his attention to my pleasure has kept my father from pressing the issue."

If only Catherine could divulge her own experience and warn Miss Sedgwick about her frivolity. Such fanciful ideas the lady had! Having no interest in being honest about why she was in Kent, Catherine offered no advice about marital attachments to her friend. Miss Sedgwick had the admiration of a worthy gentleman and would come into a great fortune upon their marriage. For a parson's daughter, it was beyond what she should hope for. Why would Virginia's parents permit such a hindrance to their daughter's future? Did she not realize the viscount could change his mind? Catherine had never considered delaying an engagement to Mr Darcy. Did ladies do such things?

"A little bit more teasing around the crown of my head, Martha."

Catherine was not surprised that Reynolds's quick education on being a lady's maid before they left Oakley had not produced exemplary results in Martha's knowledge; however, Catherine was not unfamiliar with management. She would condescend to have the girl in hand soon enough.

If only she had some additional time before they departed for the assembly.

Without her mother involved in her preparations, Catherine's tutelage for hair dressing on this day was taking a turn for the more modern. Lady Barringer would cringe, but Catherine wanted to style herself in a way in which she felt would be a more flattering.

With less height, her hair would not add to her already tall stature and would hopefully encourage a less startling first impression on the village. Only a small, local assembly it might be, but Catherine knew the importance of first meetings. If she sought friendships, she would put her best foot forward wherever she might be in attendance.

While Martha attempted to tease her hair into obedience, Catherine continued to push down on the very top of the coiffure. A few more hair pins, and it would be a much more suitable style.

"There now," she continued, "just put this last pin in here." She pointed to a stray curl trying to escape.

The diamond hairpins reminded her of all the many times she had dressed for momentous events in recent years. Here, they would accompany her once again into the unknown.

She waved off the offers to pull out more jewellery in favour of a simple sapphire necklace given to her by her father when she turned sixteen.

Catherine bent at the waist awkwardly, turning this way and that, to better see herself in the small mirror hanging far too low on the wall in her chamber. It would have to do. There was no additional time for fussing.

"You are excused, Martha," Catherine told the girl, as she too exited the room to join her aunt downstairs.

When the ladies arrived at the assembly hall, Catherine felt a wave of discomfort. Though she had understood the event to be open to the village, she had not expected to see so many people of different ranks milling about in front of the building. She could hear the music from the dusty streets and see people spilling out onto a balcony from the first floor of the modest structure. This was certainly not like the balls of the *ton* that she had once attended.

Chin high and skirts held up from the dirty ground, Catherine followed Lady Rosamund into the gathering and up a flight of stairs that opened into a sizable hall. The room was larger than she had guessed from the carriage. She knew not a soul but her aunt and perhaps Miss Sedgwick, if she were even able to find her in such a crush!

Crowded it may be, but it was only moments before Miss Sedgwick found Catherine and whisked her away from her aunt, who encouraged her to have fun with the other young people. Virginia, as Miss Sedgwick requested she call her now, tied a dance card to Catherine's wrist, and they entered the fray.

Her new friend introduced her to two other local ladies, a Miss Emilia Hawkins and a Mrs Diana Bates. Both ladies appeared to be near in age, and all three were anxious to see her introduced to as many people as possible and to see her dance card filled before the first dance began.

When the musicians signalled the beginning of the first set, Catherine was surprised to find that all but two sets had been filled on her card. Not once had she danced so much in one night, and Catherine worried she would never have the energy to keep up! Remembering the names of half the county, she imagined, would not be transpiring any time soon.

When finally she was able to exit the dance floor after four sets back-to-back, she took herself off to the refreshments table to quench her thirst. A servant held out a glass to her, and she drank it in one gulp. It was not very ladylike, but there was no one of importance watching her. She turned to ask for another and found the servant who had served her before had abandoned the table. Looking around for assistance, her eyes met those of a smiling gentleman at her side. She had not yet been introduced—she was sure of it.

The stranger was tall and lean, looming over her with a welcoming smile. He carried himself with a great amount of self-importance, which stood out from the otherwise casual crowd she had been meeting all night.

His smile adjusted slightly, his eyes narrowing upon her form, making her feel faintly like a mouse caught by a kitchen cat—almost predatory in its gleam. His manner of looking upon her was singular. He looked pleased with her, with *all* of her, and her pulse began to race. Gentlemen typically sought her out to attempt a friendship with her lovelier friends or her influential brother—but she recognized this gaze, and it was a first for her to be on the receiving end of it.

"My lady." His polite smile returned. "Shall I serve you another glass of punch?"

She blushed—she was sure of it. Even if she tried to avoid it. She could feel the heat rush to her face and pour down through her chest. He looked her over from head to toe, and a gale of excitement rushed through her body.

"Yes, sir. Thank you," Catherine finally responded.

She handed over her glass.

"Are you the famous Lady Catherine Fitzwilliam everyone is speaking of this evening?"

Embarrassment and unease overcame her. The man paid little heed to who watched his pointed attentions, and she could not help but be emboldened by his confident manner.

Without someone to officially introduce them, it was rather improper for him to state her name in that fashion, but mayhap it was the way of the country.

"I am, sir. And you are?"

"Mr Arthur de Bourgh, my lady."

Oh. "Are you any relation to Sir Lewis?"

"Unfortunately." He chuckled. "Are you acquainted with my cousin? How have we never met?"

"Sir Lewis and I have only just met. He is friends with my aunt, Lady Rosamund Raleigh."

"Oh, of course! You are Lady Rosamund's houseguest. Lovely to meet you."

He reached out a hand, took hers and bowed over it before dropping a kiss just above her wrist. Her eyes likely were bulging out of her skull at his presumption, but for some reason, she did not slap him or bat him away. It was a pleasant change to feel admiration from a gentleman, no matter how frail the acquaintance.

She slowly took back her hand and thanked him for the punch. "I must return to my friends now."

Hastily, Catherine returned to Virginia's side and decisively did not turn back to look at the gentleman after she left him at the refreshments table. Once satisfied that she was well and away from him, she allowed herself a glimpse and found him staring at her across the room.

What was it about the gentlemen in that family that made them stare so!

"Lord Metcalfe could not take his eyes off of you, Virginia!" Miss Hawkins exclaimed the next afternoon as Catherine's new friends gathered in Lady Rosamund's morning room.

"I danced two sets with him! What more does he expect of me?" Virginia responded.

"Welcoming a marriage proposal, I would wager," Mrs Bates responded.

Catherine enjoyed the ladies' casual demeanours when in company with each other. Though she had many she would call friends, most would never share such frank revelations.

Virginia laughed without restraint. Catherine liked that about her. "His attention is all good and well, but you know my thoughts on the matter. Not all of us are as lucky as you, Diana."

Mrs Bates, she had learned, had been married not six months before. She lived with her husband's parents, not five miles from Whitmore. It was a fine match, Virginia had divulged. She and her parents had been in accord when Mr Bates offered for her.

"Diana had great fortune. I should like it to happen for me just the same," Miss Hawkins said. "A handsome man of good family who singles me out over the course of a few months and makes his attentions clear from the start. A short engagement would be in order, followed by a lavish wedding breakfast where you are all in attendance. I should like most of all if I settle in our neighbourhood. Our daughters shall be the dearest of friends one day! After I produce an heir, of course."

"You only want me to accept Lord Metcalfe so that we might always be neighbours, Emilia!" Virginia retorted.

Catherine could not comprehend Virginia's reticence on the matter. If only Mr Darcy had been as attentive as Lord Metcalfe! Not only did he dance two sets with her, but he singled her out multiple times throughout the night. Her new friends had also mentioned that he regularly sent flowers to the parsonage and letters to her parents when he was travelling.

"And why would she not?" Mrs Bates joined in.

"I thought to make my own choice, and it seems Lord Metcalfe has made it for me." Virginia was suddenly serious and had the appearance of some melancholy from the subject.

It was vexing to hear someone complain of such a happy circumstance. Catherine had been so delighted to have the choice made for her. Why would someone want their future left up to fate? Fate was not always a trusted friend, and the aristocracy had little need for serendipity. Virginia would do better to be sent to her uncle, the earl, for a time. Her father had given her much too much independence.

CHAPTER TEN

MARCH 1782

Mornings in Kent were delightful. Both ladies took trays in their chambers, had leisurely meals on their own, and then joined one another in the Morning Room. Lady Rosamund had many friends indeed! They never went a day without callers, and Catherine joined her aunt to return the calls they received. It was busier than life at Oakley, for there were many people of quality in the area. After only a fortnight in Kent, Catherine was feeling overjoyed. It was a much needed respite, even if it did not solve for the problem that was her unsettled future.

One afternoon in March, Martha brought two letters when she came to dress Catherine for dinner.

Barringer House, London
March 8, 1782

My dear Catherine,

I write to inform you that your family arrived safely at Barringer House at half past eleven on the fifth of March. The roads were sufficient and the weather acceptable. Your father joined us on the seventh of March, after a stop at Pemberley. Once his business there was conducted, he followed us to London—and I shall tell you directly, the matter is settled. In preparation for the coming months, we have been to the modiste, the milliners, and the cobblers. Seamstresses have come to Barringer House also to take measurements. Your sister will attend her first ball tomorrow night and make her curtsey in a fortnight. We expect to make a special announcement in early April and host the related event by early June. My escritoire is overrun with invitations that I must attend to, so I will write more at a later date. I have directed Lady Ashby to send you a more complete letter. I am dependent on the post to know you, too, are well. Remember what you owe your family and return directly to us at Oakley in early July.

Your mother,
Lady Barringer

The letter was just as she had expected. The countess only ever wrote to her with the strictest formality and essential information. The next letter was just as her mother had directed: from Lady Ashby and far thicker and more detailed. Lady Catherine set her mother's note aside on a low, polished table next to the comfortable chair she inhabited and tore open the message from Elinor.

Barringer House, London
March 6, 1782

My dearest Catherine,
We arrived safely in London yesterday. I hope your travels were as uneventful as our own. And I am pleased to say that everyone is well and in good health. Your brother has already taken himself off to his club, and I am certain when your father arrives, he shall accompany him as well to do whatever it is that gentlemen of excellent quality do at those institutions. I shall soon follow his lead by departing after the morning meal and making a day of calling on my friends in town. My mother would like to imagine herself the first on my list of calls, but she would be wrong. Perhaps instead I shall deliver her two grandchildren to her and see if that is what she intended when she asked me to call directly upon arrival. What a scene that would be! Nanny Mary manages the boys well, but I can see that it exhausts her. When I visit the nursery, little Richard is growing so strong—much stronger than his older brother Luke at this age. The viscount says it is because he is destined to be a military man, as most second sons of good breeding are. But I also see a softness about him and wonder what he will become. Both boys will surely be happy to see your return to Oakley at the end of summer.

I must confess, you have been much on my mind.

123

While the family planned for your particular future last autumn, pertaining to a certain person who also resides in Derbyshire, I was focused only on being delivered safely of my second child. I will admit to spending most of my days resenting that I was at Oakley. I had dreamed of spending the autumn at the manor in Ramsgate or the townhouse in Bath. But of course, the countess reminded me that sons of Barringer are always to be born at Oakley.

After Richard was born, I kept much to myself. Of course, your brother kept me abreast of some details, but I have to admit, I had no notion to get involved. And, as the countess believes new mothers should not be seen until they are churched, I was left on the outside of most of the discussion as it pertains to you. I say this not to excuse my idleness, but to say that it was not truly until that guest arrived that I realized how little your particular happiness was figured into the decision. I want you to know that a husband can be of your choosing—someone you find very agreeable—and still be blessed and supported by your parents. If not, it is advantageous that you are nearly one and twenty, is it not? Be courageous, my dear. Courage, I am familiar with, am I not? For I will surely stifle my abhorrence as I attend endless musicales and dinner parties over the coming months where I am forced to listen to young ladies debut their talents on pianofortes and harps and the like, all aiming to be proclaimed the most talented young lady in all of England. I shall forbear to not

trip over lost shoe roses at balls and laugh with gen-
uine cheer when the gentlemen of the peerage make
ghastly jokes around dinner tables. Ladies are called
to abstain from opinion and acumen, but it is our
greatest secret, is it not? For we are the levers that
progress society, bending the gentlemen to our will
in our furtive little ways. You have enough pluck
to see yourself through this season of your life. Live
audaciously and listen to that unflinching voice of
hope in your mind. It shall not guide you wrong-
ly. If you will permit me one last request, do write
and tell me about Kent. You may be assured of my
confidentiality and devotion to your happiness and
should not feel you must keep any secrets from me.
You would not thank me for sharing your personal
reflections, and I shall not. You have my word.

March 8, 1782

Your mother has just asked me to pen you a long, de-
tailed letter of the state of our affairs, so I shall finish
this message today and start a new one tomorrow.
Shall I remark on the daily habit of trips to Bond
Street or the ribbons on your sister's new hat? I think
not. You can picture it well, I am sure. I hope I can
say that I have already sufficiently assuaged your
mother's request, though I feel there is little to report
on. Be well, my dear. I wish you every happiness. I
hope this letter finds you in good health and heart. I
miss you dearly.

Yours Affectionately,
Elinor

Catherine held Lady Ashby's letter to her chest. She let the tears that gathered in her eyes fall, for she could feel Elinor's encouragement all these miles away.

Coddling, Elinor Fitzwilliam would never be. But it was pleasing to have her friendship. If only she too were in Kent to better guide and direct Catherine on her prospects.

A card party held at Baldwin Manor some days later found Catherine among her new slew of friends. The ladies were lively when together, and Catherine discovered she enjoyed listening more than talking, as unnatural as it felt. She could not be but thankful to be surrounded by new people during this tumultuous time in her life. Catherine always did feel the bonds of friendship quite deeply.

She had been lately wondering if she might select a husband from those in the area and remove that burden from her parents, but no such young gentleman had caught her eye. Her parents had taught her to be discerning, and so she would be—especially if it came to selecting a husband for herself.

This night found them in the company of a gentleman she had been introduced to at the recent assembly—a Mr Webb. She had been informed that he was the heir to a small estate nearby which brought in only 1,000 pounds per annum; however, his location in this wealthy part of Kent benefited him greatly, situating him with so many people of quality. He was sure to do better finding a wife locally than making an attempt in London, though he would likely not have the means to take a house in town.

Virginia especially seemed to be pleased with Mr Webb. "Tell us, Mr Webb, do you favour card parties or musicales? I am partial to music, but I know how you like to play a trick."

An impressive flirt, she was.

"I do favour cards, as you well know. Will you not partner me for Whist tonight? I see Lord Metcalfe was unable to join us this evening."

"You should be so fortunate," Virginia replied with a cunning smile that revealed her interest in toying with the gentleman. "I would rather remain with my friends, talking, for some time. Will you not join us? We are all good friends, are we not?"

"I would be honoured, Miss Sedgwick."

"Amuse us," Virginia dared Mr Webb. She turned to Catherine to say, "Mr Webb is best known for always having an ear to the greatest *on dit* from town and abroad. He is a great letter writer, with many acquaintances across England."

"I could be compelled to think of something that would entertain you ladies," he promised. "Ah, I have it! I have had a letter from my cousin in Hertfordshire who sends a most scandalous report from his corner of England. The village is all tittering about a full young, talented flirt—of not 16 years—who has recently had her come out."

"Not sixteen? Heaven and earth! Of what are her parents thinking," Catherine responded, aghast.

"You heard me rightly, my lady. She is the daughter of a local solicitor, and very beautiful, if my reports are correct. And—hear this—she is attempting to court the interest of the principal landowner in their vicinity! Indeed, my cousin reports, she thinks very highly of herself, putting herself forward in such a way. But his neighbour, the landowner I speak of, a Mr Bennet, has better sense than to marry her. He is a Cambridge educated gentleman, a bookish sort, if a lackadaisical landlord."

Miss Hawkins gasped. "I wonder if she will be successful!"

"Unfortunately, that is the end of my tale." Mr Webb pouted exaggeratedly.

The gall of the young lady! To try and usurp the gentlewomen in her neighbourhood and attempt to take her place in the gentry. It was a shocking story indeed. Contriving, artful coquetry at such a young age! It had to be a falsity.

"You tease us," Mrs Bates responded to Mr Webb. "I am sure your cousin only writes to entertain you, or you pretend the entire farce in order to provide us some diversion tonight."

Miss Hawkins joined the fray, "It sounds so romantic!"

"Posh!" Mrs Bates responded to Miss Hawkins. "You shall see one day when you find your husband that it is not nearly as romantic as those novels you indulge in. Marriage is a sensible choice, and only a lady of low breeding would attempt to attach herself to such a man as this Mr Bennet. My mother always says, we must understand our place in the world. And she is never wrong."

Catherine agreed with Mrs Bates. It was nice to hear some sense spoken. Her mother sounded lovely.

"It is quite diverting, I think. Fiction or not, I think many ladies like the idea of a little romance." Virginia batted her eyelashes at Mr Webb as she responded. Her expression sparkled with mirth.

Catherine wondered at her new friend. Why, with such a great match nearly settled, would Virginia waste her time flirting with Mr Webb? Catherine was glad Lord Metcalfe was not present to see her performance that night.

Lady Barringer would certainly not approve of this conversation. But Catherine wondered what Lady Ashby would think. She smiled to herself, imagining Lady Ashby at the party. She would be a force to be sure. She would likely be diverted by the conversation but would never sink to participate openly. As such, Catherine would emulate her sister by marriage for the time being. She had little time for such low-brow topics, of course.

The following week, Lady Rosamund took Catherine to the parsonage to take tea with her friends. They had made the arrangements at a party the night before.

As they rode down the lane that would lead to Hunsford, Lady Rosamund pointed to the drive of the estate that they passed regularly on their way to the village, called Rosings Park.

"As I will be in Westerham for much of the day, you can walk back to Whitmore through the grounds of Rosings Park." Her aunt pointed and explained the path she would need to take to return to Whitmore.

Catherine was not fond of walking out of doors. They never had these concerns at Oakley, where many carriages were always at the ready for outings. But Catherine was determined to find her own way forward while she was in Kent, embracing new people and embarking on little adventures.

She knew her sister, Lady Anne, would laugh at such a thought. A walk of some thirty minutes would not seem adventurous to her; but for Catherine, it was unique, and as such, she would accept the task with as much dignity as possible.

"Will not your neighbour be bothered by my trespassing through their gardens?"

Catherine had yet to meet the family that inhabited the great manor. They must be in London, for their house and grounds spoke of significant importance.

"No, my dear! It is Sir Lewis who lives at Rosings." Lady Rosamund smiled and released a small laugh. "As you well know, the gentleman is in the north, and his people will not be disturbed by your presence. They are very accustomed to villagers and the like traipsing about the grounds. They are the loveliest gardens in all of Kent, I should think."

Sir Lewis. Her remembrance of the gentleman was less than positive. Petulant. Insolent. To think that he was the owner of such a property! It nearly took her breath away to consider. She would never have guessed it.

Once the ladies had finished their tea and gossip, Mrs Sedgwick directed one of their maids to accompany Lady Catherine as far as the edge of the park. While her aunt had implied that many people use these paths, Mrs Sedgwick had the good sense to ensure Catherine would not find herself lost on her first walk from their house to her aunt's home.

A canopy of large oaks and sycamores sheltered her shoulders from the sun as she walked quietly down the well-used path. The maid bowed to Lady Catherine when she left her at the edge of the grounds of Rosings. The maid, like Catherine's aunt, pointed in the direction where she might find the path to Whitmore. Her trepidation was great, but she could not let the young scullery maid know. She was meant to set an example for the worthy poor, was she not?

Large hedges banked the perimeter of the woods, opening to a sprawling formal garden. Many people might enjoy a walk through gardens in early spring, viewing new blooms and acknowledging the breaks in the earth which would soon spring stems that would adorn Rosings with life and colour. But not Catherine. She could not take many steps before being assaulted by one flying bug or another. Even with a chill still in the air, the small buzzing beasts had come above ground to take the air, much to her distaste.

It was unladylike to swat at bugs, but no one of importance was in the vicinity. Catherine picked up her skirts and increased her pace.

"My lady!" A voice carried across the grounds.

Catherine turned slowly and took in a gentleman aiming to reach her. Evidently, she had not been alone in the gardens at Rosings Park, for Mr Arthur de Bourgh was approaching her with quick, long strides.

"Mr de Bourgh," Catherine replied with a small curtsey of welcome. She had to turn her face just so to ensure her wide straw hat, set at an angle upon her coiffure, would block the sun.

The gentleman was happy, it seemed, to see her.

"Welcome to Rosings," he said. "What a fine coincidence this is. To what do I owe the pleasure of finding you here?"

Lady Rosamund had clearly forgotten Sir Lewis had a guest when she advised that no one would be at Rosings that day.

"I took tea at the parsonage this afternoon, and I am returning to Whitmore Park."

"Of course. If you will permit me, I shall be happy to escort you to your destination."

Lady Catherine was sensitive of the dangers of spending time with single gentlemen while not chaperoned, but perhaps this was the way of the country. She was nothing if not interested in fitting into the quaint and informal culture of this corner of Kent.

"You may," Catherine replied and turned to resume her walk.

Mr de Bourgh matched her strides and joined her. "It is a beautiful day, is it not? Do you enjoy walking?"

"A little," she replied.

"I find a good walk invigorating."

She murmured her assent, but she was not one to banter long about the weather or topics of disinterest to her. She was obliging, as taught, but offered little in response to his continued comments about the weather, the benefits of walking, and the grandeur that would be the gardens after some weeks. The blooms, he said, were magnificent, and Catherine realized that the gentleman must visit often, for his knowledge and comfort on the grounds were quickly evident.

"And this one," he pointed to a gnarled green stalk that climbed up from the ground, "will hold the lilies that my Aunt de Bourgh used to cultivate herself."

"I see. I am sure they are lovely," Catherine replied, though she had quickly realized the man was no horticulturist. Even for someone who preferred to spend her time indoors, she was able to identify the stalks of a rose bush. She would certainly share this little *on dit* with Lady Ashby, who was sure to laugh at the farce.

"I have such happy memories here from my childhood. De Bourgh does not devote himself like his mother did to the gardens, but the work of my aunt is still evident."

"Who do you mean? I thought Rosings belonged to Sir Lewis."

"Oh—you have caught me out! Yes, of course, he is now Sir Lewis; but I keep forgetting the King knighted him. It was such a simple thing he accomplished that I can never remember! His Majesty has become quite liberal in his knighting just about anyone who does a good deed now and again."

His flippant demeanour shocked her. To speak ill of the King and forget his own cousin's title in one breath—it was astonishing.

Mr de Bourgh must have seen the reproof on Catherine's face, for he immediately apologised and explained that he and his cousin were so close that it had been hard to remember his correct form of address. "In fact, I almost always simply address him as 'cousin.' Please do forgive my mistake."

Catherine considered his appeal but was still not certain he was truly sorry, for he wore a wide grin that matched his cheerful demeanour.

"I am sure it was only that I was so taken with your beauty and thankful for an opportunity to walk with you that I simply have forgotten how to speak."

Her reaction was immediate. A light-headed rush of embarrassment and excitement cascaded through her. She used the wide brim of her hat to shelter her reaction and provide a physical barricade to his overt flattery.

"Please do not tell Ashby of my failure," he said.

The mention of her brother startled her, and she stopped her forward motion. "Pardon me?"

"Your brother and I were great friends at Oxford. I would hate for him to hear about my blunder. Do protect me from a great teasing when next we see one another."

Her brother! The viscount was friends with Mr de Bourgh? What a laugh. She would never picture her staid brother friends with such a flatterer. It brought to mind that she may not know her brother well, and by befriending Mr de Bourgh, she might learn more about Lord Ashby through his loose-lipped friend.

Realizing the viscount would approve of the new friendship, her relief was immediate as their walk continued, and she finally espied the edge of the woods and the chimneys of Whitmore sailing above the trees.

"Thank you for your escort, sir," she said quietly and kept moving at a quick pace.

"It was my great pleasure, Lady Catherine," Mr de Bourgh replied, remaining at the edge of the woods while she continued forward.

She turned back only once, to reassure herself that he was not following her to the house and found him gone. It was a relief to be away from him. From his handsome face to his shocking and flattering words, he truly put her out of countenance in the most wonderful way.

CHAPTER ELEVEN

APRIL 1782

T he whirlwind that was Kent society was almost as exhausting as a Season in London, but much more enjoyable, to
Catherine's mind. Here, she was an illustrious lady of quality,
not only one among a sea of high society ladies.

Early April found Catherine preparing for a dinner at Diana's
house. Diana—Mrs Bates, as she had once called her—was a
nervous wreck the day before. Virginia and Miss Hawkins had
teased her endlessly about her first true dinner party. There
would be exactly nine ladies and nine gentlemen in attendance,
Catherine and Lady Rosamund among them. Catherine should
know, because she had visited to help prepare place cards two
days prior.

Diana lived with her husband's parents, who had gone to
London for two months, and as such, she was delighted to be
hosting her first true society event on her own. Even though she
had been married since the prior Autumn, she had never been
mistress of her own home, and she would not ever be, not until
her father-in-law died.

Married women should endeavour to host quality events for their neighbours, Lady Barringer had always said.

After almost six weeks in Kent, Lady Catherine had worn nearly every gown she had brought with her, with the exception of two that she was reserving for only the highest quality events—none of which would likely be held in Kent. And so, she had Martha retrieve one of her favourites for the occasion due to its flattering shape. She was in good looks that night, no doubt due to Martha's ongoing tutelage. Her new maid was indeed a quick learner, and Catherine hated to admit it, but her hair was looking better than even Jones was capable of.

It was a fine evening, the stars bright in the sky and nary a chill in the air. It was warm for early April. Catherine would know, because she had taken herself off to a balcony to escape the attention of Sir Lewis.

She knew of his return to Kent, but tonight was the first time she had seen the man since Derbyshire. Since it had been many weeks, she had put him out of her mind. But she could not deny that he disturbed her. If only it had been Mr de Bourgh invited instead.

Catherine had seen that gentleman many times on her walks in the gardens at Rosings Park, and each conversation left her feeling more and more partial to his flattering words and attentive nature. It was a pity that Diana had not mentioned his name when selecting her guests.

Catherine had been watching Sir Lewis with great care, lest she be found out. He brought out her curiosity. She had nearly succeeded in concealing her observation when, at liberty to look in his direction once again, she found him staring back at her.

Upon later reflection, it was best if she kept her eyes to herself—though she could not deny that she found him such a peculiar character!

He stood out in a crowd, with a crude sense of style and a casual manner that made her intensely intrigued. He did not behave like the other gentry; he was harsh and bold, with a laugh that nearly shook the table during dinner. But no one else seemed to find his manners crass, they simply tittered along with his revelry. He was an entertaining conversationalist, putting everyone around him at ease, with the exception of her.

Catherine was not simply hiding from Sir Lewis; she was also avoiding sitting at the pianoforte. When you tell people that you play "a little" so often, there is a danger that you may be asked to perform. Most of the ladies in attendance had taken a turn on the instrument in the last hour, and Catherine was biding her time now until tables were pulled out for cards or until such a time as her aunt called for their carriage.

The notes of a familiar song drew Catherine's attention to the opening French doors, and she found her friend Diana was joining her outside.

"Are you not cold?" Diana inquired.

"Not at all. It is a mild night; do you not agree?"

"Yes, of course," she replied. "Are you well? I worry when I find one of my guests all alone outside. Is there anything I can get you presently?"

"No, it is only that I enjoy being out of doors." Diana looked surprised by that, and she should, because it was a blatant lie built into her foundation, stone by stone, by a mother who expected her to be agreeable at all times. "I only needed some fresh air. Let us join the others."

"Well, now that we are alone, I would be happy if you would remain for a moment." Diana looked up at the sky and sighed. "Do you think the party is going well?"

"It is splendid, my friend! You need not worry. The table was masterfully set, the food appealing and diverse, and now the entertainment is just as it should be. Congratulations."

Diana blushed, but she had to know it was going well. Everyone was in such good spirits that night. "Mr Bates said as much, but he is often thoughtful in that way."

"He seems a fine gentleman, Diana. You are a fortunate lady to have found such a husband."

"You are correct," Diana responded, grasping at Catherine's elbow to lead her back inside. "Oh, and Virginia has invited us all for tea at the parsonage on the morrow. She wants to review every minute of the evening in great detail."

The ladies both laughed at that. Virginia always wanted to know all the particulars. If only Catherine could be so lucky as Diana. Her marriage was just as it should be, and the manner of marital harmony was what she hoped to one day find for herself.

The next day, after the ladies had swapped accounts of the prior evening, drank their fill of afternoon tea, and ate far too much seed cake, Catherine took herself back to Whitmore. She told Mrs Sedgwick that a maid need not accompany her, for she knew the way by heart now.

Catherine came upon Mr de Bourgh almost immediately. She had not seen him in many days, and it excited her.

"Were you out enjoying a walk, sir?" Catherine asked as he came to saunter beside her.

"I was overseeing some crop and livestock management on the estate as well as some contractual disagreements with the local farmers. There is always much to do."

"Does not Sir Lewis employ a steward for such things?"

Mr de Bourgh smiled sadly, "If only the man were to be fully trusted, my cousin would not need to call me to Kent so frequently. Besides, I am his heir. It is important I understand the responsibilities of landownership."

"Where do you hail from?" Catherine asked.

"Originally, my branch of the family is from Sussex, outside of Brighton. Are you familiar with the area?"

"I have heard of it."

"I imagine you enjoy the sea." He raised his eyebrows with curiosity.

"And why would you think that?" He was exceptionally wrong, but nevertheless, she wanted to hear his answer.

"Most ladies do, do they not? There is always so much to do in Brighton! Dancing and parties every night. Not so dull as the countryside."

Catherine thought the idea funny. She had never been so entertained as she had been in Kent.

"I can picture it now—you, walking along the beach, the wind blowing through your hair—it would be breathtaking to behold." He looked at her with suggestive, narrowed eyes. Her heart was beating faster, and her breath came more quickly.

Catherine was no accomplished flirt, but she could see right through his empty flattery, and she could hardly believe how much she enjoyed it.

He knew her preferences not at all, and yet, she enjoyed hearing his constant stream of obsequiousness. It felt lovely indeed.

An unknown man followed them, calling out to Mr de Bourgh.

"Ah, you see," he said with an exaggerated sigh. "Here comes Mr Barnes, the steward, now. You must excuse me."

While she found his attention pleasing, she was relieved to be leaving him at the edge of Rosing Park's grounds. She hardly knew how to behave around him, and it unsettled her in the best way.

With no small amount of excitement, Catherine fussed with her gloves and patted her hair into place while she and her aunt rode to a card party later in the week.

The carriage moved swiftly through the dark, carrying them to the Fuller's estate.

"Have I met Mrs Fuller?" Catherine asked her aunt.

"I am not certain. Her son, Mr Barrett Fuller, is likely the true host. But a gentleman cannot send invitations and host a party on his own, now can he?"

"I have heard of him," Catherine murmured. She did not tell her aunt that it was Mr de Bourgh who had mentioned the gentleman to her.

She had not been able to ask Diana to invite Mr de Bourgh to her event. It would have been too forward a request, indeed; but Mr Fuller was sure to invite him.

The Sedgwicks were the first family they found when they arrived, standing near to Sir Lewis and Lady Tilbury, a kindly widow who lived nearer to the village. Sir Lewis dragged his eyes from Lady Rosamund to greet Catherine. Though his greeting was all that was formal, a rogue glint in his eyes set her pulse skittering for an escape from his attention. Pulling on Virginia's arm, Catherine gently guided her friend away from the small crowd of neighbours and towards the tables that had been set for play.

All night, Catherine looked about the crowded rooms for Mr de Bourgh. When not playing Quadrille or Picquet, she was feigning interest in the people filling each room.

At last, her wish came true, as she espied him across the corridor, near the door of the salon. He was apart from the regular guests, appearing to have only arrived at this late hour.

"Mr de Bourgh," Catherine welcomed the gentleman with a curtsey.

"My lady," he said as he gathered one of her hands in his own and laid a kiss on her gloved knuckles. "I am sorry to arrive late. Have I missed all the fun?"

He grinned from ear to ear. This man made his own fun, she imagined.

"No sir, I was just about to sit down for another game."

She quickly invited him to help make up her pool of Quadrille. Mr and Mrs Bates joined them at the table. Mr de Bourgh's marked attention was a delight after years of being overlooked by the gentlemen of her acquaintance. Mrs Bates seemed to take no notice, however; her face was serious the entire game, focused only on her cards and her next trick. While it was a game where one played for oneself, Mrs Bates frequently called her husband into an alliance to prevent the others at the table from winning. In response, Mr de Bourgh would send a competitive expression in Catherine's direction, sending her heart aflutter at his generosity of spirit. She did enjoy winning.

Mr de Bourgh began a sort of secret language, nudging Catherine's elbow discreetly when he had the highest card or highest trump. In response, Catherine would play a card of lesser importance when it was her turn so he might win the trick. His smile was addictive, and she sought to keep impressing him and gaining his favour slyly through the gameplay.

Some hours later, their host served a supper for all in attendance. After many hours of imbibing and heated game play, the meal was much needed.

"Come sit here with me," Lady Rosamund called Catherine over.

To her great disdain, Sir Lewis joined her on her right.

"Enjoying your evening?" He asked her, once they had filled their plates.

"Is it still evening, sir?" She had no interest in empty banter with her least favourite neighbour.

He chuckled at her combativeness. "It is nearly midnight, my lady."

"And yes, I am enjoying myself. I do love card games." Her tone was dripping with haughtiness.

"Do you? I might have guessed otherwise."

Annoying man. "And why is that?"

"I observed you most carefully tonight," he said. "It would be a stretch to say that a lady who loses on purpose enjoys playing cards."

"I beg your pardon. I certainly do *not* lose on purpose."

Catherine grunted a very unladylike grunt. And her aunt quit her conversation with her neighbour to ask after her well-being.

Catherine responded that all was well and turned back to Sir Lewis with a reproving expression.

He seemed amused by the disruption of her pleasure. It had been such a lovely night. Why did this man seem to be waiting for a moment to pounce on her fun.

"I was surprised to see you playing cards with my cousin," Sir Lewis pointedly said to Lady Catherine.

"And why is that?" Lady Catherine realized she had raised her voice once again and moderated it as she continued, "The Fullers are generous to invite most of their neighbours."

"I hope he has not imposed himself upon your kindness."

What a vulgar thing to say about a lady! And his cousin, no less. His roguish smile increased her ire. No wonder she thought him a footman the first time she laid eyes on him. Mr de Bourgh should be relieved to know that he will take on Rosings one day. The current master was mad!

"Of course he has not. Mr de Bourgh is a gentleman!"

"Would a gentleman entice a young lady to play poorly so he might win a few shillings?"

Nettlesome man.

"Nothing to say to that, Lady Catherine?" Sir Lewis purred.

Abruptly, she felt his breath near to her right ear. "I have seen you win. It is obvious it brings you joy. Do not feign ignorance for a foolish gentleman who is undeserving of your attention. Win, my lady."

And with that, he stood from his chair and left the table.

Barringer House, London
April 10, 1782

My dearest Catherine,
I enjoyed your last letter immensely. What charac-
ters you have met in Kent! I especially would like
to meet a few of the gentlemen you have mentioned.
Would that I could be spirited away from town and
join you for a time. But, alas, you know your mother
expects me here. I am happy to report that the family
is well, and all are healthy. I apologise that it has
been more than a week since my last letter. I am
woefully behind in my correspondence. As you know
from your mother's last note, your sister made her
curtsey, and your mother hosted a ball in her honour.
It has been no great secret to the ton *that one par-*
ticular gentleman has intentions for your sister. We
have explained how grateful we are that you have
travelled to Kent to your dear aunt Lady Rosamund
given that she was in low spirits. Many remark upon
your absence and quickly applaud you for being the
most thoughtful girl in all of England for sacrificing
your Season in town. You are a hero, my dear! The
gentleman from Derbyshire calls each day and sends
flowers regularly. There can be no question as to his
intentions. It has been decided that an announce-
ment will be made among family and close friends
in the coming week, and then of course, the news will
be carried more broadly. Your mother plans to host
the resulting significant event in mid-June. I only re-
gret that it will require a longer stay in London than

I had previously hoped. I may send Nanny Mary back to Oakley with my sons before June. They are rather confined here in town, and Barringer House feels much smaller when two little boisterous boys are making noise at all hours. I applaud your courage and openness, my dear. I fear you are having much more fun than I. Please do continue to write, and do not hold back in your next letter. I expect each and every detail so that I might live vicariously through you. Please be well, and send news of good health and prosperity.

Affectionately yours,
Elinor

Catherine set down the letter. A hero, Elinor may claim her to be, but the idea of the false narrative being talked about in drawing rooms and salons across London put Catherine immediately out of countenance. The encouragement from Lady Ashby would not assuage her fear that her absence this Season would follow her for the rest of her days. Just as she was warned before she left Oakley, adept gentry would know it was a farce and would assume the worst. Whispers were likely filling the halls of town each day with talk about her—presuming her a ruined daughter or a scandal monger. Fine daughters were not sent away, and the *ton* was practiced and clever when it came to secrets. Though on occasion well meaning, they were never kept long.

CHAPTER TWELVE

S itting in the Sedgwick parlour some days later, Catherine
found it hard to focus on the latest *on dit*. It was difficult
to join her friends' debate about hat sizes when she could only
concentrate on her doubts about her reputation being intact.

"Sir Lewis said my new hat was very unique at yesterday's
garden party," Emilia said, blushing. Miss Hawkins had lately
invited Catherine to use her Christian name, Emilia. She felt
some guilt knowing she would never invite them to do the same.
Her mother would abhor it.

Virginia tittered. "And unique it is, my dear. Not many hats
require the wearer to move with such delicacy. I imagine the
gentlemen were taking great care not to get tangled up in the
ostrich feathers at your approach!"

"You jest!" Emilia pouted. "You told me you loved that hat.
You said the feathers were elegant! The milliner said it was very
modish in London this year."

"I liked the feathers just fine," Diana spoke up. "Do not listen
to Virginia. She only seeks to badger you because she is jealous of
your new collection—especially the gold wool felt and the one

made of beaver fur, for they are so large! You shall have to tease your hair to the heavens to hold up those new master-pieces."

Emilia blushed. Her mother had taken her to London for a few days of shopping, and the ladies could speak of naught but her new wardrobe. Catherine, for one, was jealous of the new *redingote* Emilia brought home with her, made of a stunning green silk with a matching striped skirt.

"I am sure Sir Lewis was overcome with admiration," Virginia conceded. "Now, let us change the subject."

"Or he was teasing you, as the officious man likes to do," Catherine murmured under her breath.

It took a moment of silence for Catherine to realize the other ladies had heard her snide comment. The silence was deafening as she took in their expressions of shock.

"Pardon?" Emilia looked stricken.

Diana spoke at nearly the same time, "Officious? But he is always so obliging."

Virginia only looked at Catherine in confusion.

"Pardon me, Emilia. I am sure he liked your hat," Catherine aimed to decrease their attention on her. "It is only—only that the man seems to have a satirical side to him."

The ladies looked at her with more uncertainty.

"But he is so helpful and kind!" Diana argued.

"And handsome! All the ladies think so," Emilia chimed in.

"If he is such a catch, why is the gentleman not married?" Catherine retorted.

Virginia was quick to answer, "He is a widower! He must be heartbroken over the loss of his wife. She was a very beautiful woman. Almost everyone remarked upon it. And she had a fabulous fortune."

Diana leaned in conspiratorially, "My parents tried every-thing they could to put me before Sir Lewis when I had my debut, but he showed no interest in me or any other local ladies. I was so relieved when it was Mr Bates who went to my parents with his intentions. Sir Lewis is rather intimidating, is he not?"

Intimidating? The man was absurd. Why were all these ladies fawning over the man? The only benefit of an attach-ment to Sir Lewis would be his fine property.

Virginia joined in, "My father often remarks that he is quite devoted to the arts and education."

Catherine could not remain silent on the subject. She did not like that he was able to worm his way into the hearts and minds of all the villagers when it was so clear to her that he was a menace. "It seems to me that the only constant object of his devotion is himself."

An immediate rush of shame ran through her. It was unlike her to be so frank, and she could only blame the gentleman in question for her flippant comments. No one irritated her as he did.

Before she could work herself into a state of distress over her loose tongue, Catherine thought it best to excuse her-self and return to Whitmore. She no longer requested the carriage, whether or not Lady Rosamund was using it. She was accustomed to making the trip on foot now, and so she would continue. She did not like to admit it to herself, but it was nearly a certainty that her ongoing walks were in the slim hope of seeing Mr de Bourgh.

Unfortunately, on this day, fate would appear to be laugh-ing at her—or punishing her, rather—for it was Sir Lewis she found as she walked through the park at Rosings.

At seeing her, he began approaching across his lawn with two large hunting dogs at his side.

"Good day, Lady Catherine," Sir Lewis greeted her.

"Good day to you, too, sir," Catherine responded in kind, keeping her distance from the animals.

"Do you like dogs?"

"Of course, I do," Catherine replied, while attempting an awkward dance around the creatures to keep them away from her skirts.

"This one is Beatrice and this one, Benedick." He pointed to the dogs, but Catherine paid them no mind.

She backed away and forced a polite smile at Sir Lewis. "Lovely names."

He chuckled and beamed a devilish smile in her direction. What nerve!

"Sit," he commanded. The creatures halted immediately and obeyed their master. He looked her over and said very seriously, "You do not like dogs."

"Pray, what is the meaning—"

"You do not like dogs." He spoke more slowly as if she were a small child.

Catherine's defences rose at his challenge.

"I heard you the first time—it is only, I do not know why you would say such a thing."

"Why do you lie about your preferences?" he asked.

"Are you implying that I mean to deceive you?"

"Not on the whole." He laughed. "However, you do seem predisposed to giving people the answer you believe they will prefer."

What an affront! "Sir, I beg you to stop this line of conversation now."

"Or what? You will be angry that I asked you to be truthful with me?"

Catherine bristled. This man never quit.

"Fine," she admitted, sighing in resignation. "I do not like dogs. There. Does that appease you?"

"You have my thanks." If possible, his smile grew. "I appreciate your honesty. You should try it more often."

"While you have proven yourself correct in this *one* instance, I demand an apology for labelling me a liar."

"I did no such thing. Do you not lie about your preferences? When Mr Hunter asked you if you enjoyed long walks in the peaks, what did you say? Or how about when I heard you agree with Miss Hawkins that her hat could in fact be larger? Or what about the time I overheard you tell Lady Tilbury that you favoured embroidery?"

She had never in her life felt such an affront on her character! She was not a liar. She was simply helping along conversation. It was polite to agree, but she never made-up stories about great hikes in the peaks or pulled out embroidery that was not her own and took credit. That is what a liar would do. And how could he know so much?

"Are you following me, sir?" She asked impertinently. "Do you hide behind the shrubberies to ascertain my preferences?"

"I do not follow you, Lady Catherine. I simply pay attention. And you have a tell."

"A tell?"

"A tell is what men who gamble call a change in behaviour that gives away the truth of things." He walked more closely to her, leaving his well-behaved dogs behind, and reached his hand up to her face, "May I?"

Catherine froze and nodded quickly. He ran his finger in a line from the top of her forehead to the top of her nose. Her entire body reacted to the attention. Every part of her being focused on the touch of his ungloved hand upon her skin.

"You crease your forehead." He ran his finger back up the same line, "—just here."

Her breath was coming short and her heart beating more quickly. She cleared her throat, and he broke the contact.

"And how have you ascertained that when my forehead, erm, *creases*, as you say, that I am lying?"

"Because I am observant. It is almost as if you consider what you should prefer to say before you give your answer." He still stood close to her. Near enough that she could reach out and touch him. "And I would dearly like to know what you really feel, rather than what you think I want to hear."

She had no answer for that. A lifetime of training had beaten her own feelings out of her mouth.

He leaned into her personal space, tipping his head to the side in curiosity. His eyes watched her intently. "Do you like dogs, Lady Catherine?"

"No, I do not. They are dirty, and I assume they carry diseases, and they make a mess of polished floors and hemlines. No matter how behaved, I cannot countenance animals permitted inside homes." Unburdening her true thoughts came rather more easily and more thoroughly than she would have assumed.

He laughed uproariously at that. "That is what I thought. Good day, my lady." At that, he tipped his hat and took his dogs in the other direction.

Catherine could not leave the grounds of Rosings fast enough. The presumption! That base miscreant!

She could not decide if she felt relief or anger at his performance. The nerve of that man!

Though, it felt rather freeing to speak the truth. To actually speak her mind and not receive judgment or redirection in return was remarkable.

When she arrived back at Whitmore, she was surprised to find Mr de Bourgh speaking to Harold, her aunt's coachman.

The men were in deep conversation until Catherine cleared her throat. She could not very well pass the stables and not acknowledge an acquaintance, could she?

"My lady! What a surprise." Mr de Bourgh approached her with a welcoming smile.

Indeed, this is how a gentleman should behave.

"A surprise to find me at Whitmore? I should think it rather the opposite. What business finds you at our stables today?"

Mr de Bourgh's smile dropped momentarily but quickly recovered. "Just a little business with some local farmers—a dispute, you see. Nothing I would want to bother you with."

"I thank you," Catherine replied, however much she would have liked to hear of it. Nothing was below her attention if it meant settling a squabble for her dear aunt.

"Shall I escort you home?"

"As you see, I have already reached my destination sir," she responded with a small chuckle. "Would you like to come inside for some refreshment? I am certain Lady Rosamund would like to greet you."

"Thank you, no. I am sorry to say that I cannot stay," he replied and then spoke more softly. "I have missed our walks of late. Perhaps I shall see you when next you walk through the gardens at Rosings."

She hung on his every word. He too enjoyed their walks and had missed her! "Thank you. I hope to see you soon, as well." "Good day!"

She nodded in his direction but had to force herself to look the other way for fear that he would see the silly grin upon her face. That gentleman was able to lift her spirits so quickly after his cousin had insulted her pride. It was like whiplash—going from one de Bourgh gentleman to the next.

"What does Lady Ashby say in her latest?" Lady Rosamund indicated the letter that Catherine had been devouring for some time.

"Anne and Mr Darcy are engaged."

Her aunt set down her teacup and did not give herself the trouble of concealing her pity. "How do you find the news?"

Catherine breathed deeply. "It was a matter of course, Aunt."

It was a nuisance, her grief over her sister's betrayal.

Catherine was decided. Rather than speak of Anne, she would prefer to finally get some answers about her odious neighbour than continue the course of their current conversation. It would certainly be a distraction from the self-ridicule that currently resided in her mind.

If Sir Lewis was going to have such an understanding of her, it only followed that she too should have as much information as possible about him. And for reasons she would not like to ponder too deeply, she could not dislodge the gentleman from her thoughts.

It was a delicate thing, asking about a man. Even with all the trust between herself and Lady Rosamund, she did not want to betray her true feelings for Sir Lewis, nor did she want her aunt thinking she might admire him.

"I came upon Sir Lewis on my walk back to Whitmore today," Catherine remarked.

"Did you?" Lady Rosamund smiled over her wine glass.

"He was walking with his hunters."

"It was a lovely day for it, I suppose. Though I know little about dogs."

"Was his wife a friend of yours before she died?" Catherine asked carefully.

"No, I never knew her. She was already gone before I moved to this part of Kent. I have heard she was a beautiful woman from a very good family. It was a prosperous match."

Catherine wondered at that. Who was this paramour?

"He was a second son. Did you know that?" Her aunt interrupted her thoughts.

"No! I had not heard."

"Yes, he was not the heir to Rosings. His parents chose his wife for her fortune because of his expectation of a military career. The death of his elder brother was unexpected, not unlike the loss of Eloise."

"I am sorry to hear it." And Catherine truly was.

"He returned home to care for Rosings, and it was during his first year of landownership that his wife died. I was not here at the time, but he lost both his brother and wife in under a year. Most of our neighbours did not know her well, for they were in mourning during their time at Rosings. I believe they made their home in London before coming to Kent, but I am not certain."

"What a tragedy. To lose your brother and wife in such quick succession!"

Catherine felt some guilt for her anger towards Sir Lewis. The man did deserve some compassion after all.

"Yes, it was a great misfortune, but no one would accuse Sir Lewis of being conquered by his melancholy. To know him now, you would never suspect it."

Catherine had to control the urge to roll her eyes. No indeed, she would never have called the gentleman melancholic. She would rather call him a pest.

"And his knighthood?"

"I have never asked directly. I was told it was granted to him in response to a heroic act while serving in the military."

Perhaps the gentleman was more worldly than she had first perceived.

The next week found Catherine at Virginia's home nearly every afternoon. She wondered at the ladies' preferences for meeting at the parsonage so often, but it did offer a slim chance of seeing Mr de Bourgh, and so she continued to agree to their afternoon teas.

Unfortunately, she saw Sir Lewis as frequently as she saw Mr de Bourgh.

On Monday, Sir Lewis came upon her, teasing her endlessly by asking her questions about her preferences. And she gave the honesty he requested.

"What think you of the gardens at Rosings?"

"The formal gardens are just as they should be, but I think some additional hedges near the lane would offer more structure."

"My steward thinks we should replace our outbuildings and stables. What say you?" He asked her.

"Maintaining the integrity of all structures on your property is a sound way to invest in the estate and the community."

And even more ridiculous, in the next breath, he asked, "Would you serve venison or duck when hosting a guest?"

"I would learn of their preferences first."

Strange man, indeed. Why he continued to pepper her with questions, she would never know.

On Tuesday, however, she was fortunate to discover Mr de Bourgh.

She felt a rush of excitement to find him not only on the grounds of Rosings, but she could almost guess that he had the appearance of having waited for her, as she found him lingering nearest to the path that came from the parsonage. She felt a rush of excitement knowing he might be paying close attention to her schedule in order to find some time to walk with her. Once they had dispensed with the necessary pleasantries, his good spirits raised her own as he escorted her to Whitmore, as he had before.

"It is so nice to spend time out of doors with a lady who so appreciates nature."

He was amiable as ever, but she felt a twinge of guilt for never telling him any truths about her preferences. Damn Sir Lewis for planting such thoughts in her head!

"Thank you, sir. The weather is very fine today."

"It is an excellent day, indeed." He smiled, and she felt her pulse race.

She could sense that he was going to say more, but they were interrupted by his cousin who was approaching them and calling their names as he came down the front steps of the house. "Lady Catherine! Arthur!"

Mr de Bourgh leaned in to whisper quickly, "I am afraid that I shall have to abandon you, my lady. As you see, my cousin is doubtful to be pleased to see me not tending to our business. I shall leave you before I hear his thoughts on my delinquencies, but I shall wish you a good day and hope to see you soon."

He was gone before she could tell him to forget his cousin altogether. He did not *work* for Sir Lewis. He was a gentleman!

"Pardon me, my lady. Where has my cousin run off to so quickly?" Sir Lewis asked.

"I am certain I do not know, sir." Catherine kept her gaze on the path and did not slow her pace for Sir Lewis.

"Shall I escort you home?" Sir Lewis joined her in the direction she was already walking.

"That will be unnecessary. I know the way."

"As you wish," he replied and bowed, turning his boots in the opposite direction.

And with that, he let her go.

On Wednesday, Mr de Bourgh and Catherine were not interrupted by Sir Lewis but by a gardener who said the gentleman was needed in the manor house. After informing the servant that he was more than aware of his duties, they spoke of the upcoming assembly, a picnic planned for some days later, and a private ball at the end of the month at Persimmon Park.

Why could not the gentlemen in London have been this easy to converse with? How much more productive her first Season would have been if Mr de Bourgh had been present—with her brother's friendship with him and his being the heir to such a grand property in Kent. Her mother surely would have been overjoyed to find such a gentleman showing interest in her.

Perhaps this is what Lady Ashby meant when she encouraged her to be happy—she could see it clearly, marrying Mr de Bourgh. Her parents would be so pleased with her choice, and she would see the earl and countess often when they visited London, until such a time as they took over the responsibility of Rosings; though it appeared Sir Lewis had much need of Mr de Bourgh's assistance, and they would be often in Kent, with her dear aunt nearby.

Unlike Virginia, Catherine had no desire to go against the earl and countess's wishes. But if she could do it on her own, that would be the accomplishment of her lifetime. Women could not pursue men overtly—but she could discreetly put herself forward as she had been taught, holding tightly to her mother's teachings, and find victory on her own. What a lark that would be!

On Thursday, it was Sir Lewis she found waiting for her.

"Do you make it a habit of walking the grounds of Rosings each day, my lady?" Sir Lewis asked.

"You know I am coming from the parsonage and only seek to provoke me, sir."

Catherine did not stop her progress as she moved through the formal gardens and walked towards the woodland that bordered Whitmore.

"Does not your aunt have a carriage at your disposal?"

"I am perfectly capable of walking," Catherine replied.

"But you do not favour the outdoors. Anyone who has paid you any little attention has noticed such."

"Are you banning me from your property, sir?" She did not turn to see his reaction.

"Until such a time as you give me a reason to, I would never do such a thing."

"You sound resolute that I shall give you a reason. Do you think so little of me?"

"You twist my words, my lady."

She peaked under the wide brim of her hat to catch his expression. He looked pleased rather than irritated.

"I do not, and you know I do not."

Such an ogre of a man! Everyone found him so obliging and helpful, but she knew the truth. He was sinister and sneaky—always waiting to bait her on her walk home from a parsonage, no less! Why could the man not simply be serious? And why could she not have seen his cousin instead?

"Why do you tease me so? Can you not simply let me pass through the grounds without following me with your absurd questions and poking holes in my character?"

"I would never deny your excellent character, I only mean to display how much I applaud frankness in ladies of good character."

"Well, frankness you have received. Have you not?" She stopped and turned back to face him.

Seeing him just there, standing over her, broody and staid, she wondered why his typical snarky grin was missing.

"Are we finished, sir?" she asked, her voice laced with a haughtiness she rarely displayed.

"Quite finished." And he turned to go.

Surprisingly, she felt his loss in an almost physical way. Her body responded to his nearness, even when she tried to deny her draw to him. She always felt some little relief to be so honest in his presence. It was as if the person she always pretended to be—the precise one with the perfect answers and controlled manners—had a moment's break that allowed her true self to shine through. But, as always, she quieted such thoughts and reminded herself that he only teased her to find fault. He was not seeking friendship, only someone to taunt.

On Friday, she asked her aunt to send the carriage after tea.

CHAPTER THIRTEEN

Martha laced Catherine's stays with expertise by the end of April. "Are we dressing for someone in particular, my lady?" The helpful maid smiled and winked at Catherine while she laid rejected ribbon and gloves aside, obviously hinting at a suitor. Catherine did not think it wise to share much with the girl. She hardly knew her. Though she missed the confidence she had once shared with Jones. There was nothing quite so intimate as one's relationship with a personal maid.

No harm could come, so long as she did not mention names.

"I do think there are some rather fine gentlemen in the area." Catherine tested the waters.

"The girls downstairs have some ideas about a gentleman who seems to follow you around with his eyes. I told them to stop their gossiping, but you do seem rather particular about your gown, hair styling, and jewellery tonight. I wondered if maybe the girls were right. A suitor! My mother will never believe me if I tell her I dressed the earl's daughter when she met her future husband!"

They were in Kent—a new place for both of them—and they had spent many hours sharing information back and forth about what they had learned about places and people. No one was better about uncovering information than a trusted servant. Perhaps it was time to charge Martha with further responsibilities.

"Tell me your surname," Catherine said.

"It is Dawson, my lady."

"Dawson. Well, that is what I shall call you from now on. You are a lady's maid, are you not? It is time others addressed you as such. I shall tell the housekeeper."

"Does that mean you will keep me on, my lady?" Dawson looked at Catherine with awe.

"It is unlikely that Jones will desire to continue on as my lady's maid, even after our return to Derbyshire. If she wants the position when we do return to Oakley, I shall provide you references to ensure you are situated as a lady's maid. However, Jones's mother continues to suffer, and I feel her place will remain at home. She will be well taken care of. Have no worries there."

Dawson smiled with pure joy.

"I think we are finished, Dawson. You are excused for the evening. We will not likely return until the small hours of the night, so you might rest now until we arrive home."

Catherine indulged in a little vanity once Dawson had left the room, staring at herself in the mirror and anticipating the dances she would share with Mr de Bourgh that evening at the assembly.

The assembly rooms were a total crush once again, but this time, Lady Catherine was not a complete stranger to the guests. She and her aunt spent more than a half hour greeting their neighbours and friends.

The dance card tied to her wrist was nearly full by the time Mr de Bourgh approached her to claim a set.

"Forgive my tardiness. I was unavoidably detained. Would you do me the honour of standing up with me tonight?"

Catherine preened at the attention. "I thank you, yes," she responded, holding out her wrist so that he might choose one of the last dances of the evening.

"You must excuse me, sir. The first set is beginning," she explained as she watched Mr Hunter approach her for their dance.

"I shall look forward to our set all night." Mr de Bourgh smiled in her direction and took himself off to the card room with many of the married gentlemen in the area. He was not dancing with anyone else! What a boon for her confidence it was to know her fondness for him was reciprocated.

The room was much warmer than she remembered from the previous month, and she rarely had a moment's reprieve from the dance floor—not that she would complain of such a thing. She was counting down the moments until her set with Mr de Bourgh, and it was nearly time. After that dance, she cared very little how the remainder of the night proceeded, frankly.

As her current partner led her off the dance floor and returned her to her waiting aunt, her heart began racing with anticipation. Her aunt handed her a handkerchief to discreetly wipe her brow and a cold glass of lemonade to quench her thirst.

"Who is your next partner, my dear?" Lady Rosamund asked.

"Mr de Bourgh. Have you seen him?"

"I am sure I am wrong, but I thought I saw him leaving not an hour ago." Her aunt's expression betrayed her concern.

"Surely not! He would not depart before our dance."

"I was unaware that you were acquainted."

Was their acquaintance unknown to her? Their walks at Rosings had not been disclosed, but her astute aunt could not have missed their other public meetings.

"We met at the last assembly and played cards at Mr and Mrs Fuller's party."

"I see. Forgive me, dearest. I had not remembered. You must be correct. I will ask his cousin where he might be found."

"Pray do not. It is not necessary—" Catherine began to say, but Lady Rosamund was already moving around the edge of the large room in search of Sir Lewis. That was the last man she hoped to see.

"Who did you say was your next partner?" Diana asked, as she stood nearby with her husband.

"Mr de Bourgh," she said, checking her wrist to ensure she was correct—and she was.

"Sir Lewis's cousin? Oh, he is long gone," Mr Bates responded with a chuckle. "A little too deep into the punch and much too short in the pockets, if you do not mind me saying so."

"What a dreadful thing to say. Of course we mind," Diana glared at her husband while he continued to look very amused. "Forget every word he said. Shall we sit together for the set? I would hazard a guess that you will not mind a rest after dancing all night. It is well after midnight, I should say."

Catherine's stomach dropped at the idea that he had abandoned her. And after all her preparations and anticipation. He over imbibed and gambled too much? That did not sound like the kind and thoughtful gentleman she was acquainted with. What a horrible thing to say about such a gentleman. There was undoubtedly no truth to it, Catherine was certain.

"Would you do me the honour of this dance?"

Catherine looked up from the chair she had claimed and found Sir Lewis standing before her, his hand reaching out to her. He was a poor replacement for his cousin. But Catherine knew she could not deny him the dance, or she would have to sit out the remainder of the night.

"Thank you," she responded. Her eyes met Lady Rosamund's, who appeared very pleased with herself for remedying the situation.

Sir Lewis led her onto the dance floor, her hand in his.

She held her chin high as she began to turn through the movements of the dance. It was one she was familiar with, and the steps came easily. She kept her gaze away from Sir Lewis and instead focused on the room and the other couples.

A terrible sound echoed through the room as one of the instrumentalists played the wrong note and proceeded to continue playing in the wrong key. Perhaps the instrument was broken—or the musician a drunkard. Catherine kept a small, polite smile upon her face, as she had been taught.

"Lady Catherine," Sir Lewis attempted to gain her attention. "What lovely musicianship we are enjoying tonight."

Atrocious, more like. "Yes, lovely," she responded.

And when she looked up to finally meet his gaze, she saw him draw his finger down from the top of his forehead to the bridge of his nose and shake his head at her. He had caught her out once again.

She whispered as the steps brought her closer to him, "Did no one teach you it was rude to speak ill of others in company?"

"I am not *company*, am I?" He grinned at this, making her want to toss him into the Thames.

"My sister Eloise used to say, 'Kitty, you must keep those types of thoughts to yourself.' And as such, I have done so. There is no harm in being polite."

"Kitty?" he mused. "You certainly have more claws than that!"

Hmph. What a ghastly comment. Though her cheeks did heat at the indirect compliment. Perhaps she did have more backbone than she often exhibited with others, but it was a part of yourself you silenced, not put on display.

"Does not your noble lineage impel you to help others? You are a clever girl. You can share what you are truly thinking. Why must you only submit to the whims of society? Those that would disagree with you are likely wrong, and others who would encourage you to tell an untruth for their own gain are selfish indeed."

Catherine had nothing to say to that. Keeping ruthless control over her emotions was a part of her. She had no experience being frivolous or flippant or fun.

"You would have me behave like a prize fool? Spouting opinions and demands wherever I went? Spurning other's thoughts and caring only of my own?"

"More fool I," he said more soberly. "I thought you were made of sterner stuff. I only want you to be yourself."

Catherine was relieved when the music came to its end and the set was complete. It was a cold comfort to join her friends who were pleased with the evening and enjoying one another's company. She deeply wanted to relax her hold on her self-control at that moment—to fully embrace how confused she felt and how deeply hurt. Sir Lewis had practically told her she was misleading, and his cousin had abandoned her. What was she doing in Kent anyway? Was she not supposed to be proving to herself and her parents that she could make her own way in the world? At that moment, she deemed all her efforts a great waste of time.

Catherine's self-pity consumed her. She recognized a familiar loneliness sweep through her—a startling realization as she stood in a sea of people who crowded the assembly room.

Some days later, Lady Catherine found herself enjoying an early May picnic at Waterstone Park, an estate not ten miles from her aunt. The property was vast, and the elderly couple that hosted the event told Catherine and her friends multiple times how happy it made them to see young people enjoying themselves.

Catherine was positioned very carefully on a blanket, propped up just so to support her tightly corseted waist, her skirts splayed out around her. Ruffles of a delicate, floral patterned lace and white silk bows decorated her low, wide neckline, protected by her wide hat, which was fixed at the perfect asymmetrical angle upon her teased hair. She knew she looked divine. She wondered what Mr de Bourgh might think if he came upon her sitting just so out in the fine weather.

She had no notion that the gentleman would join them that day, but she had taken particular care with her toilette in the case that he would. While she was still bothered by his behaviour at the recent assembly, it was only fair to allow him a chance to explain himself.

Diana shared the blanket with her, the deep rose of her gown mingling with Catherine's lavender skirts. They were the picture of propriety and good breeding; and they were accompanied by their good friends who sat nearby on their own blanket. Virginia and Emilia looked less picturesque as they made sport of each other endlessly and drank too much punch, but to Catherine, they were all becoming very dear.

Their hostess had visited with the girls for a long time, and they were finally alone in their corner of the property, enjoying the shade of a great elm.

"I am not hiding from Lord Metcalfe," Virginia interrupted Catherine's thoughts, unladylike laughter pouring out of her.

"I see. And would you say your behaviour has been welcoming?" Diana teased.

"I have not given him an answer, and so my time is my own," Virginia answered.

"I had no notion to make such a choice," Diana said.

"As you should have done," Emilia encouraged Diana. "Mr Bates was a fine catch."

"Perhaps," Diana said. "But I do wonder . . ."

"Surely you do not regret your choice?" Catherine interrupted.

"No, but I do see some sense in the concerns my sister shared with me. She wondered if our different temperaments would align when we were married, while my mother assured me they would. But I do find that we spend most of our time apart. We have very little in common. But I am sure that is usual, is it not?"

"My parents spend very little time together," Catherine responded, encouragingly.

"My father is wild for my mother," Virginia chimed in, saucily. "They eloped, you know."

"No!" Emilia responded with no little shock.

"Yes," Virginia went on. "It was quite the scandal in their day. It is why we do not spend time in town with the earl now."

"I had no notion," Diana responded.

Virginia rose from her blanket and stood before the girls, leaning over to dramatically whisper, "And that is what I want for myself. I refuse to make the right choice for only my parent's sake—or a gentleman's. My parents were able to choose, and I want the same for myself. Just because Lord Metcalfe is decided upon me does not mean I must relinquish my agency."

And with that, she sauntered off across the lawn. Within moments, she was looping her hand through Mr Webb's elbow and walking down to the nearby lake.

"Poor Lord Metcalfe. The scandal," Diana whispered. "I fear she will regret her choices."

"That she may, but I am coming around to seeing things more her way," Catherine responded, surprising even herself. "It is possible that our parents do not know what is best. Perhaps we know our own minds and should be trusted to choose our husbands."

"Do not let my earlier comments sway you away from what we both know is best. I do not regret marrying." Diana leaned closer to Catherine and rested her hand on her arm. "I see why my parents thought him a good match. He is. But sometimes it is ever so lonesome."

After checking to ensure no one had wandered over to their side of the lawn, Diana leaned in and whispered, "And his mother is a complete bore."

Catherine giggled with her friend at that and was thankful to have some ladies in whom she could confide.

"When will your sister marry?" Emilia asked Catherine. Of course, Emilia wanted to speak of Lady Anne's upcoming marriage. She was very enamoured with marriage, and Catherine's quick mention of her sister's upcoming nuptials had clearly not satisfied her curiosity. To her view, everyone was a romantic and each day held the promise of the beginning of her passionate future. Catherine did not have the heart to tell her where her dreams of grandeur could land her.

"The viscountess writes that she will marry in the second week of June."

"I am sure your mother is very busy with all the planning. Will you to go to London to witness her nuptials?"

Catherine felt some shame in her banishment from town. "No, I am quite happy here in Kent. I have no desire to cut my time short."

Diana and Emilia smiled and agreed with her.

"Do you not wish you had been given a second Season in town?" Diana asked.

"I am content," Catherine said.

She was ashamed that she had never told her new friends the truth of why she was in Kent. She had instead let them think that she and her sister had both been offered one Season in London. This approach required no effort. No one questioned her when she put it that way.

"I would give anything for a Season in town," Emilia said.

"It is not all as glamourous as you would imagine. The balls and dinner parties are quite exquisite, but you are expected to attend events every night of the week. It is exhausting, and the pressure—the pressure on some of the ladies is quite severe. Oh, to be a gentleman looking for a wife. It is much easier for them. For the ladies, there is so much sitting and waiting and conversing and waiting and sitting—on and on it goes. I would much rather find a gentleman of quality here in Kent."

This perked up Emilia. "Do you admire a gentleman in the neighbourhood?"

"I may." Catherine blushed.

"I have seen one showing you marked attention, but I did not want to speak until you addressed the topic first," Diana responded. "What I would give for you to settle here and be with us always."

Catherine replied softly, "I do hope to continue my friendship with one gentleman in particular, but one should never raise their hopes too far. It is the gentleman who must speak first."

Emilia squealed and Diana shushed her.

"Quiet now," Catherine chided. "A lady must have some secrets."

"And we are no longer alone," Diana warned and tapped Catherine's hand softly with one discreet finger.

Catherine tipped her hat to see who approached and saw Sir Lewis prowling towards the ladies. She looked around them to see if he might be approaching anyone else, but alas, they were the only people in that corner of the lawn.

"Lady Catherine, Mrs Bates, Miss Hawkins," Sir Lewis greeted them and bowed.

The ladies simpered and smirked while Catherine gritted her teeth and forced a paltry grin upon her face.

"Lady Catherine, I thought you might do me the honour of joining me for a stroll," Sir Lewis said.

A deep breath was hardly enough to settle her annoyance. That was the last thing she wanted to do. She was perfectly content as she was, enjoying the fine weather with her friends and sitting away from the sunshine.

"Thank you, yes."

She was nothing if not civil, unfortunately.

Sir Lewis offered her a hand and she placed hers delicately in his while she stood with as much gentleness and femininity as one could in such a gown.

Sir Lewis offered his arm, and Catherine set her hand upon it very gently. She had no reason to hang on him as the other ladies in the neighbourhood did. Let them all throw themselves at the chance to manage Rosings Park; they could have him. If she could get away with it, she would show him no notice.

"A fine day, is it not?" Sir Lewis asked.

"It is," Catherine replied, and quickly continued, "And I do mean that sincerely. It is not warm, and it is not cool. If the bugs would abandon the party, it would be perfection."

"Ah, she tells the truth!"

"I am capable of it," Catherine bit back.

"I am happy to hear it. And are you enjoying yourself?"

"I was." Frankness could be quite liberating!

He chuckled. "And I have gone and ruined it by removing you from your bosom friends?"

"I would not say such a thing."

"Of course you would not, but that is not why I asked."

She tilted her hat to allow herself to take him in. He was dressed very smartly, indeed. The dark blue frock coat and camel-coloured breeches—the grey eyes she would know anywhere, always laughing sinisterly—and that pleased grin of his. If she did not dislike him so much, she would say he was awfully handsome, indeed.

"I am sure you will tell me why," she finally responded, with more cheer than she expected.

"I wondered if I might steal you away, that is, if you were finding this party very dull. There is a ridge just over there, and from the top you can see the River Darent, and sometimes, on a clear day, you can see the church steeple in Westerham."

His offer was a strange one. Perhaps he had plans to take her up to that ridge so he might tell her how better to arrange her hair.

With him, one never knew. But she did know, for certain, that he seemed to always have ulterior motives. And she wondered if they were all punishment for the night she so grossly abused him at Oakley. If someone had told her to turn back into the rain and use the servant's entrance, she too might chastise them for many months.

Catherine nodded and looked back at the larger group that stood nearer to the house across the parkland, her aunt among them. Her heart sank when she saw that Mr de Bourgh was also present. He was looking in her direction, and across the field she felt their eyes meet, and he nodded in her direction. She felt a sinking feeling that she had just agreed to spend the remainder of her time at Waterstone Park kept away from the one person she had hoped to see.

As Sir Lewis led her across the lawn, they fell into a contented silence. It was far better than being teased. And when they reached the famed ridge, Catherine could see why Sir Lewis had brought her. Some miles in the distance, one could see the river and the little village.

"Just there, south of the village, there are the remains of an old Roman encampment and beyond it, a tower. When I was a little boy, my father took my brother and me there to explore." Sir Lewis pointed at his query so that Catherine might better see.

"I was never one to spend time exploring out of doors," Catherine responded.

"I know, my lady." And he certainly did. His request for honesty meant that he knew quite a lot about her. But she still knew little about him.

"Were you and your brother close?" She asked quietly.

"We were like many brothers. At odds as much as we were obliging. We were both prepared for different lives. Our parents saw to our education in an exceedingly different manner. And as such, the older we became, the less we understood one another. But I do miss him."

"I am certain you do." To be sure, Catherine undoubtedly understood it. Family, as she was learning, had its complications.

"It is easier when I remember our younger years. Life was much simpler then."

Catherine nodded and felt herself squeeze his elbow in a fleeting moment of camaraderie and support. She too knew what it was to lose a relation.

They spoke no more of his past, and Sir Lewis gave her a brief history lesson on the region. Kent was so different than Derbyshire—all lush green versus the rocky clime of her family seat. She was warming to it and to the people there.

"Shall I return you to Lady Rosamund?" Sir Lewis asked kindlier than expected.

"Yes, thank you," Catherine responded.

As they made their way back to the lawn party, Catherine was pleased to see that Mr de Bourgh still lingered near a group of gentlemen and was following her with his eyes, as she was him.

Unfortunately, Sir Lewis was leading her in a different direction, towards her aunt. If only a young lady could simply excuse herself and speak to whom she liked. She was starting to see that some of the rules that had guided her greatly principled control were perhaps not for her protection but for propriety's sake alone. And for the first time in her life, she considered the importance of caution and whether she was willing to part with her once firmly held doctrine.

The word of the day was "scandal." Virginia Sedgwick had roused much gossip the previous day at the Waterstone picnic, and after a long talk with her parents, had been warned off Mr Webb. If she would not have Lord Metcalfe, she must tell the gentleman. A private ball hosted at his home, Persimmon Park, was being held at the end of the week—and the neighbourhood had long believed that the event was for Virginia and Virginia alone. Her suitor had called in a female cousin to play hostess, and his staff had been putting in orders for weeks in the nearby villages.

"They say I must give him my answer before the ball." Virginia sniffled into her dainty lace handkerchief. "My father feels it is not right to continue in this manner."

Diana nodded along and agreed, "You must give him an answer."

"They say I made a mockery of him yesterday! Why must I make a decision about my entire future just because the viscount down the lane has made his?"

"He is a kind man. Any lady would be honoured—" Always a romantic, Emilia tried to join the fray.

"I have never said he is not kind," Virginia stammered between tears.

"If you must accept him, do it for yourself," Catherine said. She was feeling less in concert with her previous notions of blindly following one's parents. Look where it had brought her. If her friend must accept, let her make that decision with eyes wide open.

Virginia looked stunned by Catherine's response. "You have always said one should look to their parents for guidance. You surprise me."

"I am, perhaps, thinking differently as of late. I have been wondering if choosing my own husband could please my parents—and the more I think of it, the less I believe I care." Her tone was laden with boredom, but she meant every word.

It was not the working of one moment that had led her to this statement but a slow brewing resentment for her past and a desire to influence her own future—for it was truly only she who would be forced to live with the consequences or the advantages.

Chapter Fourteen

May 1782

A happy energy rushed through Catherine as she passed through the woods that bordered Rosings and found Mr de Bourgh waiting for her at the end of the path.

After dispensing with the necessary pleasantries, her potential suitor wasted no time at all in telling her how he felt.

"I was disappointed to not have a chance to speak with you at the picnic."

Catherine blushed. She too had been disappointed—in that and the assembly. If only propriety permitted her to tell him of her true disappointment and her dearest wishes.

"Would you do me the honour of allowing me to walk you to Whitmore?" He asked.

"Yes, thank you," she murmured quietly. "Your company would have been welcome at the picnic as well as the assembly. I feel it has been many days since we have had an opportunity to speak."

He offered his arm, which she took hold of with delighted alacrity. They moved in concert together easily. *What a pleasant fit*, she thought.

"Pray please forgive me for abandoning you at the recent assembly. Lewis's steward sent word to bring me back to Rosings—you know how my cousin relies on me," he said, looking a bit sheepish, which increased Catherine's pity for the gentleman.

What folly! Could not the steward beckon Sir Lewis if help was sincerely needed in the middle of the night? Could not Sir Lewis have mentioned it to her when he danced in his cousin's place? That man had all the pleasant accoutrements of his position and yet he was nothing but unpardonable when it came to Mr de Bourgh.

"And as for the picnic," he continued, "I could not have said it better than you. Your company would also have been welcome, however preoccupied I might have been by other company—I should have sought you out."

Finding him utterly innocent of any wrongdoings, it was easy to settle back into their normal conversation topics and his humorous anecdotes.

Catherine could not countenance spending more time with Mr de Bourgh without learning more about his family. At length, she discovered that Mr de Bourgh's parents had died when he was young, leaving him to spend many summers at Rosings and winters with another aunt in London. After Oxford, he had settled in town, which had the benefit of being a short ride to the family estate in Kent. Everything was as it should be. If it would not raise expectations, she would write to her brother and ask more about his friend.

"I am preparing to take over management, so I must be close at hand," he said.

"Why would Sir Lewis pass over the obligation to you?" Catherine asked.

"He is bored of the country and feels overwhelmed by the responsibility. He never plans to marry again, so he knows it will be me rightfully taking over the estate at a later time. He hopes to speed that transition. My cousin was never overly fond of Kent to begin with."

"I had no notion of his plans!"

"It is why I am here now. He wants to travel the continent and shall be handing me my inheritance sooner than ever expected."

"He puts much trust in you." And rightly so. Mr de Bourgh was plainly an attentive representative of Rosings Park. Lady Barringer would approve. It was not correct to shirk one's responsibilities. And it was no surprise to Catherine to learn that Sir Lewis was lacking.

"He need not—I have been managing his properties for some time."

Catherine felt a strange excitement to know that should she and Mr de Bourgh continue this discreet courtship, it could one day lead to a proposal in truth—and Rosings! Her parents may not like her making a choice for herself, but once they saw the vast property, they would surely come around in some time.

They could be engaged before she returned to Derbyshire in July and then marry from Oakley in the Autumn. It could be done before year's end, and she would no longer be required to fear the future. Removing that uncertainty was paramount to her happiness.

The possibility of resolving difficulties for herself made her walk in even a more enthusiastic manner. She felt a weight of worry lift. Even if her mother could not bother to write her, she would have to respond if Catherine were to write with such happy news. Mr de Bourgh's situation in life was quite suitable—grand, rather! Pemberley was nothing to Rosings Park!

"What think *you* of Rosings, my lady?" Mr de Bourgh asked rather pointedly.

Catherine felt the weight of the question and turned her head, angling her hat so that she could take in the gardens and fine house. "It pleases me very much. It is a testament to your devotion, surely."

Catherine spent the next few minutes answering questions about Derbyshire, Oakley, and her family's house in town.

"Barringer House is in Grosvenor Square. Where is your house in town?" she asked him.

"Very nearby—assuredly, one could walk."

That pleased her too. Rosings and a house in town. She could not but keep the smile from her face.

When they reached the hedgerow that lined Whitmore, Catherine stopped and thanked him for taking the time to accompany her.

"There is no need to thank me. I take much joy in walking with you," he responded. "Perhaps we might see one another tomorrow? Have you seen the folly at Rosings? We could meet there after your daily sojourn to the parsonage."

Catherine's heart sank at that. A walk through the gardens was one thing, but a clandestine meeting was quite another.

"I am not certain my aunt would approve. She will worry when I do not return at the designated time."

"Your aunt need not know, my lady. You are a woman grown. Are you not? You might simply tell her that you plan to remain at the parsonage an hour longer than usual."

His words soaked into her being. They clawed at her deeply held desire to be taken more seriously. It was just what she had lately been thinking on. She was grown, if not of age—but that hardly mattered. She knew her mind and was capable of telling her aunt she would be at the parsonage longer through the afternoon.

"I shall think on it." She could hardly make him a promise.

"And I shall wait all day."

That made her laugh. "No need for that. If I am able, I shall meet you at half past three."

That made his grin grow even wider, his eyes alight with joy.

She could hardly wait. That future—the answer to all her questions—felt once again within her reach.

"Lady Catherine! You came." Mr de Bourgh made his way across the lawn and reached for Catherine's hand. He bowed over her wrist regally and laid a kiss upon the back of her hand.

"I said I would try."

Catherine was already nervous. It was not like her to make secret plans of this nature. What would her aunt think of her? What would Lady Barringer say? She should have at least brought Dawson along. She had lain awake well into the night contemplating whether to meet him.

It was one thing to allow him to guide her across the grounds of Rosings once or twice, but quite another to plan a tete-a-tete in a quiet corner of the estate.

Mr de Bourgh appeared elated, and for now, that would have to be enough for her. She would reap any consequences at a later time.

"The folly is quite lovely. Did you have some larger part in seeing it built? I did wonder about you bringing me here."

"A perceptive woman you are." He smiled that expression that made her stomach flip.

"Will you attend the ball that Lord Metcalfe is hosting?" Catherine inquired.

"That I shall. I had hoped to claim your first set, should you allow it," Mr de Bourgh said.

"I would be honoured." Her face burned and her cheeks ached from smiling. After he left the assembly early, she had been hoping to have another chance to dance with him.

Mr de Bourgh took Catherine's wrist and spun her around with a flourish. His light-heartedness warmed her.

When he had finished spinning her about, he pulled her wrist just a touch and brought her closer—so that she was standing directly in front of him. His joyful and jubilant spirits were contagious.

"I have a question of some importance that I would like to ask you." His smile remained, but his voice took on a more serious tone.

She nodded. She would welcome any entreaty today. He was ever so kind to her.

"I have told you about my inheritance and my plans for Rosings," he said, measuredly.

"You have." She felt out of breath and body, filled with an unfamiliar anxiety.

"But I was remiss to leave out the most crucial part." At this, his gaze sobered, and he looked her in the eye. "I should like a wife and a family, and I feel I have met the right lady to be mistress of Rosings."

Catherine's breath was coming and going ever so quickly.

"Lady Catherine Fitzwilliam, would you do me the great honour of becoming my wife?"

If Catherine thought she could not breathe before, she was sorely mistaken. Her entire world tilted on its edge as the question she had most wanted to hear for many months had finally been asked of her, and for some peculiar reason, her immediate thought was *run, run, run*. That nagging voice inside that turned her stomach and made her breath catch was back. That voice that told her no—this is not right. It had returned, and it was screaming at her.

She wondered how much of that voice was truly her and how much was her mother. If it were the latter, she was just coming around to the possibility that ignoring that voice might be in her best interest.

And yet—there he stood—a smiling, kind gentleman that she had been eager to imagine a future with, putting himself before her as a match. An exceedingly suitable match. With a very happy future.

And she hesitated.

"The earl—my father—" It was all she could think of to say. "My family has not met you."

Mr de Bourgh pulled her closer, setting his hands on her shoulders—nearly an embrace, and as close to one as she had ever experienced.

"My darling, how could your father object? Look around you. Is not Rosings enough proof of my worth? My cousin has dined at your father's table, has he not? And your aunt approves."

"Does she?" Her aunt had never spoken about Mr de Bourgh to Catherine.

"Are we not friendly neighbours? I am certain all will be well."

Catherine was not certain. She was, frankly, understanding Virginia more than she ever had before. This felt fast—faster than she had imagined. While she had hoped for his attentions, it did not follow that she had been prepared for a proposal this quickly. His admiration, she had sought and conquered, it seemed.

"I have not reached my majority."

"Once you tell your father that you have made a promise to me, he will see that it cannot be undone. Be brave, my lady."

And she wanted to. She dearly wanted to be brave. But this did not feel courageous, it felt reckless.

He must have noticed her fear, for he spoke quickly and re-assuringly, "Graham will surely approve. Give me your word. I love you. Let us be married at the first possible moment."

Graham. That one word shocked her more than he could have known. Lord Ashby, the viscount, Graham Edward Luke Fitzwilliam. Mr de Bourgh had called her brother by his Christian name. It was a rare occurrence. She herself had never called him Graham. *No one* called her brother Graham. She did not know whether to rejoice that their friendship allowed such an oddity or to be frightened for her suitor, who was conceivably out of his depth. Once again, he shirked the responsibility of addressing someone by their title and it confused her.

"Listen to me, Catherine," he interrupted her thoughts.

There it was again—a frankness and freedom she permitted *no one* in her sphere. She was always Lady Catherine, even with her closest friends. If he thought showing this informality would endear her to him, he was working under false presumptions.

With her guidance, she could help to manage these near blunders in the future.

He continued, "All will be well. We can announce our engagement at the ball and then send a letter to your parents. We need not wait for their approval to begin making plans. I have no apprehensions. We shall have their support once they hear the good news."

In the end, Catherine had left Mr de Bourgh with no certain answer. She promised to give him one at the ball. When they danced the first set.

She felt overwhelmed with emotion as she walked with purpose back to Whitmore. On the one hand, she felt she had solved all of her problems. Mr de Bourgh had chosen her—not Anne, not any of the other beautiful ladies in the neighbourhood. He selected *her* and appeared to favour her above all. It was a thrilling sensation. She imagined Emilia squealing with joy about love and romance, and a chuckle bubbled up in her.

She did not love him, nor did she feel that any notion of romance was necessary. But he had been fairly passionate in his sentiments. Above all, his interest would increase her importance, and it felt fine to be desired for the first time. She had never felt this way during her first Season. Most of the gentlemen who had asked her to dance in London had only been in pursuit of gaining favour with her brother or the earl—only seeking a closer connection to her family, not Catherine.

She was lucky, then, that her mother had been focused on Eloise and told her particularly that no suitors would be considered for her at that time. Elder sisters married first, and she was merely in London that spring to make friends and be seen.

She had enjoyed the sights, the theatre, and all the lovely balls. She had little interest in the gentlemen and now had absolutely no practice in knowing what was up or down with men in general.

Knowing that she and Anne would be engaged the same Season, however, did increase her pride. She could hold her chin high if she said yes. No one would dare say that the de Bourghs of Rosings Park were not a fortunate alliance.

But perhaps they might. She wondered if that sick feeling in her stomach was her concern for her parents' approval. Anticipating the needs of her family, their guests, and greater company was the education of her lifetime. But, in this moment, she could not guess. Accepting him before calling on her mother's opinion had the potential to be the most detrimental choice of her life.

And yet, she felt eager to see the deal done. Even the apprehension pouring through her veins could not stop the joy that ran in parallel. All of her dreams for her time in Kent were coming true. She would be a married woman, a woman of great property, soon and hopefully one day, a mother and a principal lady in the neighbourhood.

It was that thought that carried her into Whitmore with a smile upon her face and a lighter step.

She would soon be Lady Catherine de Bourgh.

CHAPTER FIFTEEN

"**A**re you *humming*?" Lady Rosamund looked aghast at Catherine.

A giggle that felt especially foreign indeed fell out of Catherine's mouth. She was, frankly, elated.

"Apologies, my lady. I am only excited for the ball tonight."

Her aunt looked to the time piece on the mantle. It was half past five, nearly the hour to abandon their places in the drawing room in favour of getting ready for the ball.

It was a rare day indeed when her aunt had no callers at Whitmore during receiving hours. But it must be that the ball being held that night at Persimmon Park was at the forefront of everyone's minds. After a quiet afternoon, they had shared a small repast ahead of the night's gaiety. As it stood, for all her anticipation, Catherine had little stomach for it and could hardly wait to abandon the drawing room for her chambers.

"Have you any particular gentlemen you hope to dance with tonight?" Her aunt was nothing if not perceptive.

"I may." Catherine turned to avoid her aunt's knowing gaze.

"I shall not force it out of you, but I know there is something you want to say. Do not fear my reaction—out with it!"

She had not planned to tell Lady Rosamund until she had accepted Mr de Bourgh, but she could not contain her joy at that moment. It had been the work of her lifetime to stifle her emotions, and yet, this pleasing news, she could not keep quiet.

"I have received an offer of marriage."

Lady Rosamund gasped—and it was a sight to see! Catherine could no longer deny her cheerfulness.

"Have you? I had no notion you had a suitor in the area. Will you not tell me who?"

"I have not given him my answer, but I feel certain my parents will be pleased with the prospect."

"Do you?" Lady Rosamund did not seem convinced. "I would caution you to continue to delay any reply and let me send a note to London. Your parents would not appreciate your giving any young man—pleasing or not—an answer without their knowing him and providing you with their guidance."

"I had thought the same," Catherine replied. "And yet, I believe I shall give him an answer tonight. He has secured my first set, and I fear if I do not answer him this evening, he shall be hurt."

Lady Rosamund looked exceedingly concerned at that statement. "My darling, but you must delay! Any gentleman worthy of you would understand my caution."

"Then send an express, Aunt, and we shall have my father's blessing soon enough," Lady Catherine said with some newfound authority. She stood and made to leave the room. "I must go start my toilette. Dawson will be preparing my bath now, as it is nearly five."

Her aunt stood and followed her, "Please, dearest. I beg you to hear me in this—the earl's attention is required. He could deny the release of your dowry if he objects. And you are in no position to legally accept. You have not yet reached your majority. Surely your young man knows this. Any gentleman who would ask you to forgo your father's permission is not worthy of you. Do you not see?"

This irritated her to no end. "Do you not think I have considered all angles of this? I am a woman grown. And my parents have abandoned me to focus only on my younger sister. If I do not seize this opportunity, I shall be a spinster before long!"

"How can you say such a thing?" Lady Rosamund asked. "You are conscious that your parents have not abandoned you. It was your choice to accompany me to Kent. I am not suggesting that I or my brother would impede an engagement. I am not suggesting a delay of great length nor promising that your parents shall not be in favour of the match. Only that you must see that consulting with the earl is imperative. You are my responsibility, and I take that seriously. Where is this coming from?"

"Abandon me, they have." Catherine jutted out her chin. "And for once, I shall take control and see to my future on my own."

"The earl will not appreciate my allowing this type of secret courtship. I had no notion! Catherine, I beg of you—"

Catherine stood tall, rising far over her aunt's shoulders and looking down at her with a defiance that was new and thrilling. "You shall not be held accountable. I shall explain the entire situation when the earl arrives." Catherine smirked and whispered, "He shall forgive me all my impertinence and eagerness to answer my suitor when he hears that I shall be the future mistress of Rosings Park."

Lady Rosamund's eyes grew at that information. "You cannot be serious."

Catherine held her gaze and saw her aunt's approval softening her demeanour. She understood now. And she seemed pleased. Her aunt would be happy to call her neighbour.

Lady Rosamund replied, "Do not take my reaction for approval. The earl is still required. I shall send an express directly, but pray, please tell your suitor that a delay is necessary so that he might take an audience first with the earl. I know he shall understand completely. He is not without propriety nor good manners. And let us pray that your father travels with haste. He is required at Whitmore immediately."

Her aunt left her to go straight to her desk at the back of the room. Once Catherine had seen her pull out a clean sheet of paper, she excused herself.

Catherine had saved her favourite ball gown for a special event and was exceeding pleased to have done so. Imagining Mr de Bourgh's reaction made her smile as she approached the carriage. A stranger in Whitmore livery stood at the front of the coach. Dawson had not mentioned anything about Harold, her aunt's driver, being replaced. And Dawson always gave Catherine the latest information about the estate.

A footman approached and handed her and Lady Rosamund up into the darkness of the carriage. It was not five miles to Lord Metcalfe's home—very little time, ensuring that her skirts remained untarnished from the ride. The gown was done in the softest pink with gold embroidery, opening at her waist to reveal a white silk skirt with flounces of the finest lace, displaying her wealth and importance. It would indeed be the finest gown at the ball, of that she was certain.

When the ladies arrived, a footman handed her down, and she waited for her aunt. After visiting with their hosts in the receiving line and greeting a few friends in attendance, her aunt took her arm and led her into the great hall.

It was decorated with fresh flowers, and the candlelight bounced off of all the polished surfaces in the room.

Catherine could hear the musicians tuning their instruments for the first set. While her aunt guided her across the room, she could not help but seek out her suitor with her eyes. She looked in every direction and finally found him—smiling and serene, standing near an open door that must lead to a balcony or terrace. He was surrounded by other gentlemen from the neighbourhood, some known and some new to her. But his smile was for her alone, and she returned the gesture. It would be only a few moments until their set began and she gave him her answer.

Her aunt was still leading her about the room and came to a stop in front of Sir Lewis, who greeted both ladies with a welcoming smile and a deep bow.

"I saw you across the room, sir," her aunt said to Sir Lewis, "and thought I should bring my niece to you for your dance. I understand you have claimed her first set."

Oh dear.

Sir Lewis looked at Catherine with a question in his eyes. He almost seemed to be asking her if she wanted him to pretend that he was indeed her first partner. How had her aunt misunderstood her this greatly? *Sir Lewis? Of what was she thinking!* Of course, she would not be considering marriage to a man with an unhealthy proclivity towards seeing her uneasy and bewildered at every turn. Did not Mr de Bourgh say that everyone in the neighbourhood understood he was here to take his inheritance?

"You misunderstood me, Aunt," Catherine said quietly to Lady Rosamund. "Sir Lewis did not claim my first set."

Her aunt looked back and forth between Sir Lewis and Catherine in great confusion.

"I would be honoured to dance with you this evening, Lady Catherine," Sir Lewis offered. "May I claim your second?"

She thanked him for the honour and wrote his name down.

Her aunt's confusion was replaced with astonishment when Mr de Bourgh approached to claim her hand in the first set. As she let her suitor lead her to the dance floor, Lady Catherine looked back at Lady Rosamund and nearly laughed. How could her aunt think that it had been Sir Lewis who had proposed to her? Surely, as the closest neighbour to Rosings Park, her aunt was conscious of *both* gentlemen in residence! Besides, it was Mr de Bourgh who oversaw the property in the most meaningful way and handled disputes! And his inheritance was soon coming. Could she not see that it was *he* who was the prize?

"You seem in rather high spirits tonight, my lady." Mr de Bourgh beamed. He inferred he understood her good humour, and he was right.

The dance did not allow any privacy in the way Catherine had hoped, so the next time the steps brought her closer to Mr de Bourgh she simply said, "I have given your question much thought and have come around to seeing your way of things."

His smile was such that it lowered her typical guard, and she allowed a giggle to escape.

"Do you mean to tell me your answer is yes?" Mr de Bourgh looked thrilled.

She nodded.

"Thank you for your trust in me. You will not regret it."

Their shared joy and boisterous attitudes were gaining notice from the other couples on the dance floor, and so Lady Catherine stifled her delight for the remainder of the set, but her happy eyes never left Mr de Bourgh.

She had done it. She had accepted his proposal and would soon be his wife. It would be the culmination of all of her parents' wishes and teachings.

It was only her aunt's confusion now that brought some concern to Lady Catherine. She informed Mr de Bourgh that his cousin had secured her next set, and so her future husband led her off the dance floor in the direction of Lady Rosamund and Sir Lewis.

He said very little in the way of farewells, simply nodding and excusing himself, not even greeting her aunt or his cousin. Catherine was conscious that Lady Rosamund was holding her tongue while they were in company, and she looked forward to easing any of her aunt's concerns when they returned to Whitmore.

While she waited for the second set to begin, other gentlemen from the neighbourhood joined their small, gathered party and requested the honour of dancing with her.

By the time Sir Lewis led her onto the dance floor, she had four additional partners that would follow this dance. She was pleased, indeed.

Sir Lewis looked stern this evening, not quite his typical smirking self. She wondered at it. Could he already know about his cousin's proposal and not approve of his cousin marrying? Did Sir Lewis disapprove of her? It would be no surprise considering the fact that he was constantly baiting her and taunting her. The thought made her enraged. He had better not get in the way of her joy. She was a Fitzwilliam! How could he deny that she was the ideal person to oversee the de Bourgh properties? It was he who had decided to abandon Rosings to his cousin, and surely he would not begrudge Mr de Bourgh a partner at his side.

She had no interest in pretending friendship with the man.

"You look tired, Sir Lewis." It was his own fault that she told him the truth of it.

That comment seemed to lighten his mood. "And *you* look beautiful, my lady," he said and then followed with a quieter answer near to her right ear, "And no honorific is necessary between friends. My name is Lewis—just as I told you when first we met."

After four more partners, Catherine happily escaped the warm ballroom, exiting through the French doors that led outside. Couples were arranging themselves on the dance floor for the supper set, and she was pleased to find a moment of quiet and fresh air before the meal. She had hoped Mr de Bourgh would approach her for another set, but she had not seen him since he took himself into the card room some hours ago. It was flattering, though, to know that she was the only young lady he had asked to dance.

She found herself very alone outside on a long terrace that ran nearly the length of the house. Four single torches glowed along the stone railings, permitting more shadow than light. More torches were placed throughout the lawn, lining the paths of the formal gardens. A group of gentlemen gathered down below and in high spirits, puffs of white smoke encircling their heads. It made her chuckle. While the ladies grouped in the corners of the great hall for whispered conversation behind their embroidered fans, the gentlemen lit cigars and had their own private chats outside in the open air. What folly.

"My target is caught, my boys. You must congratulate me." A voice filtered up through the garden that Catherine would know anywhere. Mr de Bourgh.

She did not much enjoy being called a target, but she did relish knowing that he was sharing their joy with Mr Fuller and some other gentlemen from the neighbourhood. She moved more fully into the shadows so she might hear more of what he had to say without being seen.

". . . the unsuspecting, naïve daughter of an earl with a pretty portion—40,000 pounds to be exact. All of my debts shall soon be paid in one fell swoop. I dearly hope I shall have some money left in my purse when Sir Lewis dies and I finally get Rosings for myself, which cannot happen soon enough."

Catherine froze. Her hands began shaking, and she could not catch her breath. A spinning sensation overtook her that nearly made her faint outright. But she would not swoon. Not yet. If she had learned anything in Kent, it was that she had a voice, and she would use it now.

She was moving towards the light, taking herself closer to the railing to better see the men below.

". . . her aquiline nose is too much like a hawk for my taste."

"A goose, more like," Mr Fuller chimed in.

"And so tall—" another voice rang out.

"Too masculine by half."

All of their voices were mixing now. She could not ascertain which was Mr de Bourgh's, for all the vitriol coming from the garden was enough to make her stomach roll in defeat. She hardly knew what to do—and it felt suddenly like a great punishment for making a decision on her own, for once in her life. Hands shaking and her breathing uneasy, she finally reached for the railing—to say what, she did not yet know.

She wanted to rail at the man and stomp her feet and scream at the unfairness.

Strong hands grabbed her by the shoulders, rubbing her upper arms. A voice reached her, whispering. "Hush now," was murmured on her right. The stranger pulled her back from the railing, sinking them into near darkness. She turned her head to take in the strong, stern face of Sir Lewis. "Do not say anything just now. You have not been seen. I know I have encouraged you to speak your mind, but now is not the time. Let me return you to the party."

Catherine turned in the shadows of the terrace to look Sir Lewis in the eye. "You know I cannot resume my evening as if naught has occurred."

"Of course you might. I am the only other person here. No one of importance heard it. You can be assured of that. Everyone has taken themselves into the dining room for supper."

"It is not that which prevents me from returning! I care not *who* heard—did you not hear what your cousin *said*? I have given him my *word*! I agreed to marry that horrible man."

He sighed, resigned to her words and becoming visibly angrier by the second.

"I hoped I heard wrong," Sir Lewis said gravely.

"You did not—surely you understood which daughter of an earl was being spoken of! For he described me quite specifically. Why must I be compared to a goose or a hawk? Only large birds with hooked beaks—why not a songbird with a pretty little bird call? Why do only the petite and dainty ladies receive such compliments?"

This seemed to soften him. "Your noble nose is just as it should be," he said, running a finger from the top of her forehead to the end of her nose. "My cousin is not worthy of your notice and never will be."

Mortification flooded her being. She was angry and hurt and felt a defeat that she had never known.

"I am nothing, sir," she said so softly that she had to wonder if he would even hear her.

"Do not say such a thing."

"It is true!" She spoke more loudly now. "Mr Darcy chose my sister over me with less than a fortnight of acquaintance, and now Mr de Bourgh was going to use me to raise himself up in the world! What more proof do you require?"

This time his finger set upon her lips, quieting her and ending her ramblings.

"You are not nothing! You are Lady Catherine Fitzwilliam! Daughter of an earl! Great niece of a duke! You are *everything*." He told her.

At last, the emotion of the evening overtook her, and she fell against Sir Lewis's chest. The sobs that escaped her felt foreign and embarrassing, but she had no power to stop them.

"I will help you out of this mess," he said into her hair. "Whatever I can offer, it is yours."

His gentle touch—arms wrapped around her shoulders and chin set upon her head—softened her. It awoke something in her that felt like home—like safety. She felt comforted by his nearness. It was a softness she had not expected from him.

"Promise me," she whispered.

"I pledge my fealty to you." She felt his beard move against her forehead as he answered her.

It was a relief to know he might help her, but it did not stop her unseemly weeping.

"Hush, little songbird. It only becomes a scandal if you allow it to be so. Hold your tongue, woman, and plan your fearsome retribution for another day. How many of your friends know of your promise to him?"

"Only my aunt," she said after a rather unladylike hiccup. "But the identity of my betrothed was a mystery to her before the ball."

"Lady Rosamund will protect you. And it is only his word against yours. I knew he was up to no good! I had seen him in my gardens with you, but I could not stand guard each hour of each day. Even my gardener and steward attempted to keep him away from you, but we could not be watchful at all times. How he came to find you so often, I shall never know. I should have spoken to your aunt of my concerns ages ago, but I let my pride get in the way. I did not want all of the neighbourhood to know that I did not trust Arthur. She will not forgive my lapse."

"She will not hold you responsible. You knew nothing."

"I knew enough. And while many in this county know my cousin's honour is flimsy at best, he remains a favourite of many with whom he spent his childhood. I was right to worry about his fascination with you and attempt to keep him away."

"How does one go about banning their guest from walking in the garden?" Catherine laughed lightly at the absurdity of it all.

"He is *not* a guest in my house."

Mr de Bourgh was not allowed on the grounds at Rosings? She could barely comprehend the new information sinking her further into desolation. Her breath quickened once again, sobs pouring out once more, due to the enormity of her blunder about the worst gentleman in all of England.

"If he is so untrustworthy, if he is not even a *guest* in your home as I was led to believe—then I have been a supreme fool. He told me you were handing over Rosings . . . that he was receiving his inheritance early so you might travel the continent . . ."

"Hand over Rosings? My grasping cousin has not been invited to Rosings for many years. And yet I found him staying in a guest chamber, managing my staff, when I returned from Manchester. I sent him to the Green Lion in Hunsford weeks ago! I could not for the life of me determine why I kept finding him wandering my grounds regularly like a rat. I told myself I was overreacting when I saw him trotting you about the gardens. When I worried his objective could be *you*, I reasoned . . . well, I had hoped I was interpreting his actions wrongly. I assumed it was me—something to do with *me* that kept him returning to the estate."

Mr de Bourgh had her convinced that he had the full run of the estate! Her foolishness was only the beginning of her defeat—her unfounded, naïve trust, her complete stupidity, her ill-advised belief that a man could care for her, could choose her. It was all too much.

"If he is a known rogue and you attest that he is not permitted at Rosings, then why is he here in the neighbourhood? How has he been allowed at all of the events of such quality people?"

"His charm and our shared name allow him far too much latitude. And he was a favourite of my elder brother. He never did see our cousin's shortcomings. I do not trust him, but I never thought him a villain—just a selfish creature who liked to take advantage of his relations. I thought him an idle man with delusions of becoming rich with little to no effort. I never thought the young ladies in our neighbourhood were at risk. I would have warned you. I assure you, I would have." He ran a hand down his face and through his beard, "And I do not like to speak ill of my family publicly. I thought it was best, but I was wrong. This is all my fault. I take full responsibility, my lady."

Despite her great dislike of the man, she once again found herself wrapped in the arms of Sir Lewis, clawing at his lapels and wishing to God that the events of the past hour had never happened. Unsure if she had reached for him or he for her, she found herself clinging to him—praying the consequences would disappear—hoping beyond hope that it was all a bad dream.

"Shall I find your aunt and bring her to you?"

"No, sir," she whispered, taking a step back. "Perhaps you could call for our carriage and carry word to my aunt that I am feeling poorly. I cannot return to the ballroom in such a state."

"Of course. It is the least I can do. Wait here. I shall speak to a footman about your coach and then find your aunt. Once I have done so, I will return and walk you around to the front of the house myself. I would not want you to encounter any of those gentlemen in the garden on your way."

Catherine sighed and thanked him for his kind attention.

Lady Rosamund said very little on the drive back to Whitmore. She was holding her tongue, and Lady Catherine was conscious of it. Every time her aunt looked at Catherine in the darkness of the cab, she felt the weight of her aunt's disappointment. Apparently, they were not going to speak of her behaviour that night. And that was just as well, because Catherine could not make heads nor tails of her decisions at that time. She wondered what Sir Lewis had told her aunt. Did he confide the truth in his old friend? Would she be punished come morning? And what of the earl? What would he say when he arrived?

Catherine had thought she knew disappointment in herself, but nothing could be worse than the self-defeat she felt on that ride to Whitmore. When last she was brought this low, her sister and Mr Darcy could share the blame. What had felt like a short ride on their way to the ball felt like an eternity upon their return.

Once they arrived back at the estate, Catherine quickly took herself to her chambers. If her aunt could not be roused to speak in the carriage, it would not do to have this conversation in the small hours of the night with servants greeting them in the main entry.

Dawson was ready to help Catherine dress for bed when she arrived in her room. Evidence of her ruined evening must have been unmistakable on her face, for even in her exhaustion, Dawson clearly saw the truth of it.

"What has happened, my lady? Are you unwell? Shall I call for a sleeping potion?"

Catherine stopped Dawson's speech, holding up her hand. "I do not require any potion. Please, help me undress and that shall be all."

Dawson looked uneasy and worked quietly. She removed the gown and then her beautiful skirts—visibly noting the mud on the hem but never saying a word. After she helped her from her stays, she brought in a fresh chemise for Catherine to sleep in.

She looked bewildered. Catherine was under the impression that the girl was staying her tongue—fighting against the desire to know more.

After Dawson released perhaps her twentieth sigh, Catherine finally gave in, "I confess, it was a terrible evening."

"My lady! What can I do for your health?"

"I am not ill. A gentleman I had considered a friend spoke unkindly of me tonight." It was not all, but it was the truth.

Dawson was clearly shocked. "Who would do such a thing? And on the night of your engagement!"

"My engagement?"

"My apologies. I am ashamed to say that the servants have been gossiping all night. A footman overheard your conversation with your aunt earlier today. The kitchen girls have been making guesses at the fortunate gentleman."

Mortification upon mortification.

"I promise you I took no part in it," Dawson declared. "I would never divulge what we speak of behind closed doors, though I can assure you I had not a guess at the gentleman. But you did seem rather enthusiastic this evening."

"It was Mr de Bourgh—Sir Lewis's cousin. But I trust you will not repeat it."

Dawson looked confused.

"He was also the gentleman who insulted me this evening, so I hope I can convince my father to ask him to go quietly. I wish nothing from him at all."

"What a snake in the grass!" Dawson cried out, followed by a vastly unladylike curse.

Catherine was shocked by her candour.

"My lady, you could not know this, but he was involved earlier in the week in a scheme that saw the coachman, Harold, removed from his post with no references and sent away."

"What can you mean by that?" Catherine queried.

"Mr Allison—the butler—discovered the scheme. Harold was taking money from a man for information about the goings on in the house, my lady. We had no notion of why the man sought these reports, only that he was paying rather handsomely for details about the family and your movement in the neighbourhood. The man was a Mr Arthur de Bourgh."

CHAPTER SIXTEEN

As it was, Catherine did, in fact, require a sleeping potion. And she hoped it would do more than help her rest—she wanted it to erase the events of the past week and settle her into Kent before—before she had made the worst decision of her life.

First her sister had made a fool of her, and now Mr de Bourgh. She had been gravely mistaken, and as it happened, a proposal of marriage had not solved all her problems or brought her any happiness—only misery.

She was wrong to trust him. She was wrong to not confide in her aunt. She was wrong to not delay her answer and await the earl. She was wrong to make her own choice.

The only person who did not make her feel additional shame had been Sir Lewis. To her unmitigated surprise, she had felt comforted and even relief from a man she had incessantly cast aspersions on. He had not scolded her, only his cousin. He had even taken the burden of fault.

Catherine's conscience reproached her. Remarkably, the world was a much scarier place than she had once thought. She had led a sheltered life, indeed. Every tutor and governess and even her mother's advice could never have prepared her for the life-altering ordeal that was Mr de Bourgh's deceit.

She had no idea how to move forward now. She had thought only the morning before that marriage would solve everything. But she saw now that a proposal was nothing to a partnership that could bring stability and trustworthiness and steadfastness. It was not promised. The pain of her self-reproach seeped into every inch of her being. She could find no interval of ease.

And even she could admit that a little voice inside had told her to *run*.

That feckless dolt had her convinced that everything she believed about the world was upside down. When Dawson brought her some tea and a tray of food around ten, she was no closer to any solution that might save her reputation and punish Mr de Bourgh as she hoped.

"Lady Rosamund will see you in the morning room," Dawson said as she stirred Catherine's tea and placed it before her.

Catherine ate quickly, for she had little appetite. Walking down the stairs to her aunt, she felt the squeeze of anxiety in her chest.

"Catherine," her aunt called to her. "Come sit here with me."

Catherine did as told and took a seat next to Lady Rosamund.

"I am sorry, Aunt—" Catherine began.

Lady Rosamund raised a hand, halting her apology.

"No. Pray pardon me. This is as much my fault as yours." Her aunt loosed a frustrated sigh. "I had not realized you had been much in company with Mr de Bourgh—certainly not enough to be entertaining such an attachment. Had I realized, well, that is to say, I might have warned you that he would not be an ideal partner for you."

"His ghastly ways have become known to me. That is why I requested we leave the ball early last night. I overheard him—" Catherine could not finish the sentence. Tears began to gather in the corners of her eyes, and a sob bubbled up in her throat.

"I am aware," Lady Rosamund said, patting her hand in a comforting manner. "Sir Lewis told me all when he came to me last night."

"I can assure you I had no idea that his attentions were motivated only by my fortune."

"I am at fault as well. Mr Allison recently discovered a scheme with my coachman. It seems Mr de Bourgh was paying Harold to track our movements. Even after Harold was dismissed, I could think of no reason why Mr de Bourgh would desire to learn information about my household. It had not even occurred to me that his efforts were about you. I did not think you had been much in company! I should have gone to Sir Lewis. Their dislike of one another is well known, but he is still family to my friend. I did not know how my concerns would be received," Lady Rosamund continued. "Mr de Bourgh was a favourite of Sir Lewis's brother, and he continues to have many acquaintances in the neighbourhood who are more than happy to welcome him into their homes."

"I see. Sir Lewis did tell me some of the same . . ."

Lady Rosamund cleared her throat and turned to Catherine. "We must talk about your future."

Catherine nodded.

"Your father has by now received my summons. Because of my misunderstanding, I wrote to him that it was Sir Lewis that you had received a proposal from. I have no notion if he knows of Mr de Bourgh or what Mr de Bourgh has to offer you—I cannot say what my brother's reaction will be when he arrives.

But, know this, dear: the earl is a compassionate man. We shall tell him all, and he will not force your hand—not for a scoundrel. He is too protective of the Barringer name and especially his beloved daughters. He will not allow you to be taken by a rogue gentleman and whisked away to an unknown life without protections."

Catherine hoped her aunt was right.

"You look as if you need rest."

"I do, Aunt."

"I will not take more of your time. Return to your chambers, and we shall await the earl."

Dawson sought Catherine at half past three, telling her that the viscount had just arrived.

"My brother! It was supposed to be my father," Catherine thought aloud.

What would it mean that Ashby had come in her father's stead? Her future was looking bleaker and bleaker still. Her own father could not be bothered to travel to Kent on her behalf? Not even for a marriage proposal? Perhaps it was better that she knew now how little she meant to the earl—for her distress was now absolute.

"The footman overheard the viscount telling your aunt that he carries settlement papers on the earl's behalf. He will take them back to London for his father's signature post haste," Dawson explained.

A sickening feeling crawled through her stomach and almost had her calling for a chamber pot. If she could keep her breakfast down, it would be a great feat.

"Has my brother asked for me?"

"He has not. I came as quickly as I heard," Dawson said. "I knew you would want to be prepared."

Her aunt was informing him of her dreadful choices now. What would he think of her? Would he carry word of her stupidity to Elinor? Would she too ridicule her?

Would he possibly force her to marry Mr de Bourgh? Ashby had shown no compassion for Anne only a few short months ago. And she felt certain, in that moment, that he would not want his time wasted and could possibly insist on her following through with this marriage to preserve the Fitzwilliam name and avoid a scandal. And what of her brother's friendship with Mr de Bourgh? Did that exist or was it another falsehood? The latter was more likely, but the thought of Ashby knowing his true character, and perhaps reacting with indolence, frightened her. His quickness to boredom bordered on distasteful. And now she would be the recipient of his lassitude.

That thought spurred her into action.

She grabbed Dawson's shoulders and spoke quietly, checking the door to ensure she heard not another soul nearby. "I need you to listen to me very carefully."

"Yes, my lady," Dawson replied, evidently surprised by Catherine's fervour.

"I need you to find Sir Lewis de Bourgh."

Her lady's maid's eyes grew into large saucers.

"No one else should be informed. You will leave without telling Mr or Mrs Allison where you are going." The butler and housekeeper would no doubt interrogate her if they thought she was up to no good. "And if anyone stops you, you tell them you are on a private errand for me. Do you understand?"

She nodded in agreement.

Heart hammering wildly, Catherine wondered if this would be the next unpardonable decision she made in a lengthy list of recent poor choices.

"Find Sir Lewis—not his steward and not his housekeeper—you find the gentleman *himself*, and you tell him you have a private message for his ears only. Do you understand? *No one else must hear you.*"

"I understand." Dawson nodded emphatically.

"You tell him that the viscount is here with settlement papers and might mean to make me go through with a promise I made last night. He is here to determine consent, you see. And you tell him that I need him to honour a promise *he* made last night."

"Yes, my lady."

Catherine made quick work of going to her escritoire and tearing a new sheet of paper from the stack. She wrote only "You pledged your fealty," and folded the note quickly before handing it to Dawson.

"Go at once—make sure he understands that I need assistance *directly.*"

"Of course."

"Go now."

Catherine watched Dawson quickly disappear out of the servant's door.

He promised. He said he would help her out of this mess. And even if she had never liked the man, at this very moment, he seemed her only hope.

Not an hour passed before the housekeeper, Mrs Allison, came to Catherine's room and asked her to join Lady Rosamund and Lord Ashby in the drawing room.

Her hands could not stop shaking, and she nearly tripped over her own skirts as she made her way downstairs. She hoped Dawson would find Sir Lewis in time, because her fate was riding on this upcoming interview with the most mercurial member of her family. She hoped dearly that Lady Rosamund remained with her. Her brother had no appetite for emotions, and she was unsure if she would be able to keep hers under regulation.

"There you are. It took you long enough," the viscount said in place of a greeting.

His cold demeanour increased her agitation.

"Is our aunt correct in telling me that you have attached yourself to the neighbourhood scoundrel? How could you ask this of me?" he roared. "He is known in London for being a fortune hunter with less than savoury acquaintances. No one of quality would call him friend. Although I have never made his acquaintance, even I have heard of his brazen past. Of what were you thinking?"

Catherine could not stop her shaking and saw that her aunt, too, was agitated. Lady Rosamund's hands were tightly wound in her skirts, and her look of disappointment was heartbreaking. Lie upon lie upon lie was compounding, and an exceedingly unladylike sob was begging to be released from her chest.

"Speak now!" Her brother demanded. "I have little patience for theatrics."

Catherine could not find it in her to answer him. Her shame was immense, so large it felt as if it swallowed her whole. She swayed on her feet, reaching for something to hold and found a ready hand at her side, grasping her fingers tightly and squeezing her hand.

When she looked to her right, she found Sir Lewis. *When did he arrive?*

His grip felt like a steady promise. He had come! He would help her, she knew it. Surely he would not press his cousin's suit. She felt fortified with his presence. In her desperation, he seemed the only haven for safety. He can call it off—he is the man's relation, after all. He could hush up Mr de Bourgh, could he not? He could send him away and beg his silence on the matter.

"Lord Ashby, Lady Rosamund," Sir Lewis greeted the others in the room. "Catherine."

His look was intense. He looked resolved about something, and she knew not what.

"I hope you will wish us joy," he said to the viscount and her aunt.

Everyone's confusion was great, especially Catherine's. She looked at Sir Lewis for a clue as to what he was saying, and he simply lifted her hand to his mouth and kissed it.

"We hope to marry within the month. Is that not right, my dear?"

Catherine nearly fainted outright. The alarm of his statements shocked her into silence. Stunned, but also for the first time in weeks, she felt some relief pass through her. He would make sure this is all righted. They need not go through with the deed. He was only helping her remove herself from his cousin's hold. She pressed her lips tightly together to repress her own physical reaction to his statements. Whatever his objective, she must go along until they were able to plot in privacy at a later time.

"Where is that cousin of yours?" Lady Rosamund asked.

"What need have we for my wayward cousin? I saw him off myself, just this morning. He caught the morning post and is bound for London."

There was a silent conversation that was passing between Lady Rosamund and Sir Lewis. Her aunt seemed satisfied with him and nodded her agreement; but no one was looking to Catherine for hers.

Sir Lewis addressed her aunt. "Can you be happy for us, old friend?"

Lady Rosamund smiled and curtseyed. "I am overjoyed."

Lord Ashby looked amongst the others in the room and finally settled on Sir Lewis. "You have proposed marriage to my sister?"

"I have."

"And she has accepted?"

"She has."

Lady Rosamund intervened for a moment, "Lord Ashby, it appears I was under the wrong impression when you arrived. Is this not happy news? It is just as I said in my letter to the earl. Sir Lewis has offered for Catherine."

Lord Ashby looked to Catherine for her assent, but Catherine was too astonished to respond.

"You must forgive my forwardness in joining this conversation without an invitation," Sir Lewis addressed her brother. "Catherine sent for me as soon as she heard of your arrival, and I knew it was best to rush over and inform you of my intentions.

There it was again—her Christian name. Solidifying to all in the room that he must be her betrothed.

Ashby appeared sufficiently more relaxed. "The ladies ought not stay for this conversation. Sir Lewis and I will handle the contract from here."

215

It was done. Not only was she safe from Mr de Bourgh, but her future was again her own.

Mrs Allison found Lady Rosamund and Catherine in the library to inform them that the viscount had departed. Lord Ashby quit Whitmore without even saying goodbye. Not the earl, not her brother—no one in London cared about her well-being.

Lady Rosamund thanked her and turned to Catherine, "You deserve a private audience with Sir Lewis, I should think. I must go dress for dinner. You will not find me interfering."

And with that, she led Catherine back to the drawing room.

Sir Lewis was standing by the fireplace staring into the flames. When he faced her, he looked tired. Dark circles revealed he had slept as poorly as she had.

"I cannot thank you enough for coming," Lady Catherine said to him.

"You need not thank me for that which I would happily do." For the first time since meeting Sir Lewis, the gentleman appeared skittish and apprehensive. He moved his hands from his pockets to clasp them behind his back and then rested them on the back of a nearby chair. Was he nervous? Did he fear she would hold him to this promise?

"Nevertheless, I am eternally grateful to you." She sought to reassure him.

"Are you? I had thought you might enter this room and rip me to shreds." The uncertainty in his smile endeared him to her.

"How could I? You have saved me from a terrible fate. I had no idea what a scoundrel your cousin was. I am ashamed of myself."

"I am glad you see it that way. I had not thought you would appreciate me tying myself to you without your consent."

"I do not see why that would be necessary. We both know that a marriage between us would be a great folly. We shall wait a couple of days, or weeks if necessary, and then I shall tell my brother that we have decided against the match. No one will be the wiser. It is only the two of us who know about today's interview. My aunt will not press the issue."

Sir Lewis looked weary. "Lady Catherine, my friend, I hope. We must marry."

Catherine gasped. "We shall not!"

He eyed her warily. "We shall. And soon. Your brother has my word that it will be within the week."

"The week! What authority has he over you?"

"He has my signature on the settlement papers, Catherine. Your dowry will be released by early next week. It is done."

The room began spinning as it had done earlier that day, and this time, Catherine could not stop the inevitable from happening when her vision departed swiftly, and the world went black.

When Catherine came to, she found herself lying on a nearby sofa with Sir Lewis kneeling at her side. He looked at her with such pity that she was forced to cover her face with her hands. She could not have him see her in this vulnerable state. Not again. She must ensure some dignity prevailed.

"Are you well?" Sir Lewis asked delicately.

"I shall be. Do not worry overmuch. I slept little last night."

He smiled at that and took one of her hands in his. "I, too, found little rest. I shall find Lady Rosamund and bring her to you. And I will return on the morrow. We can discuss more details then."

"I beg you, no. I shall see you to the door and take myself upstairs for a rest. I have no desire to speak to my aunt at length about my stupidity."

Ah! Another truth divulged to Sir Lewis.

He seemed unsure but agreed shortly.

In the entry, the butler handed him his hat and she bid him goodbye.

Once he departed, she raised her chin and returned to her chambers where she would spend the afternoon in tears, comforted by little, and feeling all alone in the world.

After taking a tray at dinner and again for the morning meal, Catherine was resigned to join her aunt in the drawing room for morning callers. She could not avoid her any longer.

Lady Rosamund rose at her entrance, relief apparent on her sympathetic face, and greeted her with a kindness she did not deserve.

"My dearest, I hope you are well. I know you have had quite a scare."

"I am not certain how I feel today. Could we not pretend none of this has happened?"

Her aunt chuckled at that. "We could, but it would not last for long. I have had the knocker removed. Only Sir Lewis shall be admitted. I am not certain how many people were told of your engagement to Mr de Bourgh at the ball. In that vein, I fear what guests might say if they were admitted. It is more important that you and I and your future husband come to a decision about how we might further protect your reputation ahead of the wedding. Sir Lewis is to visit this afternoon, and once you two have had a chance to speak, we will set the date."

Catherine felt a sinking feeling about her life once again being out of her control. She was a prize fool.

"Perhaps we can marry from Oakley this autumn?"

Lady Rosamund's expression was one of sincere pity. "No, my dear. I am sorry to say that you shall be wed by the end of the week."

"Sir Lewis spoke the truth," Catherine murmured as her heart began to pound in her chest.

"Yes, my dear. I suggest that we decide upon a date this afternoon once Sir Lewis arrives. Naturally, he shall have to travel to London for a license. He can visit Mr Sedgwick before he departs to secure a morning for the ceremony."

Catherine's mind was swimming in the many details she had not yet considered.

"Once the rector and he choose a date, we shall call on our neighbours to begin sharing the good news of your engagement."

"And what if they have heard it was Mr de Bourgh and not Sir Lewis?"

"Well, then," Lady Rosamund said, a conspiratorial look gleamed in her eyes. "We shall do what ladies always do. We shall laugh and titter and appear amused by their confusion. And then we shall graciously invite them to a luxurious wedding breakfast at Whitmore."

Catherine hoped her aunt was correct—that it could be that simple.

"No one shall desire to upset Sir Lewis, nor you, once you are his bride. They will go along."

Catherine examined the lace on her sleeves, finding a study of the fabric far easier than forming a response.

Her aunt's encouragement continued. "We could visit a modiste in a neighbouring village to begin choosing some of your wedding clothes. We will not have time to make all your purchases for a trousseau, but you can send to London for more—perhaps your mother would be so kind as to make some acquisitions for your wardrobe on your behalf."

Catherine could hardly keep track of all that must be done.

"You shall be married from Whitmore by the week's end, and then you shall go to Rosings after the breakfast."

Silence was her dearest friend in that moment. She had nothing to offer and no hope of her own—but this time, she could blame none but herself. It was she who had sent for Sir Lewis yesterday morning. In her desperation, she had determined to accept whatever choice he made in order to save her from a life with Mr de Bourgh. She had trusted him, and now she wondered how dearly she would come to regret it.

Sir Lewis looked especially handsome upon entering the drawing room. He had clearly had more sleep than she, and he was dressed impeccably. His beard was trimmed, and his hair oiled. If she were not so angry at his high-handedness, she would say he looked quite spectacular.

Lady Rosamund left the two alone and departed with a warning that she would return within the half hour.

Catherine herself was to blame for sending the note to Sir Lewis, but he had decided her entire future without her input.

"How do you do?" Sir Lewis asked.

"Do not play nice with me now."

That appeared to amuse him. "How should I behave?"

"Be honest, just as you have always asked of me. Are you not pleased with yourself? I would be. You have secured the hand of the daughter of an earl. What a lark! And without ever having to court her or even ask."

His expression betrayed his mortification. "Catherine—"

"I do not give you leave to call me by my Christian name," she said abruptly and rather harshly.

"My lady, I am sorry if you are upset—"

"Upset?" She laughed almost maniacally at that! "You think me upset? I have ruined my entire future. I am certain there is a stronger word for the way I feel, only I cannot think of one just now."

"I see that you are—*not upset*—and I would not dare assign a word to your temperament without your permission, but I would have you tell me the truth. Are you angry with me?"

"Angry is also not a powerful enough word. You have forced me into a marriage I never asked for!"

"And what would you have had me do when your maid found me, out of breath and begging for assistance?"

"I know not, only that I had no say—"

"Should I have let you marry my cousin? Could you be contented living in his rented rooms in London? Many miles from the comforts of Mayfair, I should add. Or would you rather be the mistress of Rosings Park? I could see no other option as I rode as quickly as I could to Whitmore. And when I heard the viscount's stringent set down—"

"And now you shall have my dowry, shall you not? It seems this has all worked out rather well for you." She eyed him with contempt. Her hubris knew no bounds.

He looked at her aghast. "Obstinate, headstrong girl! Arthur pursued you only for his purse. Is that what you would have preferred?"

"Certainly not!"

"He has not a farthing to his name!" His tone was laced with astonishment at her ongoing fervour.

He came closer and stood before her—looking deeply into her eyes. "Would you like to be the mistress of Rosings Park or follow my cousin to London? I shall give you this choice while we have not yet announced our engagement. But I offer it only one time. And I shall assure you that while the chimney piece at Rosings cost me 800 pounds to rebuild, my cousin has not seen 800 pounds in his lifetime. And he will swindle away your fortune at his earliest convenience. Do you not remember what he said about you in the garden?"

"I would *never* elect to tie myself to that man. I only wanted *some* choice in my future. You took that possibility away from me."

"And when, pray, did you imagine we would have had time to come to a decision together?"

That she did not have an answer for.

"Listen to me," he said more gently. "I shall not be heavy handed. You shall be my wife, and I will ensure you are afforded everything that comes with that position. I will not make any future decisions that affect our lives without consulting you. I have faith in you and respect you. But you must put some trust in *me* now."

Catherine was once again against the wall with no place to run. First Mr Darcy, and now Sir Lewis. She was tired of men choosing for her. But they could not take away her agency. She would be mistress of Rosings Park, and no one would force her hand ever again!

He continued when she did not respond. "I have married for fortune once before, and I have no need for it this time around."

"What need have you this time, sir?" She asked apprehensively.

"Only your happiness, my dear girl."

CHAPTER SEVENTEEN

T hey were married in a small ceremony three mornings later. Catherine participated in the movements of the ceremony with little emotion. She held her chin high and repeated
Mr Sedgwick's words when prompted.

She brought her dowry to the union, but little else. No father,
mother, brother, or sister was in attendance, and no trousseau
would follow her to Rosings Park. She had opted to wear a
favourite gown rather than have some local woman put together
a hasty wedding ensemble.

When they returned to Whitmore after the ceremony, the
formal parlour was decorated in flowers chosen by Lady
Rosamund, and the breakfast that followed included all of Sir
Lewis's favourites. She had provided no guidance and held her
emotions in check at every turn.

After her argument with Sir Lewis some mornings before, she
had resigned herself to her fate and had simply gone through the
motions.

The gentleman across from her smirked when she promised
to obey, and that was the only moment during the ceremony

when she felt some semblance of levity. Perhaps he would be a reasonable husband.

Ashby's man of business, Mr Fraser, had stayed for the ceremony in order to report back to the viscount that the wedding was completed. He was the only symbol of her previous life.

At the wedding breakfast, her friends were quieter than she had become accustomed to. All three had been wide eyed and surprised when she had announced her engagement the afternoon before over tea, although they each wished her well. Virginia had been contemplative and more quiet than usual, Diana pleased for her, and Emilia elated.

They were likely displeased that they had been kept in the dark about the circumstances. No doubt, there were whispers of some scandal or compromise that had led up to it. She hoped her friends thought better of her. Although, if they believed it had been Sir Lewis who stepped outside of propriety, they would be extraordinarily wrong.

After the breakfast and all the well wishes for a happy future, Sir Lewis handed his new bride, Lady Catherine de Bourgh, up into his carriage. She sat in the front facing seat, and he took the rear. They were quiet for the ride that took under ten minutes by carriage and might have been managed in the same amount of time by foot.

When she arrived at Rosings Park, they pulled up to the front, and she saw a bevy of servants awaiting them on the steps, ready to greet their new mistress. Dawson was a friendly face among them and allowed Catherine some little confidence as she took her place next to her husband and ascended the staircase that led into the hall.

The grandeur of the house, at first notice, was reminiscent of Oakley. At the very least, she had not married below her station.

Oak panelled walls lined the receiving corridor, and the floor glistened from a fresh polish.

Introductions to the butler and housekeeper complete, she was shown to the mistress's chambers and told that dinner would be served at half past five.

Her rooms were lovely. Every surface polished to a pristine gleam, and a palette of light blues and creams covered the walls and furniture. She could see that it had been aired and cleaned for her use. She wondered at his previous wife who had likely decorated the rooms. It was Catherine's right to request her own renovations, but for now, she was content. Before starting any changes, she would write to the housekeeper at Oakley and request that the rest of her things be sent to Rosings Park.

Her chambers included a large bedroom and private sitting room. She began exploring where the other doors went—the servant's corridor, a large dressing room, and finally, a door that led into a masculinely decorated room—that of her new husband. That door was shut very quickly, and her breath was caught in her chest knowing of his easy access to her now.

In the early morning hours after Lord Metcalfe's ball, in the privacy of only her own mind, she had returned to that balcony and thought of the physical comfort Sir Lewis had given her. His strong arms and kind words—the murmurings of a friend who would help her find a solution. The physical reaction she had to him. It had all meant something—she knew it—it had been sufficient that when she had felt entirely trapped, she had sent for him the next day. And it would be this night that she would see an intimacy with that same man that she had never shared with another living being. And it frightened her.

She had always imagined the marriage bed to be a duty, but something about Sir Lewis told her that it would be unlike her expectations.

Lady Rosamund had cautioned her to be open and trusting with her husband. She had explained some of what would occur on a wedding night, and if anyone knew, it would be her—for she had had three wedding nights of her own. Of her three different husbands, Catherine hoped Sir Lewis would be gentle and sensible, as Lady Rosamund's first had been. Her second husband sounded quite the rogue, if she could trust her aunt's description. And her third a beastly predator—though her aunt explained all with a snicker and a look of fondness. Catherine was not prepared for such theatrics.

She returned to the dressing room, where she had found Dawson already unpacking her things.

"Are they treating you well downstairs?" Lady Catherine asked Dawson.

"Yes, my lady. Everyone is ever so kind."

"I know your time with me was supposed to be of a short nature, but Jones will undoubtedly not join me here. She likes to be of use to her family and had arranged to return to Buxton at the time of my marriage. So, consider the position of lady's maid permanent, should you wish it."

Catherine hoped she would stay, otherwise she might feel woefully alone in this mysterious house.

Dawson grinned and accepted quickly. She had hoped the same, and it was a great relief to Catherine.

Instead of resting, she sat at the fine writing table in the corner of the room and wrote a letter to Lady Ashby. She knew, of course, that her brother would have told everyone of her marriage, but she wanted Elinor to hear it from her—to not fear for her. If she were to be truly honest, she was sad to see that Elinor had not joined her husband when he rushed to Kent. Lady Ashby would have known the correct path to take, and Catherine wondered if her sister by marriage would be disappointed in her now.

Lady Barringer, she had no desire to write. She had not received a letter from her mother in above two months. If one really considered it, it was her mother's interference in her life that had led her to this point. If she were to bother herself to write, perchance it was best to relinquish anything that arrived by her hand to the fire anyway.

After her letter to Elinor, it was nearly time to dress for dinner, and she felt strangely obligated to stay in her rooms until that time. She had never been in the house before, had not been offered a tour, and would surely find herself lost. It would be better not to delay her first meal as mistress.

The two removes of the meal were taken in near silence. Only mentions of passing different food at times and pleases and thank yous were murmured. If she would live her life at Rosings Park, it was best to begin how she planned to go on—and so she began with quiet dignity and polite silence. She would much rather be taking a tray in her room, but the mistress of such an estate must show her face on her first night. It would not bode well to have the servants whispering about her so quickly.

The butler oversaw the serving of a custard tart, and Catherine picked up her fork, eager to see the dinner come to a close.

"Leave us," her new husband commanded.

Sir Lewis's demand, said rather more loudly than was necessary, shocked Catherine out of the oblivion of mindlessness that she had settled into.

At his command, the butler and the footmen promptly left the room.

"We are capable of serving ourselves, are we not?" Sir Lewis asked her. "And I can see that you are uncomfortable."

"I certainly am not!" Lady Catherine was affronted by his suggestion.

"You have said less than five words all night. You have been cloistered in your chambers all day. Surely you do not wish for a silent, solemn meal?"

"Not solemn—I have been perfectly dignified! What would you have me do instead, sir?" she demanded.

"Speak, my dear. This is *your* home. You are its mistress."

She let out a long sigh. "You want the truth? Do you want me to say everything on my mind when I think it? I have no words to say. It has been a long week. My life is suddenly changed—my name, my home. I do not rejoice in it."

He smiled at that.

"Is that really what you want from me? To defame you in front of your servants?"

"Certainly not," he responded. "But when it is just us, I want the truth."

"And I have given it to you," she responded.

He seemed pleased with himself, and that made her irritated. There was no one else she had ever met whose happy expressions irked her more.

After their desserts were finished, they sat in a more companionable silence for some moments before Lady Catherine remembered that as mistress, the meal was finished when she indicated it was. She stood from her chair, and Sir Lewis followed her action.

It was a rather silly thing, then, that upset her. She had no idea where to go! The housekeeper had brought her directly into the dining room at half past five, and she had no notion of where a drawing room or parlour might be—or if even that was where Sir Lewis spent time after dinner. Perhaps he typically retired to a billiard room or his study? A library or a morning room or a private sitting area . . . the possibilities were endless, and she had no idea what came next.

He grinned as he watched her contemplate her next move.

"Will you stay here and take some brandy, or should we adjourn to another room?" she asked.

"I could show you the library."

She nodded and followed him out into the large entryway that housed the principal staircase that led to the family wing of the house. From there, he opened two French doors and began a short, impromptu tour of the house.

"My mother called this the morning room. The easterly windows are large and allow for an abundance of sunshine. The space is quite dated. I rarely use it."

The room was stuffy, and no fire burned in the grates. She could see the outline of many fine pieces of furniture and a lightly coloured stucco on the walls.

"You may update it as you like," he said casually as they moved into an adjoining room. "This is one of the drawing rooms. When I was a child, my mother held receiving hours in this room. As you can see, it is used very infrequently."

White sheets covered the furniture, but she could see from the light in the corridor that it was a large space with big windows that overlooked the darkened garden. It would be a pleasant aspect by day.

They departed the drawing room through a small antechamber. From there, he turned down a long corridor and began pointing as he walked. "My study is here, a small parlour is there, billiards in here, and we have small summer breakfast parlour through those doors where we shall break our fast tomorrow . . ." And then he stopped and turned to face her. "And here we are . . ."

He opened the doors with a dramatic flourish that nearly made her laugh. "The library, my lady."

But the laughter that was bubbling up stopped in her chest when she took in the room. It was the largest of the principal rooms she had seen. Polished wood gleamed on nearly every surface, and small conversation sets of furniture were placed throughout the space. It was beautiful—far lovelier than the library at Oakley or her parents' house in town.

"It is beautiful."

Sir Lewis looked pleased. "There are other rooms in the west wing that I can show you at a later time—another drawing room, a parlour where you might host friends and have tea—oh, and a room my mother used as a study but was later turned into a music room."

The house was vast, and she was suddenly excited to see more of the manor. If she thought some renovations to her room in Oakley pleasing, revitalizing Rosings would be the making of her—she could feel the creativity simmering inside her, seeking a release.

Sir Lewis stood next to a pair of chairs and waved his hand to invite her to precede him in sitting.

"I usually read in the evening. What did you and Lady Rosamund do?"

She took a seat in the chair he had indicated.

"We often retreat to her drawing room to read or talk."

"Which would you prefer tonight?"

Catherine had no interest in talk. She was uneasy about what was to come later, and any conversation she had with him now would be a poor reflection of her nerves. Catherine immediately stood and announced that she would find something to read.

And so, she did. Grabbing the first book of any familiarity and bringing it back with her, Catherine spent her first evening at Rosings pretending to read a book.

After bathing and dressing, Dawson left Catherine with a kind smile and wished her a good night's rest. Catherine sat by the fireplace for some time awaiting Sir Lewis.

And then she paced back and forth across the room.

And after, she sat on the bed.

Later, she stared out the windows into the darkness of the night.

Where *was* her husband?

It felt like one of his taunts—letting her squirm in worry and self-deprecation in the mistress's chamber while he chuckled to himself next door. He likely had a wicked little peep hole where he was watching her pace and laughing maniacally at her disquiet. Naughty boy.

Finally at her wits end, she opened the door to his chambers to find it empty. The fire crackled in the grate, and his bedclothes were turned down, but there was no husband to be found.

She was not sure whether to be relieved or offended that he had forgotten it was their wedding night.

In the end, she exited his chamber and was too exhausted to determine his motives, falling asleep as soon as her head hit her pillow.

They broke their fast in the quaint breakfast parlour he had pointed to the night before. At least she had known how to find it and did not require a chaperone in her own house. And yet, she itched to see the remainder of the house that morning. It was only that she first must get through a meal with Sir Lewis before she might find the housekeeper and beg her assistance in becoming acquainted with the place. There would be meals to plan and fabrics to order and rooms to open and air. She felt enlivened by the possibilities.

"Did you sleep well?" Her thoughts were interrupted by her husband.

"Yes, thank you. I am eager to engage the housekeeper to see more of the house today."

"I am sure Mrs Owen would be happy to give you a more thorough and thoughtful tour."

That she hoped.

Sir Lewis continued, "Please make any changes you see fit, open any room you like. It will be awfully obvious which rooms have been in use and which have not."

"Thank you."

"Before you go in search of Mrs Owen, might we have a quick chat in my study?"

Hopeful prospects for the day fizzled out of Catherine. Meetings called in a man's domain often were foreboding. She had no interest in receiving a set down on her first full day at Rosings.

"Of course, sir." She responded and followed him out into the corridor they had walked the night before.

Once in his study, Sir Lewis began opening a safe and removing boxes.

"For you—" he said, waving at the small containers as he continued removing more. "There is another safe in your dressing room where these might be better stored. Or you can advise Mrs Owen which ones you are most fond of, and she can move only those."

Catherine opened the first box to find a necklace of sapphires with intricate gold detailing surrounding each jewel. "Oh," she gasped, running her fingers softly on the delicate piece. "How beautiful."

"My mother wore that one often; there is a matching set of earrings somewhere."

Catherine gently opened another box, finding a dainty hair piece—woven metal meant to look like leaves and diamonds for flowers.

"I shall send Mrs Owen to you now so you might direct her where you would like them."

She turned to her new husband, wide eyed. "These were all your mothers?"

"Some were gifts from my father to her, but many have been in the family for generations. These are the de Bourgh jewels—some date back centuries."

A small sliver of jealousy wove through Catherine's chest at the idea that she was the second woman to have been presented the de Bourgh jewellery by Sir Lewis. "Were many of these your first wife's?" she asked carefully.

He looked surprised at the mention of the lady. She bit her lip in contemplation as she awaited his answer.

"Caroline. Her name was Caroline," he said quietly. "And no. The jewellery she brought into our marriage was returned to her family. None remained here."

Catherine could only nod at that.

"I rarely speak of the past, you shall find, for I am always focused on enjoying the present and looking to the future. But do not let that stop you from inquiring. If you have any questions about her, you are free to ask."

It seemed their brutal honesty went both ways. "No. Not at this time."

But she did have one more question—not about his wife, but about why he had not come to her the night before. And for a reason she could not fathom, she did not want him to leave.

"Was there something else?" He had a way about reading her expressions that never ceased to shock her.

"I wondered if you want an heir," she said quietly, and then with more confidence, "How quickly do you require an heir?"

He approached her slowly, coming around his desk to stand before her. "It could be an heiress. My family does not see the necessity of entailing properties from the female line."

He moved closer to her, looking her up and down, breathing more slowly, more decisively. She glanced at his lips, and he caught her. He must have felt the same pull that she had, wanting to be nearer, for he took a step forward and leaned into her, pressing the back of her legs against his desk and lining his body up with hers.

She could feel the fabric of her skirts shift against her own legs as he moved into her space, and his breath on her neck as he whispered into her right ear, "How quickly do *you* want a child?"

Catherine was frozen in time. She had forgotten how to breathe or speak. It was taking all of her power to keep herself from shaking or from pushing herself even more closely to him. The memory of nuzzling his neck and folding herself into him only days before came rushing back to her all at once. His comforting hold and welcome scent were once again at the forefront of her mind. Where once her body told her to *run, run, run*, she now felt a sense that she wanted to be *closer, closer, closer*. No echo of warning sounded in her mind.

"I—I do not know."

He backed away slowly, taking with him every semblance of intimacy he had instigated. "When you know the answer to that question, you tell me." And he departed the room.

She could only catch her breath once she was well and sure he had gone.

CHAPTER EIGHTEEN

Mrs Owen gave Lady Catherine a more substantial tour of the house that afternoon, and they made a plan to meet after breakfast each morning to review menus and discuss household business. This, she was comfortable with. This, she had been prepared for thoroughly. To run her own home would be a pleasure, and it seemed that even if her marriage were one in name only, Sir Lewis had told Mrs Owen that Catherine now had the run of the house.

The knocker had been removed from the front door the day before and would be reinstated in three days' time. It was appropriate and typical for newly married couples to have some time to themselves before they received morning callers or guests. It was not entirely enough time for Catherine to feel she had the house in hand, but it appeared from what she had seen so far that Mrs Owen was managing just fine on her own.

After some adjustment to the upcoming week's menus and requesting changes for refreshments during receiving hours, she sent Mrs Owen on her way.

She had finally seen the west wing of the house. The drawing room and great hall there were in remarkable condition and up to date. So, it was to her to consider reopening the east wing's principal rooms. She was most excited about the morning room and drawing room she had seen the night before.

When she entered the old morning room his mother had used, she was again impressed. Even in the darkness the night before, she could see that the room was well furbished.

A light-yellow stucco covered the walls, integrating a Neo-Palladian wall scheme with delicate ornaments in the spirit of the French Rococo. White moulding complimented the yellow walls, contrasting smartly with the mahogany furnishings and oak floors. The dark stained doors and shutters were equipped with gilt-bronze hardware that reminded her of some of the fixtures she had once removed from the attics in Oakley to update her own room. Before she could start with renovations, she would first have to ask Mrs Owen to air out the room.

The adjoining drawing room was going to be her masterpiece—she knew it. The detailed, plaster ceiling with ornamental wheel moulding and garlanded trophies was just to her taste. A rose-coloured paper covered the walls and was the backdrop to large murals of classical myths symbolizing the elements. It was extravagant, and she would embrace that theme as she made her own decisions to update the room.

As there was another drawing room on the ground floor, she decided she would begin calling this one the Rose Room, with its soft pink walls and sharp details. The contrast from the rich colours and the oak floors was dramatic, but one did not replace flooring like this—it was likely cut from trees felled on the estate, which made it all the more notable.

The Rose Room would take much more time than the morning room, for under the white sheets she found solid, well-made furnishings with worn fabrics that would require replacing. She could hardly wait to explore the warehouses in London for materials that would be equal to the beauty of the two rooms. It would take more patience than she possessed.

When Lady Catherine arrived at dinner that evening, Sir Lewis stood at her entry, pulled back her chair, and told her how lovely she looked. What a show he was putting on for his servants! She pursed her lips at his flattery.

This evening was much more pleasing than the previous, for they spoke about their days, and—bless him—Sir Lewis appeared enthralled by her animated descriptions about her future renovations. It was rather a treat to have a gentleman who shared her interests—or if he did not share them, he was doing a remarkable job of appearing to care.

After dessert, they both adjourned to the east wing so she could continue telling him about her plans. He followed her around both rooms, giving attention to all of her ideas and agreeing to each of her schemes. She was elated that her updates might please him too.

She was standing on her toes, showing him a small rose painted into a mural in the Rose Room, for which she was planning to base the remainder of her decorating scheme, when he came up behind her and said, "If I give you a compliment, will you give me your word that I will not suffer for it?"

She laughed at her husband. "Do you admit to being afraid of me? Do I treat you so badly?"

"No, not as such. But I have seen the way you react to flattery."

He was correct. "Of course," she said and held up her hands in submission. "You have my word. You will not be punished."

His smile created a buzz all its own that worked its way through her body from her shoulders to her toes. Why would he not simply say it? His delay was beginning to vex her, and she was certain that was by design. "Out with it," she finally said.

"It is lovely to have a lady in the house again. And not just any lady—you."

Well.

There were no retorts for such thoughtful words. She had been prepared for some flavour of mockery, not the kind courtesy which found her instead.

"I bid you good night," he said simply, his voice laced with sincerity.

He had no need to ask her permission, she would never have given him trouble for such kind words. And he could never know how much she had a need to hear them.

On the third morning after marriage, Lady Catherine de Bourgh woke with a start. A strange sound had stirred her, and she flinched when she found herself in an unfamiliar room. It took some moments to remember where she was. Tucked under the luxurious bedclothes, Catherine calmed immediately as she remembered she was mistress of Rosings Park. It had taken some time, but the last two days had given her a surge of energy. At last, she had a purpose.

No longer the girl waiting for a future to find her, she was a wife and the mistress of one of the largest estates in Kent. She had heard mention of other properties as well and would look forward to learning more about her new life.

She had little reason to imagine they would become close friends or confidants, but that was not what made a marriage, and she did trust his word.

She broke her fast with her husband, met with the housekeeper, and created lists upon lists of work for herself. Just like when Eloise died, finding a task and a purpose in her ever-changing world felt grounding.

When she met her husband in the dining room that evening, he looked tired. Had he not been sleeping well? She never heard him in his bed chamber at night and wondered how little he was sleeping. The Catherine of last week might have said something unkind, but since he had been magnanimous in welcoming her into his home, she, too, wanted to show some compassion.

"Are you well?" she asked him sincerely.

"Yes, and you?"

"I am, though you look—"

"Say it, Kitty," he said with a smirk and then shovelled a large forkful of beef into his mouth.

Catherine groaned audibly at the audacity of her husband. "I loathe being called Kitty."

"Really? What shall I call you? The Right Honourable Lady Catherine de Bourgh feels slightly formal, does it not?"

She rolled her eyes. Her ladylike composure that had been driven into her all her life was nearly a memory after a few months of sparring with Sir Lewis.

"You may call me Lady Catherine, or my lady, or your ladyship." Her voice was saturated with irritation.

"Fine. Now tell me what it is you mean to say, Minx."

Heavens above! "Did you study the art of conversational redirection or was it born of your peculiar temperament?" He studied her intently, his grin widening with amusement. "I was going to tell you that you look dreadful."

At that, he nearly choked on the beef. His laugh boomed through the dining room, surprising not only herself but apparently the footmen in attendance too, for they were struggling to maintain their solemnity. Propriety be damned, she wanted to laugh too.

"Might I ask Mrs Owen to prepare you a sleeping draught tonight? It is obvious you have found little rest of late."

"How perceptive you are, my lioness."

First a small feline dependent upon field mice and now a comparison to an exotic, wild animal. He lived to rile her. "Lioness? Do you expect me to answer to your ridiculous nicknames? For I shall not."

"Much more suited to you than Kitty, if you ask me." He smiled around his fork.

Catherine stood then from the table, abruptly, even as her husband was clearly not finished with the second remove and long before dessert would be delivered. But due to her position in the household, Sir Lewis was forced to swallow quickly, abandon his cloth napkin, and join her in standing.

She smiled at her small victory. "Shall we adjourn to the library, sir?'

From his smug smile, you would think he was enjoying her little prank as much as she was.

"Please give my gratitude to the cook," Catherine told the butler who attended over their meal. And then she left with a kick in her step and a smile on her face.

Point, Catherine.

The sun shone abundantly through the large, extravagant windows in the old morning room the next day. Catherine was pleased with the quick work of the servants to open the two rooms and told the housekeeper as much. She still had much to do, but not on this day, because she was on her way to the parsonage.

It would be the first time she was seeing her friends since her marriage. They would place the knocker back on the door that day, but she asked Mrs Owen to delay. For instead of waiting on callers of her own, she only wanted to visit the parsonage. There would be many days for receiving guests.

Catherine hurried down the steps, adjusting her hat and pulling on her gloves. When she reached the drive, she found Sir Lewis walking with his hounds.

"Sit," he ordered the dogs. "See here? This is my new wife who has relegated you both to the stables for the remainder of your days."

"Oh posh! I did no such thing." Catherine did not stop walking. She had time in abundance for her husband's goading, but not today.

"I seem to remember you saying that dogs do not belong in the house," he said, coming to walk beside her down the drive, his hands clasped behind his back in his casual manner.

"I am not so highhanded."

"I do not mean to say you are highhanded—you are mistress of this house."

Catherine had no time to play his games today. "When I mentioned that I did not think animals belonged in houses, I was not speaking of your dogs specifically, and that was long before I was mistress of Rosings. Now, I am off to visit Miss Sedgwick. I shall return in time to dress for dinner."

"Shall I have the carriage brought around?"

"That is not necessary. I am perfectly able to walk. It is only half a mile across the park."

"I am aware of your abilities, but that does not signify that you should walk if it is not your preference. You should know that I ordered a second carriage, and it has arrived. Walk if you must, but I know you are not fond of being out of doors."

A new carriage! She finally stopped and turned towards Sir Lewis.

"A new carriage?"

"It is only right that you should have one. It arrived from town today. The new coachman is called Marley, and he shall be at your disposal."

She hesitated. It would be rather lovely to call for the carriage, but she did not like to delay. She had sent a note ahead to tell Virginia of her intentions and expected arrival time.

She looked back to the stables and then to her husband. "I thank you. I shall call for the carriage on my next visit."

She returned his smile, and he nodded to her. "It is no more than you deserve."

A blush warmed her cheeks at his praise. He was truly charming when he wanted to be. His short brown hair was slightly mussed around the edges of his tricorn hat, and his commanding tone only increased his handsomeness. She was staring at him too long. It was time to go.

"Please do try to stay out of trouble, Catherine." He yelled after her, and the bubble of admiration she had just felt for his person popped and faded as she rolled her eyes and turned towards the path that led to the parsonage.

After crossing the lawn of the church and walking through the garden that surrounded the rectory, she felt she was taking her first breath since the ball.

Virginia's parents were in the small parlour in the back of the parsonage when she was announced by their maid.

Mrs Sedgwick stood upon her entry and offered congratulations on her marriage and wished her well. She excused herself to find Virginia while the parson invited Catherine to sit.

Mr Sedgwick was an educated man of middling fifties if she were to guess. By the look of him, he had something he wanted to share with her before Virginia arrived.

"Well, well, you look in good health, my lady. It appears that marriage agrees with you."

"Thank you," Catherine gave a gracious and demure response to his flattery.

"I was surprised when Sir Lewis approached me with a special license last week. The entire village was. I am sure you comprehend that I should not like my Virginia to have any false admiration for a quick run to the altar. A lady's reputation is as fragile as glass—what begins as a small sliver of a crack often leads to its inevitable demise. Rumours can just as swiftly blacken the name of a genteel lady, no matter her position. As the parson, I take the sacred oaths of marriage exceedingly seriously, as do my parishioners. I alone hold the responsibility to set an example for the parish."

Their efforts to hush the rumours surrounding her engage-ment had obviously been thwarted. No matter, the deed was done. She was married. And Mr Sedgwick, as he had so finely put it, was the head of the local parish, and his interests were tied to quelling such allegations about her and her husband.

Catherine was not a stranger to proud gentlemen. "I thank you for the well wishes, sir. Of that, we are in accord. It is cer-tainly an auspicious day when your *patron* takes a wife. And speaking of responsibility, as the *principal* landowners in the neighbourhood, my husband and I also understand the impor-tance of setting an example."

It was good for Catherine to remind him of who she was to him. She would not be pushed to reveal personal information about her marriage to a man whose living depended on her estate. Did he not realize her position in this community now? He would do best not to accuse her of any wrongdoing.

He held her gaze, clearly deciding whether he wanted to con-tinue the conversation he attempted to begin. "Blessings on your happy marriage, your ladyship. If you will excuse me."

He stood and informed the maid by the door that he would be in his book room.

If Catherine lived long enough to see the living at the Hunsford rectory vacant one day, she would certainly choose someone who would know their place.

When Virginia entered, she brought good cheer and happy wishes. So, too, did Emilia and Diana when they arrived. After some time was spent discussing the preparation of tea, and the selection of cakes and biscuits, the ladies finally came around to discussing Catherine's quick marriage.

"We were so surprised!" Emilia cried. "Why did you not tell us of your engagement?"

Virginia and Diana sent quelling looks at her, asking her silently to stop her line of inquiry.

Catherine reached out a hand to Emilia and patted her arm. "Your questions are acceptable. We are friends, are we not? You can ask me anything you like."

The three ladies all looked to her to continue.

"The engagement was of a short duration, but I am happily married. And I am thankful to have all of your support—especially yours, Diana, as I am new to being a married woman."

"Of course!" Diana cried. "You may rely on me."

"I think it all very romantic!" Emilia joined in, just as Catherine could have expected.

"It is all as it should be," Catherine said. She would not divulge any details to her friends. "Sir Lewis met my family at Oakley before I came to Kent. We were certain of their esteem for my husband then, and our friendship grew accordingly once I was in the neighbourhood."

Catherine turned to Virginia. "I did not have the pleasure of speaking to you overmuch at the ball. Have you given Lord Metcalfe an answer?"

"Oh!" Virginia exclaimed. "I had nearly forgotten that you had not heard. Yes, I have agreed to marry Lord Metcalfe."

"Have you?" Catherine was surprised.

"I cannot imagine why I thought to toss away such a good prospect over a flirtation! I did not answer him that night, but when I heard of your wedding, it helped me come to my senses! I could not become the future Mrs Webb! It would be unseemly."

Diana frowned at that. "Mr Webb is a kind gentleman."

"To be sure! But a life with Mr Webb would not compare to being a viscountess." Virginia sounded convinced, but there was less certainty behind her smile. Catherine wondered how many ladies made their marital decisions with such little conviction. "I see now how clever you have been, my friend, and it helped me see to my future. And we shall be neighbours always! Just think—soon I will be serving tea from my own drawing room. It will be far grander than this little parlour my mother allows for my use."

Catherine hoped, for Virginia's sake, that she would enjoy her new life. Heaven knew, she was realizing it was not promised for all married ladies.

CHAPTER NINETEEN

"I meant to tell you," Sir Lewis said over breakfast some two weeks later, "I have recently commissioned an artist from London to visit later this summer so you might sit for a portrait."

The gentleman certainly had a manner of surprising her with some consistency. Their lives were made up of two types of interactions—those where he shocked her with the outrageous things he said, and the other half, where he appeared to be a very fine husband. For the former, she had learned her own manner of retorts, and for the latter, she often knew not what to say.

"Why?" she asked softly.

"My father always had a portrait of my mother in his study, and I should like to do the same."

If it were not for her staunch hubris, she would tell him that this news increased her affection for him. His piercing gaze held her own, and she was finding it harder and harder to look away from him when he said such lovely things—when she forgot he had a first wife and thought that one day she might be the centre of his world. But that was not what this marriage was.

This marriage was an alliance that saved her from a much worst fate, and she would be forever grateful. But she must be careful not to project her growing feelings onto him. He should not be repaid for his good deed with a romantic wife full of delusions of grandeur about their partnership.

Lady Rosamund had visited four times since she began sitting for receiving hours at Rosings, and each visit her aunt spent the entire time speaking of Sir Lewis's past charitable deeds, family, and known history. She had an obvious sentiment for the gentleman and wanted her niece to feel the same fondness. It warmed her heart to know how greatly her aunt wanted her happiness. Letters from London arrived from her mother, Lady Ashby, and Anne with congratulations, though Elinor's words had carried more warmth and candour.

After the morning meal, Catherine sat down with Mrs Owen per usual. She had found some growing confidence in her interactions with their servants. Watching as Sir Lewis scolded his servants into harmony increased her desire to be worthy too of her position. Where once she found him self-important, she now found him formidable—and likewise, where she once found him a scoundrel, she now found him exceedingly droll.

The previous night, they had spoken of some ways she might involve herself in the community. He felt the neighbourhood would desire her guidance and management. Initially, when he would make recommendations to her that suggested he found her worthy, she responded defensively—for she assumed he was aiming for a laugh. But she was learning to accept his flattery without rolling her eyes or scolding him.

It was only late at night that she still felt some sadness over her circumstances. She had indeed been abandoned in Kent by her family. If it were not for Lady Rosamund's dedication to her happiness and Lady Ashby's regular correspondence, she would assume her family had all forgotten her existence.

Barringer House, London
May 22, 1782

My dearest Catherine,
I am much obliged to you for writing to me again so soon. Your letter yesterday was quite an unexpected pleasure. The London air is thicker now that the cool, spring breezes have passed over and sunshine now abounds. I believe most of the city has been abandoned in favour of the countryside, with the exception of those waiting to see the earl's youngest daughter married in three weeks' time. The viscount says we can depart London for Oakley as soon as your sister is married. We have already sent the boys ahead with Nanny Mary. The event will take place on the morning of the eleventh of June. Lady Anne will be married from St George's in Hanover Square. I should ask your sister to sit down and add to this letter, but alas, she is out of doors, for she always rides Rotten Row at half past four. While I am certain the event shall be one the grandest the ton *has ever seen, it is your wedding that I have been much thinking of. I deeply regret that I was not able to stand up with you on your wedding day. I do not regret, however, that you have already found a partner in this life. I am relieved that I will not have to chaperone you through the squeezes next Season where you would be forced to flirt and seek a hus-*

band. Next time we are together in town, we shall be required to attend only those events that will bring us joy. Friday last, we attended a ball at the home of the Earl of Grover, marking the engagement of his eldest daughter, Sarah. The dancing was held in a lavishly gilded Great Room on the first floor, with an exquisite, ornate Neo-Classical ceiling that spoke to their great wealth. I know you appreciate a rich scheme of architectural decoration, and I wondered what you might have thought of it—you have such an eye for ornamentation. Rumour has it, there were near to four hundred of our closest friends pressed into their home, and I can believe it. At one point I found myself nearby an open window and considered leaping into the formal garden so I might take a full breath. The servants were forced to open the state rooms downstairs, including the earl's library, where they hosted supper at half past two in the morning. We shall be very glad to see you whenever you can get away, but I have no expectation of your coming to Oakley until Autumn—or perhaps we could find time to open the house in Bath? Or we might persuade our husbands to London, for which we both agree is the most advantageous. I found the loveliest rose patterned fabric this week that I must send you for your newly styled "Rose Room at Rosings." Do say the word, and I shall have some length cut for you and sent to Kent forthwith. Take care and be well.

Your affectionate sister,
Elinor

Lady Catherine carried the letter from Elinor with her as she entered her husband's study. She had lost her fear of his domain very quickly, for he often invited her in to give her opinion on estate matters.

"Lady Ashby has written," Catherine walked around his desk, rather than taking a seat. She leaned against the large mahogany desk, her skirts spilling around her. "She carries news about my sister's wedding which will be held on the eleventh of June in town. At St. George's, of course. And she speaks of when we might see one another. Do you think we might travel to Oakley before year's end? We could also meet in London. You know how I want to visit the warehouses. Or we might invite Lord and Lady Ashby for a visit? It could be this summer or later in the year—"

Busy re-reading the letter to ensure she shared the most vital information, Catherine had not realized Sir Lewis was not responding.

She finally looked up to see clear amusement on his face and returned his smile. "Are you out of countenance or simply neglecting me?"

"I was only listening. I look forward to meeting the incomparable Lady Ashby again, for if she always makes you smile like this, we shall be ready friends."

"You tease, but I hope it shall be so," Catherine responded.

Sir Lewis leaned back in his leather chair, the ends of his long legs hidden under her skirts.

"Then it shall be."

Then he added quietly, "Would you like to attend your sister's wedding?"

Guilt squeezed at Catherine, for her first reaction was resoundingly in the negative, however selfish that would sound. She could not imagine finding any joy watching her sister marry

Mr Darcy, no matter how settled she felt in her new life. Even for her sister, with whom she had always held some little affection, the chasm between them now was too great.

"I think not," she replied without meeting his eyes.

He sat forward and reached out a hand to cover Catherine's free one. "Write to Lady Ashby and make whatever plans you like. Our servants are capable, and we are free to travel."

The smallest touch from Sir Lewis had been setting Catherine into a frenzy for days. A brush of her hand here and a pat on her shoulder there. It mattered not how long or short the duration, it was affecting her. She could no longer deny that she desired to be near her husband.

She lifted her thumb to brush over the top of his hand and held his gaze. She still wondered at his failure to visit her at night. When he found ways to physically interact with her so often throughout the day, it led to even more confusion.

She had not mentioned the conversation of an heir again. Conceivably, her happy mood may be what she needed to find the courage to ask again.

"If we have no children together, does Mr de Bourgh stand as the only living heir to Rosings Park?"

She had clearly surprised him with the change of subject.

"He has a younger sister. If he were to perish before I, she could inherit. She is not constituted of the same wickedness as her brother, but she is a social climber just the same."

"I see."

"He is only my heir on paper, but he is not worthy of the position. He would drain the coffers at Rosings in under a year, mark my word. A responsible landowner understands the full weight of the ownership—from his duty to care for the land and livestock to the people who depend on such."

"Yes, of course. And you remind me how important it is that we have a child of our own," she said measuredly.

He sat forward in his chair, pulling Catherine's hand into both of his. "That is what I want." His thumb was moving back and forth over her wrist in a manner that was distracting. The intensity of his gaze was appealing all on its own. Her breath began coming short and fast, her entire person desiring to be *closer, closer, closer.*

She felt nearly ready to vocally agree with him—to say something that might entice him to come to her that night. But they were quickly interrupted by Mrs Owen, who had just admitted a guest for her husband into the drawing room.

She knew Sir Lewis noticed her hesitation to leave him. And she hoped he understood what she sought without telling him directly.

Catherine never made small demands or asked trifling questions now. She had found her voice, as Lady Ashby suggested, and as Sir Lewis encouraged. No one wondered at what she meant or how she felt any longer. She had been Lady Catherine de Bourgh for nearly a month, and she felt the weight and triumph of the position.

After receiving or visiting hours were complete, her previous habit of many years was to adjourn to her chambers for some rest before dressing for dinner. But in the intervening weeks of becoming a wife, she had begun seeking out her husband for some conversation. They often spoke of the estate, the events being hosted in the neighbourhood, or of how they spent their mornings. It felt a true partnership and something she had never experienced nor expected for herself. This was not the way of the earl and countess who seemingly lived incredibly separate lives, often dwelling in different homes and having opposite sched-ules. This was not the marriage she had prepared herself for, but she was warming to the idea that Sir Lewis, being the unique gentleman he was, might be perfectly suited for her.

Today they walked to the folly in the warm, late afternoon sun. A new hat, sent from London by Lady Ashby, was propped at a very fashionable angle upon Catherine's coiffure.

Her husband carried shears so Catherine might cut some roses for the front hall.

"When are you going to explain to me why William cannot cut your flowers? I seem to remember a time my gardener was ex-pected to do this work." Sir Lewis smiled at his wife and handed her the shears.

Catherine bent to examine the newest blooms from the rose bushes that curved around the folly. While beautiful, the hat was an imposing creature, getting in her way of making her cuttings expediently.

"I require your assistance," she said to her husband. Taking his hands in hers, she guided them to her head, showing him that she could not succeed in removing the hairpins that secured her hat. His fingers moved nimbly, releasing each one. "William is perfectly capable of cutting flowers, but his eye for balanced arrangements is lacking. I prefer to choose the colours and vari-eties myself."

Her husband removed the hat and stood back, and she walked around the structure to examine the blooms. As she made her first cuts, he was at her side, ready with a basket to carry them back into the house.

"So, William is removed from his duties, and I have been promoted to flower mule," Sir Lewis teased.

"An apt description." Catherine smiled to herself and looked back at her husband to see his reaction. "Mules are well known both for their stubbornness as well as their strength."

His smile did peculiar things to her, especially when he approved of her retorts. She felt seen and appreciated.

The basket near full, she approached a bush with light creamy coloured blooms but was so caught up in watching Sir Lewis that she pricked herself in her distraction.

The thorn was a sharp pinch on her skin, and a bubble of blood rose from the tip of her finger. "Ouch," she said, bringing her hand up to examine it.

Sir Lewis set the basket down and put her hat upon it, coming quickly to her side. He reached for her hand and pulled it to his chest. It was quick work for him to remove a handkerchief from his breast pocket and cover up her blunder. "All is well. It will stop bleeding if I keep some pressure."

For all her efforts to not stare at her handsome husband, it was moments like this—standing close, with her wrist being cradled in his hand—where she was unable to do so. A light laugh escaped her. Only he had ever been capable of disrupting her equanimity in this way.

He tugged playfully on her arm, bringing her to stand much closer. She now stood inches from her husband, and that longing once again made an appearance. She wished to be held by him, like the night of the ball, but she did not know how to ask for it. She had too much dignity to beg.

He held her gaze and smiled, removing the handkerchief and kissing the tip of her finger. "All better," he whispered.

Her breaths were coming in and out frequently, and her body warmed rapidly under his gaze in combination with the sunshine.

His attention and her growing attraction made her uneasy, and so she removed her hand from his grasp and picked up her hat.

"I have enough roses. Shall we return?" Her breathless response was evidence of her desire, and she picked up her pace to ensure her husband would not notice.

Upon arriving at the house, she handed over the flowers to Mrs Owen and told her to put them in water until she could arrange them in the morning. Her hat was given to a footman, and she took herself upstairs to dress for dinner.

Entering her room, she was quickly taken aback when she saw herself in the mirror. Physical changes in her were so obviously on display. Golden streaks swam through her tresses—a shimmering blonde that must have appeared for all her time spent out of doors—brazenly joining light brown hair. One obstinate curl, striking out on its own, refused to bend to the will of her hairpins. The sun-lightened hair and new freckles across her nose were not only evidence of time spent out of doors but of her recent happiness. And yet, only some weeks ago she would have found it especially appalling. Lady Barringer certainly would have. But how it suited her! She looked more alive than ever before.

Later that night, after dinner, Catherine and Sir Lewis took coffee in the library together as had become perfunctory.

"I wished I had learnt to better play the pianoforte so I might supply us with some entertainment in the evenings," Catherine lamented.

Musicianship had always come so easy for Eloise and Anne. Sir Lewis deserved a wife who might play for him.

Sir Lewis stood and approached her, leaning over to kiss the top of her head. "No one in England shares your true enjoyment of music or has such natural taste, my dear. If you had learnt, you would have been a great proficient."

She batted him away, always uncomfortable with his flattery.

"And we shall have plenty of music on the morrow at Whitmore," he said as he took his closed book and returned it to a shelf. He was a much faster reader than she.

While their evenings mostly looked like this, they did partake in some neighbourhood events. And her aunt would host a musicale the following evening. Sir Lewis was right, she did enjoy music more than most. Perhaps that was enough.

"You are correct, of course." She stood to join him, placing her book on the low, polished table beside the settee to finish at a later time.

He reached for her hand and placed her arm on his. This had become their habit. They would take coffee and read for a time, and then he would accompany her to her chamber door.

There was always an intense feeling swirling in her belly when he brought her to her door each night. She longed to pull him inside, and yet, she always hesitated. She needed more proof that he would welcome her attentions. She was certain she had felt it—more than once. Catherine wondered too if he was waiting for her to make an advance. In all of her education, this was never discussed—the ways of husbands and wives.

On this night, she held onto his arm even after they arrived at her chamber door. She thanked him for a pleasing evening and for transporting her flowers that afternoon.

"Your flower mule, my lady," he responded and bowed to her with a regal flourish. Always making sport.

And this night was like so many others. He pulled her close and raised her hand to his mouth where he left a burning kiss on the back of her hand. She nearly asked him to join her. Instead, she simply bid him sleep well and bemoaned her cowardice once behind her closed door.

A few days later, the fabric arrived. After many quick letters back and forth, and an embarrassingly unfortunate sketch on the part of Elinor, Catherine was finally in possession of the fine, brocade fabric that would soon be upholstered on all the seating in the Rose Room. The light and dark pinks were divine, and the cream-coloured roses, tied in a bow, were just as she had pictured.

Dawson and Mrs Owen helped carry the large packages into the room so she could lay out one of the swatches upon a chair.

"It is very beautiful, my lady," Dawson told her.

Catherine nodded but was immediately drawn to the sound of loud boots outside the room. Her husband!

"Sir Lewis!" she called and walked towards the front hall. "The fabric has arrived."

His smile reflected her own as he followed her into the room and praised her good taste. Soon she would be hosting guests before dinner in the Rose Room, just as his mother had.

"I think this calls for a dinner party soon," her husband said. It was just like him, these days, to say what she was already thinking. They were in such delightful accord.

"Perhaps something small? Some dinner and cards?" she wondered aloud.

"Or something grander, my dear. What say you to hiring some musicians to come perform?"

She beamed. Hosting her first event at Rosings Park would be pleasant indeed.

"Excuse us, if you will," he said to the servants. Both Dawson and Mrs Owen dispersed quickly, closing the doors behind them.

He was still smiling at her—he looked so pleased. His hands came up to both of her cheeks, framing her face.

"It is beautiful."

"Thank you."

"Truly. I have long hoped that Rosings would feel a family home again, and you are bringing it back to life."

His expression was so full of awe that she could hardly contain her happiness too. She was content—fully and wholly blissful, if she were honest.

He was looking at her so intently, and then his gaze shifted to her mouth—and quickly back to her eyes. Hands shaking and pulse racing, she smiled in response. If he was looking for permission, she was only too happy to grant it in that encouraging manner.

"Catherine, my girl," he whispered, and then his lips were on hers.

His mouth was softer than she expected and a lovely dissonance with the roughness of his beard. She moved her lips against his, eager to learn the correct movements with him leading the way. His kisses were delicate, and she could scarcely believe how deeply every inch of her was affected by his interest. No part of her body, from her fingers to her toes, was not altered by his touch.

His breath mingled with hers, each kiss promising another, it seemed. Her body softened at his attention, and she melted into his embrace. It was the moment she had been waiting for—a signal that he welcomed her attentions and an opportunity to show she would welcome his.

A soft knock on the door had them stepping back from one another, but not too quickly, and not before she saw the disappointment cross his expression.

"Come," he said, once they were at an appropriate distance.

The butler entered the room and handed a letter, edged in black, to Sir Lewis. "This just arrived. The rider said it must be passed directly into your hands."

Sir Lewis looked at Catherine in concern. The blackened edging on the correspondence indicated that the letter carried news of someone's death.

"Does he require a response?" Sir Lewis asked.

"No, sir."

"See that the rider has a meal before he departs."

And with that, they were once again alone. Sir Lewis crossed the room to stand more closely to the sunlight coming in from the windows. Catherine followed, her hands shaking vaguely, though she tried to hide it. Her husband skimmed the letter quickly, betraying no emotion.

"Your ladyship," he said formally, looking into Catherine's eyes with sadness. A sense of foreboding pooled in her stomach. "I regret to inform you that the Earl of Barringer has died."

Father.

Catherine reached out for the nearest seat and sat herself. She was in a daze, her mind reeling from the news. Suddenly, Sir Lewis was at her feet, kneeling before her and asking if he could provide her anything—some tea or he could accompany her upstairs—she heard not what else he offered. Her thoughts were in such disorder that she could not comprehend the news.

"Tell me what else the letter says," she finally said.

"The letter was sent from an inn outside of London. Your mother and your brother travel now to Oakley to bury your father," he said.

"I see."

Women were not often invited to burials, but they would be expected in Derbyshire as soon as possible. "Does mother want us at Oakley?"

"It is not your mother who writes, but your brother," he murmured, looking up from the letter with a gentle gaze. "He does not mention our travelling, but we can leave at first light if you wish it."

"He does not mention us travelling to Oakley? Does he mention what happened to father?"

She pulled the correspondence from her husband's hands and skimmed the missive herself. No details on her father's death were included or her brother's expectations of her—only that Anne and Elinor remained in London for some days to close up the townhouse before following their party to Derbyshire.

She looked up at Sir Lewis's kind eyes. "He mentions that Elinor and Anne are prepared to welcome us in London."

"Was not your sister's wedding to take place this week?"

Oh, Anne! Only four mornings away.

"Should you like see your sisters?"

"Yes." It felt wrong to remain in Kent and mourn alone. She should be with family if they were not expected in Derbyshire.

"Well, then, let us to London."

After a rest and some private weeping, Catherine took a tray in her room. It arrived with a note from Sir Lewis that informed her that he would be in the library after dinner. As she had requested, her husband had personally gone and told Lady Rosamund of the earl's death.

When she joined him, he approached her with some hesitancy but, in the end, he held her in his arms like he had at the ball. His physical touch was a deep comfort to her.

Sir Lewis pulled back to ask her, "Shall we stay with your family at Barringer House, or should I send ahead my man to secure rooms in town?"

"You do not have a house in London?" Catherine was surprised at that. Her husband had mentioned many properties.

"I do, only it is leased through Michaelmas. Remember when I travelled to Manchester? I have leased the house to a businessman—a Mr Bingley. He has done well for himself in textiles—a real innovator. And he means to find himself a gentlewoman for a wife."

Catherine chuckled. "Good luck to him in town. The gentry will not take lightly to an unknown man coming to London to purchase a wife."

"There will be some ladies for whom marrying a man like Mr Bingley will mean keeping herself in the manner to which she is accustomed. He is a good man. Not all fathers plan so well for their daughters as yours."

"You mean to say you are in support of his efforts? To bring himself up in the world by way of a marriage to a lady of the gentry? Is that not the same as what your cousin attempted? You cannot imagine he will be welcome in most good homes."

"I mean to say that Mr Bingley is an excellent man—more so than I can say of many so-called gentlemen in London, my cousin included."

She pondered that.

"So not Barringer House?" He asked, uncertain still of her preferences, for she had never given him an answer.

"No, no—We shall stay with my family. It is only that so much has changed. I will hardly know what to say to any one of them."

"You have changed, too, my dear," Sir Lewis said, smiling at her with great fondness. "And they will love you just the same."

CHAPTER TWENTY

JUNE 1782

C atherine woke in a daze. Dawson was carrying a candle and attempting to gently coax her from slumber.

"My lady, it is time to dress," she said lightly.

It was difficult that morning to go through the motions. Without Dawson, she would have been lost. Catherine had slept fitfully, and while she moved her arm when needed and stepped into her skirts as directed, she did not fully feel herself. She had chosen three of her least favourite gowns to be died black until they could procure bombazine and crepe in town.

Once her hat was secured and her gloves pulled on, Dawson informed her that all was in readiness for removal to town.

Catherine had begun a note to Lady Rosamund the evening before but had been unable to finish it. She wished she had accompanied her husband on his visit to Whitmore the day before. Lady Rosamund had always been fond of her brother. Seizing the unfinished letter from her escritoire, she handed it to Dawson.

"Please see that this note reaches Lady Rosamund today and give her my apologies for my correspondence not being complete. Any other details she requires, I hope you will provide. I do not want to worry her," Catherine said numbly.

"Yes, your ladyship." Dawson curtsied and added, "And please accept my condolences. The earl was a fine master. He will be missed."

Catherine swallowed hard. She did not have it in her to respond and instead nodded and departed as quickly as possible.

Sir Lewis was waiting outside of her chambers, and she felt an instant relief at seeing his lovely face. The tension in her shoulders immediately dissipated. How had he become her dearest friend in such a short amount of time?

He held out his arm, and she took it, leaning into his sturdy frame more than was necessary. His steady gait was reassuring and his strong arms at the ready, she knew, if she needed more comfort.

He led her out into the darkness of early dawn to their waiting carriage and four. All was in order, and she silently thanked her husband for his efficiency. She could not have done this on her own.

Sir Lewis helped her into the carriage. And instead of taking his customary place on the backward facing bench, he took the seat next to her and held her hand in both of his as they departed Kent.

The de Bourghs arrived on the outskirts of town by mid-morning. Sir Lewis had sent fresh horses ahead, so they were not forced to stop for long. Mrs Owen had packed a basket, too, that carried sustenance. Sir Lewis had thought of each detail to ensure her comfort and ease their travels.

Catherine held tight to her husband's hand as they made their way through the crowded London streets. While it was still morning, the city was alive with activity and noise. She felt an ache of longing to be back in the country that amazed her. How had Kent already begun to feel like home?

When they reached the front of Barringer House on Grosvenor Square, Catherine closed her eyes and took a deep breath. She would have to face the truth of her changed circumstances. She was a daughter without a father in this world. And while daughters might logically always know that this day could come, no one could have prepared her heart for the loss. Only Sir Lewis's strong grip and steady nature urged her to make her way up the lavish front steps.

A barouche better suited for use in town had followed their closed carriage, carrying Sir Lewis's valet, Elliott, and Dawson. She watched their conveyance continue past them and turn at the end of the block to enter from the servant's entrance near the mews.

Barringer House had a fashionable address and a pristine reputation. Nothing to Oakley or Rosings Park, the house had a few reception rooms on the ground floor, rooms for entertaining guests, a music room, and a great hall on the first, and the bed chambers and a private family library on the second. There would be little room for privacy, save for their bedchambers.

Lady Ashby had written about the heat, but the prevailing winds in London tended to blow eastward, bringing a soft breeze that made being out of doors tolerable.

A mourning wreath was suspended above the front doors. Because the knocker had been removed, Sir Lewis announced their arrival by banging his gloved fist on the door. Mr Porter, the butler, answered wearing black gloves and a black band tied to his sleeves. He welcomed them into the hall, taking their hats and gloves and asking them to wait in the Blue Reception Room. "Lady Barringer will be with you shortly," he told them.

It was a strange thing to be a guest in your own home. Sir Lewis and Catherine were not forced to wait long. Soon enough, Elinor arrived to greet them.

Catherine greeted her sister by marriage with enthusiasm, holding tight to her and exchanging a perfunctory greeting.

"You know my husband." Catherine stood back to acknowledge him saying, "Sir Lewis."

"Of course, my dear. It is lovely to see you again, Sir Lewis," Elinor replied.

"And you, Lady Barringer," Sir Lewis replied and bowed.

Lady Barringer. Elinor was no longer Viscountess Ashby, but The Countess of Barringer. The thought had not yet crossed her mind. And her mother, now The Dowager Countess of Barringer. The realization seemed to steal away her breath and thoughts in rapid succession. Had not Mr Porter just indicated they would be received by Lady Barringer? Due to the familiarity of such a statement, she had not particularly noticed what he said. But this, too, was another of the very great changes that her father's death would initiate.

"I am relieved to finally see you both in person so that I might offer my sincere congratulations on your marriage," the new Lady Barringer said. "And it appears that marriage suits you."

She beamed at Catherine. Wishing them joy, while welcome, felt peculiar under the circumstances of their meeting.

"Thank you," Catherine responded.

"I wish you were here under more favourable conditions." Elinor began walking out into the hall, and they followed her. "I am sure you will want to refresh yourselves after your journey. Mrs Price will show you to your chambers. Once you are rested, I shall be in the drawing room or the library and ready to receive you. I have not seen Lady Anne today, but she might be found in the music room this afternoon."

Catherine swallowed her response. When did her own family begin to feel so foreign? The formality. The empty etiquette.

"Thank you, your ladyship," Sir Lewis answered for them both, offering Catherine his arm as they followed Elinor into the front hall.

The housekeeper, Mrs Price, met them at the bottom of the principal staircase and asked them to follow her. Thankful for her steady and solid husband, Catherine leaned on him for genuine support. Everything felt so wrong, except for the gentleman at her side.

Shock upon shock, the housekeeper stopped in front of the Ashby Apartments on the second floor. Her mother had redecorated the set of adjoining guest chambers upon Lord Ashby's engagement. These rooms had been used by Catherine's brother and Elinor for these past five years.

"Why are we staying in my brother and sister's apartment?"

Mrs Price's gaze betrayed her displeasure. "The new Lady Barringer ordered her things and her husband's moved to the master and mistress's chambers. Her ladyship requested that we prepare these rooms for your use."

Catherine gasped. Her father was not even laid to rest, and Elinor was having the servants rearrange the house. She felt the sharp sting of betrayal from the female in her family that she had felt the closest to.

Catherine had begun to realize the plight of a lady living with her husband's parents. Through both Diana and Elinor, she had seen clearly that they were not mistress of their homes—their husbands' mothers were. And she could understand their frustration, but this felt cruel. Her mother was being moved where? Had she even been notified? Would her brother remove her mother from her chambers in Oakley upon their arrival to Derbyshire also, or had he sent a messenger ahead to begin airing the dower house? The entire situation made Catherine feel more sickened than she had upon learning of her father's death. If Catherine bore a son one day, would she too be swept away upon her husband's death?

All her life, Catherine had listened attentively as her mother and tutors and governesses explained her place in society. The social structures were in place for a reason, she had always been told. And Catherine had listened and honoured those practices and rules without question.

And now she was seeing it for what it really was—and unending cycling of power and wealth that left dreadfully few happy or content in their lives.

And she did not want any part in it.

After changing her clothes and washing the dust from the road off her face, Catherine paced her chamber with angst and resentment. After many months of longing to see Elinor, she now did not wish it, and visiting with Lady Anne was no better. If she had been put in her typical chamber, she would feel some greater comfort. But God only knew what the new Lady Barringer had planned for that space. Catherine wanted to throw something—something sharp and fragile that would break into hundreds of little pieces. But to punish the servants for her family's failings would be unkind, she knew.

A soft knock on the door interrupted her heated thoughts.

"Come," she said a little more sharply than she meant to.

But it was not the door to the corridor that opened, but the adjoining one—from her husband's room. He was wearing new clothing. A pair of tight black breeches under tall, polished boots and a loose-fitting linen shirt opened at his neck with the sleeves rolled up. She had never seen him in such a state. And he had never looked so handsome.

Her expression must have betrayed her emotions, for his gaze held such sympathy and kindness. "Are you well?"

"No," she said. "How can I be?"

He nodded. "I thought I heard you pacing the floor, and while I have always allowed you your privacy, I could not abide knowing you were uneasy. I had to see to your welfare."

She felt the tears welling in her eyes. She bit her lip in some embarrassment for her dramatics, trying hard not to weep in front of her husband. But his sympathetic expression did her in. At his approach, with open arms, ready to hold her and carry her through this, she became a well of emotions needing to overflow. She had been trying not to drown from the weight of it. And those arms—solid and abiding and comforting—pulled her to his chest, finally allowing it overtake her.

Some while later, Catherine woke in a bleary-eyed state, confused about where she was. Until she realized she had fallen asleep on Sir Lewis. They were seated side-by-side on a sofa in her bed chamber, and she must have dozed off on his shoulder. After holding her for nearly half an hour while she exorcised all of her emotions, he had gently sat her down and told her to rest while he read. And here they were. Him, reading, and her, waking feeling much clearer minded. She was tempted to hold still so that she could prolong their closeness, but he had hearing like a hawk and had already noticed her waking.

She sat up, straightening her bodice and brushing her hands down her skirts in a failed attempt to smooth out the wrinkles. It was no use; she would have to change once again.

"It is nearly time to dress for dinner," Sir Lewis said quietly.

Catherine gasped and laughed. "Are you teasing me?"

"No, madam. It is past four in the afternoon. What time does your family sit to dine?"

"I slept all day!" It was a shock. Her neck would surely ache for it later, but she was not certain she would regret it.

She hurriedly pulled the bell to call Dawson while responding to her husband, "At Oakley, we dine at half past five. But I cannot know if we are keeping to country hours here in town. I will ask Dawson, and then we shall know how to proceed."

Dawson entered and relieved her nerves. Dinner was at six, and so she sent her away and asked her to return in an hour.

It did not go unnoticed, however, that Dawson was surprised to find Sir Lewis in Catherine's chamber—in his shirtsleeves no less. What Dawson would never know is how novel it was to Catherine as well.

Sir Lewis reached out to her, and she gave him her hand. He pulled her back down to sit with him. "Let us rest a little longer, hmm?"

Sir Lewis tucked her in close to him, his legs hidden under her wide petticoat. And then he raised his arm on the back of the sofa

and nodded his head at his shoulder—an invitation for closeness that she deeply desired too. And so, she rested in the arms
of her husband until it was time to dress for dinner.

Catherine left her chamber with five minutes to spare and
found her husband awaiting her just outside their rooms.
Though he leaned against the wall in the most informal
manner, his dress was the complete opposite. It was rare to
see her husband in evening wear. Even when they attended
parties in Kent, he often chose tall, polished boots rather
than the white silk stockings and low-heeled, buckled shoes
he wore this evening. Though the black silk was subtle, his
double-breasted waistcoat was indeed fashionable.

"You forgot your powdered wig, my dear," Catherine said,
her tone saturated in sarcasm.

That made him chuckle, and the enjoyment she gained
from making him laugh was shameful.

She had, at first meeting, found him crass and casual. And
now, seeing him dressed like her brother or father felt all
wrong.

"Shall we?" He offered his arm, and she took it, leading him
down the stairs and into the drawing room.

Elinor was present and waiting when they arrived. She
looked beautiful, and Catherine forgave some of her anger
when her sister by marriage pulled her in for a very unexpected hug, kissing both of her cheeks and inquiring if she and
her husband had settled in.

Catherine was about to answer her when Anne entered.

Catherine turned to greet her and was suddenly surprised to see her sister so changed. Where her face had been round and freckled, she appeared to have slimmed, and her unblemished, porcelain skin was astounding. From her gown to her hair, she was everything a woman in her first Season in town should be. She looked grown, and it tugged on Catherine's heart in a way she would never want to admit aloud.

Catherine curtseyed to her sister and began making the necessary introductions.

"May I present my husband, Sir Lewis de Bourgh of Rosings Park in Kent. Sir Lewis, this is my sister, Lady Anne Fitzwilliam."

"Sir Lewis," Anne said. "It is lovely to meet you."

"And you, Lady Anne." His manners were impeccable. She was relieved to have him by her side.

"Shall we go through to dinner?" The new Lady Barringer halted the tension in the room with remarkable aplomb.

Being the highest-ranking lady present, Sir Lewis offered Elinor his arm and led them into the dining room. Sir Lewis took a seat at her left, and Catherine at her right. Lady Anne pondered her options and selected the seat next to Sir Lewis.

Dinner was a strangely quiet event. Once the necessary pleasantries were dispensed with, the small party found little to speak of. Catherine thought the silence unnerving and decided to seek answers to some of her questions.

"Do we have word from my brother?" she asked.

"They should reach Oakley tomorrow if the weather and state of the roads did not impede them," Elinor replied.

"And then you will follow them to Derbyshire?"

"Yes. I have been tasked with closing up the house. There was much to do with the wedding breakfast cancelled."

A small sound—almost a whimper—escaped Anne's mouth.

Catherine turned to Anne and asked delicately, "Have you discussed when you will marry?"

"In December. As soon as six months have passed. I begged Darcy to consider a quiet, private country wedding later this summer, but he will respect my mourning period." Her shoulders slumped. It was obvious that she was hoping he might bend the rules for her.

"Does Mr Darcy remain in London?" Catherine asked.

"Of course!" Anne responded. "He shall not depart until we do. Lady Barringer has agreed to permit him to visit the house, discreetly of course, in the late mornings and after dinner until we depart for the country. I cannot go on our daily rides or expect to see him at events, so I am grateful for her granting his visits." Anne nodded to Elinor in appreciation.

Elinor leaned to Catherine to further explain, "Your sister had a habit of riding at Rotten Row with Mr Darcy each afternoon. We delayed dinner until nearly seven each evening so they might enjoy some time out of doors."

Catherine nodded. Hearing about her sister's courtship did not appeal to her.

Anne went on. "I tried to explain to Darcy that people in the country are more forgiving. No one should have to know that we have wed . . ."

"Mr Darcy is very correct," Catherine responded, appalled at her sister's lack of sympathy. "Our father has died. His death deserves respect." This, she said unabashedly, looking to both Elinor and Anne.

"You must forgive me for bringing up such a topic at dinner, but no one has explained what happened to my father," Catherine said with care.

Elinor's fork halted in the space above her plate. "My apologies, Catherine. Of course you deserve to know. Your father had been somewhat unwell for a period of a month. Your mother requested that I not mention it in my letters to you because your father wanted privacy. Two doctors visited, dispensing tinctures and attempting other procedures. This is why your brother rushed to Kent instead of your father when you received your proposal from Sir Lewis. It is also why he did not stay for the wedding and instead left behind Fraser in his stead."

"I see," Sir Lewis responded solemnly.

Catherine joined in, frustration fuelling her honesty. "I understand not wanting to spell out my father's private business in the post, but why could my brother not tell me the truth of it in Kent?"

Elinor's attempt at a sympathetic expression failed to dissuade Catherine from anger. "I cannot speak for your brother."

"Of course, you cannot," Catherine blustered, setting her napkin on the table and rising.

Sir Lewis immediately stood.

Catherine placed her hands on the table. "And then? He continued to become more ill, and you did not think to call me to town?"

"No, dear," Elinor responded. "It all happened so fast. One day he was feeling much better—attended dinner and sang with your mother while she played the pianoforte. The next morning, he did not wake. The doctor said it was apoplexy."

Catherine's heart surged in her chest, beating with grief in a profound way that brought her to mind of the days that followed Eloise's death.

Catherine wondered why they had even come to London. No one here was mourning her father. Her own brother had made no mention of the de Bourghs traveling to Oakley to see her father buried. Not one person in her family had sought to call her to London when he was ill. Whereas she had heard of his death and made immediate plans to depart for town, Elinor and Anne appeared as if nothing had changed except a shift in power and foiled plans.

The weight in her chest began to ache. She sought the gaze of her husband and nodded in the direction of the doors. She was finished with the meal.

She felt lost in her own family and wanted only to return to Kent.

CHAPTER TWENTY-ONE

The next morning found Catherine and her husband attending church with Elinor and Anne. All eyes stared from the pews as they entered like a dark cloud, sombre and clad in black. The whispers and tittering followed them until they took their seats near the front. Unfortunately, when they arrived at their pew, Mr Darcy awaited them. Catherine had hoped to avoid him and had not considered seeing him so soon. Though her husband knew about their thwarted engagement, she had never told him of the resentment that still lingered.

Her bitterness then followed Catherine to Barringer House where she was forced to introduce Sir Lewis to Mr Darcy and dine with the gentleman. She kept her eyes and her attention away from her near-brother, seeking to keep herself composed. She refused to let his presence ruffle her, even as the bitterness boiled underneath her perfunctory additions to the conversation.

Once Mr Darcy had gone and Sir Lewis was attending to some correspondence in his chambers, Catherine sought out Anne.

They were long overdue for a conversation, and Catherine could not see a way forward without having words.

She found her sister in the music room, sitting in front of the pianoforte, but with the appearance of someone who had no intention of playing the instrument.

"Lady Anne," Catherine said as she entered the room.

With equal formality, Anne responded in kind, "Lady Catherine."

The sisters stared at one another for quite a long moment. Neither wanted to speak, and since it was Catherine who had desired this chat, she would have to begin it, it seemed.

"How was your Season?" Catherine asked.

Anne shrugged and crossed her arms across her chest. "Busy. But you already know that."

"Did you attend the theatre much?"

Lady Anne pursed her lips. "You know I did. I am not unaware that you and Lady Barringer exchanged letters frequently."

The use of their mother's old title made Catherine flinch. How did Anne find it so easy to replace their mother's title so quickly? "It is not easy for me to call her that, yet."

"And why not?" Lady Anne pressed. "It is her place. It is the correct form of address. She has been waiting many years."

"It feels wrong—like we are erasing our mother right along with our father."

Anne's expression betrayed her distaste. "Our mother would not have waited any longer than the current Lady Barringer. I am certain her father-in-law was not long in the grave before she began making changes herself. It is the way of things."

"And the way of things feels wrong," Catherine argued. "You—you of all people, who has flouted the rules of propriety since you were born—"

"I do no such thing. I am only realistic. You—on the other hand—you followed the dowager's rules like they were your religion."

"Mother did not raise us to—"

Anne laughed heartily. "I cannot imagine how you plan to finish that sentence, because in any way you do so, it would be wrong. *Mother* did not raise us at all. We were raised by servants, Kitty!"

Catherine flinched at that. "How dare you—"

"No!" Anne did not allow her to finish again. "You put too much faith in her. You always have. Look at what she allowed to happen to you this winter past."

"That was *your* doing, and yours alone. She wanted to see me happily married, as any good mother would."

"Good mother—you exaggerate, and you know it. She cares nothing for our happiness, only our reputations, and you would do well to finally see her with eyes wide open."

Catherine felt torn. The directives of her childhood had begun to lose their sharp rule over her thoughts, but she was too angered by her sister to relent. Anne was the cause of her pain and suffering—was she not?

Always a selfish girl, now only concerned with taking her place as mistress of Pemberley and having no apparent sorrow for their shared loss. Just like Elinor, Anne cared only about herself, it appeared.

"Pemberley is nothing to Rosings Park!" she declared.

Anne's eyes widened with confusion. "If you think I desire Darcy for my husband because of his home, you know me little. I care not if Rosings Park was larger than any home in England, and I assumed that you felt the same."

Confusion plagued Catherine.

"I assumed you loved Sir Lewis," Anne said softly.

"And why would you assume that?"

"You married him, did you not?"

"Marriage has very little to do with love, sister—as I am sure you will soon find out. But, of course, that is not the sort of story people like to tell, is it? Life is not a romance novel, Anne! Marriage is an alliance. It is dignified. I have a place now, and a purpose. But I do not flatter myself beyond that. And neither should you."

The pity in Anne's expression enraged Catherine further. Could not Anne sense the pain she had caused Catherine?

Catherine scoffed. "Forget our mother. Eloise would never have done such a thing to me. Did I mean *nothing* to you?"

Evoking Eloise's name to support her argument finally broke the hold Anne had on her temper.

"Our sister loved you for who you *were*, not what you would become or what name you would take when you married. And she certainly would never have compared residences in place of the gentlemen who dwell in them. And you know this. She loved you. Deeply."

This nearly broke Catherine. Tears welled in her eyes.

"And I loved you too," Anne said. "I did not mean to cause you pain. You must see it now—Darcy and I are so suited. Neither of us wanted to hurt you, but surely you did not want to marry him. You found it difficult to even speak to him. I was there—I witnessed your discomfort. You were only parroting our mother and seeking her approval, not seeking happiness. I have seen you with your Sir Lewis. You are content. I am certain of it. Why do you bring this argument to me now? I was supposed to marry this week—to a man I love and respect, a man who I imagine building a life with and having children with.

Children I plan to nurture and love, rather than scheme and manoeuvre to my own will."

Anne finally took a breath. Catherine could not hold back the tears that were falling down her face as a physical sign of her inadequacies and failures. It was the least dignified moment of her life—and Anne was witnessing it. Was it true? Had she only been a chess piece in her mother's game? The thought sickened her.

Catherine could not respond. Instead, she took herself quickly out of the room, up the winding staircase, and into her own bed chamber.

Catherine could not settle herself. An equal rush of resentment and shame poured through her, and she felt woefully alone. *If only Lewis had been there. He would have said the right thing.* She trusted only him to fully understand her.

Hearing some sounds coming from her husband's neighbouring chambers, she felt awash with relief. She knocked and immediately walked into his room, already speaking as she entered. She could barely catch her breath as she hurriedly attempted to update him on her latest mistakes. She had given her younger sister a set down, before their father was buried in the ground—days before what was to be her wedding day—and she was not even sure if she had accurately communicated why she had been so distressed, nor if it was even necessary.

"I am such a wretch, am I not?" She asked her husband with a very undignified pout.

"I would never say such a thing," Sir Lewis responded.

"Not out loud." She laughed.

"Not even in my dreams. You are as dear to me as any person has ever been."

"Cease with your empty flattery. I am trying to be serious. I need you to tell me how horrible I am."

"I *am* being serious." *That grin—that smug, delicious smirk.* Catherine rolled her eyes.

"You can rail at me and call me names for the remainder of our lives, and I would still choose you," he said, soberly now.

"You never *chose* me," Catherine said.

"Of course I did."

She was uneasy with the direction of the conversation. It was one thing to be happy in their current situation and another to rewrite history.

Catherine replied, "Regardless of how we came to be together, I am happy you are my husband."

It was significant for her to admit that much.

"We came together because you sent your lady's maid to me. And because I could not refuse you. I will never deny you anything."

If he would not agree that she was the worst possible human in all of England, she had better change the mood to something more playful. She was not comfortable with his empty worship. Flattery aside, his intent gaze and serious words made her physically anxious.

"Anything?" She grinned *his* grin.

Feeling slightly emboldened by the direction of their conversation, she approached Sir Lewis and stood very close, tilting her chin up and daring him to step closer. If he would not agree to punish her, she would tease him and goad him until he understood how she often felt at the hands of his own provocations.

"Anything, Catherine." And she realized too late they were playing very different games. For his expression was as sincere as she had ever seen him, and it ignited a small spark of longing in her that she had been trying to silence for weeks now.

His dark eyes were watchful. His gaze was weighing her down.

His earnestness notwithstanding, she could no longer play at being lively. His eyes told her that he was not going to join her game. Catherine's heart stirred at his words—traitor that it was. She could not fall in love with her husband! It was unseemly! Love was for ninnies and empty-headed debutantes.

Closer, closer, closer, that voice inside her head called. Sir Lewis appeared to be answering the same call, for he wrapped his arms around her waist and looked her intently in the eyes. The space left between them felt like an ember, ready to ignite the world and burn it down. Her hands itched to touch him and her lips to kiss him.

She could wait no longer.

Sensing once again that he waited for her, she finally answered the demand flowing through her, surging onto her toes to kiss him.

His body went rigid for a moment—and she nearly backed away in defeat. But just as quickly, he appeared to make a choice. His hands moved to the back of her neck, holding her still, and he slowly ran his thumbs across her jaw until they met her lips. A wicked grin overtook his face, and she felt nearly giddy. That mischievous grin that had irritated her for months was now the dearest smile she knew. His eyes dropped to her mouth, and Catherine's entire body turned warm under his inspection.

He slowly began inching the two of them backward until Catherine's back was against the wall. One hand remained holding her cheek while the other began an exploration of her hair.

He stood back with an expression of awe that felt so natural that she wondered if it was reflected in her own gaze.

He brought his lips to hers, angling her face for a deeper kiss, and she parted her lips. Their breath, intermingling, became faster and warmer.

After many minutes of gasping and frantic exploration, his tongue slid into her mouth and ran along hers. The movement was so small, and yet, it felt another world had opened up to Catherine—a sensation yet unexplored, a well of emotion that had been hidden away. A warmth spread low in her belly, an indication, she wondered, of things to come.

"Is this what you want?" He broke the kiss to ask her.

She was not interested in conversation, and nearly panted her response, "Naturally."

"My girl." He took her face in his hands. "Tell me how you would like this marriage to be. And be very clear."

As usual, he asked for honesty, so she answered as such. "I wish to be your wife. Fully."

And that was all it took.

His hands tunnelled through her hair, sending hairpins in all directions. With each *ping, ping, ping* she heard as they hit the oak floors, she grew more eager.

She gripped the lapels of his frock coat—to pull him closer or to steady herself, she did not know. And she began to feel a great loss of control—her inhibitions dwindling with every moment that passed. Her hair began falling down in long, golden curls that felt as intimate as the kisses. No one, besides Jones or Dawson, had ever seen her in such a state.

Hair down, her reticence collapsed around her.

He tasted like he smelled, like the gentleman who had become her closest ally and friend. And she kissed him with an abandon yet unknown to her, learning the shape of his mouth and the feel of his breath.

He moved to brush his lips on her cheeks and then lower, down her neck, urging her on and opening new doors in her mind.

"My lioness," he purred, and she chuckled in a haze of want. She would accept the ridiculous moniker now, for she did feel wild.

Closer, closer, closer that feeling inside her shouted. And as if he had heard the demand, he began to tug at the closure of her *redingote* just above her waist. She reached between them and began to show him how to remove the hooks from the eyes, and then pulled at the concealed lacing beneath, opening her gown to reveal her chemise and petticoat.

If she had felt on display before, it was nothing to the way he looked at her now. He was wild too, and she felt every bit his prey as his eyes danced riotously upon his target. She knew not whether to cry in relief or laugh in amazement at their behaviour.

His frock coat and waist coat joined her clothing upon the floor, followed by his boots. He stood before her in only his breeches and shirtsleeves, his shirt opened to reveal his lean, muscular chest. She could see the outline of his strong arms. His masculine form and height made her feel more feminine than she had felt previously in her life. She felt emboldened by his interest in her and could no longer deny their shared desire.

She expected to feel more defenceless or exposed in this moment, but she only wanted to pursue these new instincts further—to coax them out and see them to completion. Regardless of her shaking hands, she was resolved to be his wife in every way.

She dropped her petticoat and lifted her chemise over her head, leaving her only in the barest of underclothes. He joined her in removing his slim breeches.

Catherine took in their new state of undress and smiled. She trusted him and herself in that moment as he pulled her closer and led her to his bed to lie down upon it. He moved to brace himself above her—gently, almost reverently.

Towering over her now with his solid arms beside her head, Catherine whispered that she was glad she sent for him that day in Kent. She would trust none other with her future than him.

He kissed her softly then and promised that he could have done no less than he had. That he had wanted her long before that moment.

When at last they came together as husband and wife, Catherine felt equally a sense of awe and comfort and passion that was foreign to her. He was her home. Wherever he went, she would follow. He had helped her find her voice, and in him, she found a shelter for her orphaned heart.

They lay together for some time afterwards, until their breathing regulated. Her head resting upon his chest, Catherine's fingers still discovering the feel of him, his hands running through her hair—and she wondered if she would always be this happy.

And ever so quietly, Lewis increased that joy tenfold. "I love you, Catherine, my girl."

An immeasurable pulse of comfort shot through her and left her without any reasonable response. She moved against him, holding him more closely and kissing him on his chest. She hardly knew how to suppose that she could be the object of admiration for so great a man. His bewitching good humour. His kind eyes. He saw her as worthy, and the novel feeling overtook her. Her affection was also secured, but she could not find it in her to voice that thought—the moment felt too precarious, too precious.

"It is a rare occurrence indeed that causes you to be speechless, my dearest," he whispered. "Perhaps I shall tell you that I love you more often."

They both dissolved into laughter that eventually led to the soundest sleep of her life. Her last thoughts before drifting off were, *I love you too.*

Catherine woke in her husband's arms. A soft knock from the interior door had roused her, signalling that his valet was going to enter.

"One moment please," she called out. It must be nearly time to dress for dinner.

She was not eager to leave the warmth of the bed, nor the comfort of Sir Lewis's arms wrapped tightly around her.

"Sir Lewis," she whispered, and he squeezed her more tightly. His possessiveness forced a laugh from her.

"Lewis," he growled.

"Fine. Lewis," she said, kissing his neck and giggling against his rough beard. "Elliott is outside waiting to dress you for dinner. I need you to release me so I might return to my own chamber."

"Tell him to leave," he grumbled, moving against her and laying his face across her stomach. He kissed her belly in long, languid, open-mouth strokes. "I am going nowhere."

"After my performance earlier, Anne will think I am hiding from her." She attempted an escape but found herself sinking deeper into his embrace.

"Let your sister think what she will. Now that I have you in my bed, I shall not let you go."

Catherine felt breathless against his ministrations. Her mind and body were in a peculiar battle for victory over the other.

"Stay," he commanded, rising off of the bed. Catherine turned her face to avoid the sight of him with no clothing on. She heard the door crack open to the servant's corridor, and Sir Lewis spoke in quiet tones to his valet, Elliott. The door shut quietly after a brief exchange.

"There. It is done," he said smugly. "You shall not run from me now."

He returned to the bed, and instead of crawling under the bedclothes, he pulled the blankets back. She fought against it, pulling against his efforts—and lost. She was left exposed, un-clothed, and under his intent inspection.

Fondness and mischievousness permeated his expression. She felt her cheeks heat under his gaze and flipped over, turning her face into the pillow, attempting to hide herself from him. But that only seemed to rouse his interest. He lay on top of her, surrounding her from behind with his body, trapping her under muscled legs.

He moved to whisper in her right ear, "They will send a tray for us at six. I have no intention of leaving this bed until then."

The whisper-soft promise of what was to come made Catherine's body react in the most unladylike way—brazen and hungry and frantic. In that moment, she barely recognized herself. And she closed her eyes against the expectations of the world to embrace this new life fully.

CHAPTER TWENTY-TWO

After many hours alone, and a meal shared in bed with her husband, Catherine snuck into her room and called for Dawson. Sir Lewis was slumbering soundly, but she was too restless to sleep.

The fulfilment she felt in that moment was everything she had ever wanted and never knew she did. It was a shock to learn that such intimacy was possible with another person.

She was in love with her husband—something she never imagined.

Dawson came to dress her in a simple gown that Catherine could remove later on her own. She excused her lady's maid for the night and slipped out of her room.

Her mind was too full of reflections and sentiment to rest. And while she knew she would not find any meaningful distraction, she went to the library to read.

Entering the library, she walked directly to the shelves she knew would hold something of interest. She ran her fingers across the leather-bound spines. Fielding. Bacon. Defoe. Locke.

She found herself too preoccupied by her own thoughts to make a choice—and too distracted to notice she was not alone.

A gentleman cleared his throat, causing Lady Catherine to jump. She covered the small scream that escaped her lips with her hand.

"Mr Darcy!" she finally said when she noticed the gentleman sitting on a large leather chair in the corner of the room.

He stood and bowed. "Lady Catherine, how do you do? I did not mean to startle you."

She moved her hand to her chest, willing herself to calm quickly. "I am well sir, thank you. Whatever are you doing in here?"

It was after ten o'clock. She had noted the time when she crept out of her bed chamber.

"I am waiting for Lady Anne. I believe she went to fetch something from the music room just now before I took my leave of her."

"And the countess?" Catherine could hardly allow that Elinor would leave Anne and Mr Darcy alone in the library at night.

"The housekeeper came to fetch her. I am sure she, too, will return soon."

"Oh, well, please do not let me interrupt." Catherine made to leave the room.

"You do not interrupt. I am thankful, frankly, for this opportunity to speak to you," Mr Darcy said.

He gestured for her to sit in a nearby chair, but Catherine jutted out her chin and remained where she was.

"We spoke earlier today. You congratulated me on my marriage. We pondered on the weather. I do not imagine we have more to discuss."

Catherine felt ignited with confidence. She had Sir Lewis by her side and a love she could never have imagined. She felt emboldened and cared for. Mr Darcy had only sought a wife, and Sir Lewis had wanted *her*. The difference was so obvious now.

Mr Darcy took a few short steps towards her, "I wanted to apologise for any pain I caused you this winter past."

"Oh, would you now?"

He looked confused at her response. "Of course, we are to be family, and I wish to—"

"Wish to what? Be dear friends?" Lady Catherine laughed heartily. "Mr Darcy, we shall never be friends. What woman would find friendship with the man who jilted her? Cuckolded her with her own *sister*!"

He looked stricken by her outburst. Emboldened by Sir Lewis's love, she felt the confidence to finally say all she wished she had at Oakley months ago. Mr George Darcy had not cared how his actions would affect her reputation, and he deserved to know the harm he caused her.

"I could have been ruined! I was forced to make difficult decisions about my future under the threat of scandal! I abandoned a second Season in town and fled to the country. I very nearly ended up married to a scoundrel and was forced to marry Sir Lewis. All because of your selfish choices."

"Sir Lewis seems a fine gentleman." Mr Darcy eyed her warily.

She was tempted to tell him that Sir Lewis was twice the man he was and that she loved her husband with all her heart, but something inside her wanted to harm Darcy the way he had injured her. "He is tolerable, to be sure, but I certainly would not have gone looking for a no-name widower in the back country of England. My parents had a plan, and you ruined it!"

She let the silence sit quietly between then. It was something she had seen Sir Lewis do, and she emulated him now. Let Mr Darcy wallow in bewilderment and anxiety for once. Let him feel the confusion and humiliation she felt for nearly a month in her own home due to his disinterest.

He nodded and said quietly, "I am sorry. Sincerely. Please excuse me."

It was not nearly as fulfilling as she had imagined, railing at Mr Darcy. Neither had arguing with Anne been earlier in the day.

It left her feeling rather empty, to be truthful. She should have remained in bed with her husband. Mr Darcy and her sister would never understand the distress they caused—and even if one day they did comprehend it, that would alter nothing.

Instead of finding a book, she too escaped the library and returned to her bed chamber to sleep.

Catherine woke to a rare feeling of complete contentment. She stretched her arms across her bed and smiled into the soft morning light filtering into her chamber. Memories of the prior day were already playing through her head, and she could barely keep from giggling outright. Who had she become?

Happy.

She had become happy.

She had a man who loved her—a steady, clever, strong husband.

And she loved him too.

It was a startling thought, but she was becoming increasingly accustomed to the idea.

Dawson joined her some time later, and Catherine could not contain her joy. She smiled and thanked her maid more than once, and two times she tripped trying to step into her skirts.

She was completely mad. All sense of propriety and decorum had fled.

Unburdening herself to Anne and Mr Darcy had also created a lightness in her. She had said what she needed to say, and now it was time to go home. Following her sisters to Derbyshire did not interest her. She and her husband could visit later in the year—stay for a few months and attend Anne's wedding. But, for now, she felt a stranger in a place that had once been home, and all she wanted now was to wrap herself around her husband and tell him she wanted to remove from London directly.

"Has the family already broken their fast?" she asked Dawson.

"Lady Barringer took a tray in her room, and Lady Anne is in the dining room now."

"Has Sir Lewis awoken?"

He was the only person she was really concerned with that morning. And why was she asking Dawson when she could find out for herself by opening the adjoining door? She began to move in that direction when Dawson answered her.

"He left at first light, my lady."

Catherine stopped, frozen in her misunderstanding.

"Where has he gone?"

"Back to Kent, my lady. I assumed you knew. I was only told this morning."

"No—no, I did not know." It was beyond embarrassing to learn such a thing from one's servant.

"Did he leave a note?"

"I was not passed a note—but I can check his bed chamber, if you like."

"That will not be necessary. I shall check myself," Lady Catherine said.

Dawson added, "A footman told me that he woke Mr Elliott around half past ten last night, and they were gone before the sun rose."

Catherine took herself to the window and searched the streets of London for an answer and found none. Her expression must have betrayed her thoughts for Dawson began to ramble.

"It was the night footman; Griffith, I believe he is called. He was stationed near the main staircase last night. He was waiting until Mr Darcy departed, he said. And Sir Lewis woke just after ten o'clock and was walking the floors, first going downstairs, and then up to the library. Then he returned to the footman. He asked him to wake his valet and send him to his chambers immediately. Mayhap he received a letter of some importance?"

"Did an express arrive?"

"No, my lady." Dawson looked at Catherine sympathetically.

And then it hit her. *The library.* Just after ten. And he was gone before the sun rose in the sky.

"Oh no," Catherine whispered. He must have heard her—and she could not even remember the exact words she had used, but her stomach dropped at the memory of calling him *tolerable.* She said she was *forced* into the marriage.

Her husband could never understand that those words for Mr Darcy had naught to do with her relationship with Sir Lewis now. She was resentful and hurt, and Mr Darcy had caused her so much self-doubt. She had wanted to hurt him, and instead, she had hurt the man she loved.

And yet, she had never told her husband that she loved him. Catherine had offered herself wholly to him but had not uttered the words.

Mr Darcy did not hold a candle to Sir Lewis. But her husband could not know the truth of her feelings, because she had never divulged them as she should have. No one could compete with Sir Lewis de Bourgh! And now she was on the precipice of losing the one thing she desired more than anything else in the world.

It was time to leave London. Now.

Dawson was efficient as they began packing her trucks. It was the work of minutes to send word to the housekeeper that she would depart by mid-morning. As it happened, she learned that her husband had taken the barouche and left her the carriage and four. Always putting her above his own needs—that was her husband. And that knowledge, of his unfailing solicitude, heartened her desire to depart with even more haste.

She took a seat at the escritoire in her chamber, writing quick notes to Elinor and Anne straightaway. It was a cowardice, indeed, to slink off without a formal farewell, but she had little time and insufficient concern for the others in the house and their feelings.

Just as she was preparing to depart, Anne let herself into Catherine's chamber, beholding her with obvious contempt.

Dawson immediately acknowledged the tension in the air with a smart nod and excused herself.

"You are leaving London," Anne said sharply.

"I am."

Anne fidgeted with her hands and appeared unsure of herself. It was a rare thing to see her sister flustered.

"I do not wish you to leave while we are on bad terms," Anne finally said.

"We are not. We are as we always were." Catherine avoided her sister's gaze, continuing to gather her belongings about the room.

"If this is what you wish—for us to be relations in name only, I shall leave you. But that is not what I want."

Catherine knew not what to say to her, but finally she faced her younger sister. "I wish you no ill will. My emotions got the best of me yesterday. I had not seen you in so long and—and even before then, we were speaking infrequently. We have lived much of our lives apart."

"I could not agree more. I know little of you . . . but I would like to change that. I have always looked up to you."

"Have you?" Catherine was amazed to hear it.

"Of course I have."

"I did not know that was promised. You have always seemed rather set apart."

"Just because we are not alike does not mean I did not envy you in many ways. I did try to emulate you and our mother, but it did not come easily to me."

"That is an understatement," Catherine retorted.

Anne laughed uncomfortably. "Mr Darcy sees me for me. Like I believe Sir Lewis views you. And when I found so many things in common with him, and our dreams were so alike, I—I could not watch him marry my sister. No matter how much I respected you and desired to see you happy. And I am sorry. I should have taken your feelings into consideration. I ought to have spoken to you directly. I know it was not easy."

"It was not."

"I want to do better," Anne said. "I know that one conversation cannot change the past, but I hoped we might exchange letters."

"We may."

Anne sighed, seemingly relieved. "Thank you. I should like to have a sister—in blood and in my heart."

The thought warmed Catherine, but she remained wary. "We could try."

Anne nodded and wished her sister safe travels to Kent.

As it happened, Lady Catherine was unable to slink out of London without speaking to the new Lady Barringer either. As she descended the main staircase, the lady of the house awaited her near the entry.

"I am conscious that you are hurt and did not feel at home here," Elinor began, "But I want you to know that you are always welcome—here and in any of our homes. You are dear to me, and I have been so pleased by our friendship."

Lady Catherine could not comprehend all of her mixed emotions well enough to explain her unease to her sister by marriage.

"Thank you," Catherine responded. "I welcome your continued correspondence and hope to see you again soon."

Though more formal and less friendly than Catherine would have imagined the visit, the hostility between them would soon wane, and she did deeply want to continue their friendship.

The road was dusty, and Catherine had not the faintest clue how to send ahead for fresh horses like her husband had done on the trip to London, and so she directed the driver to stop in Bromley at the Bell as she had with Lady Rosamund many months ago on their trip into Kent. Catherine shook the dirt from her skirts and took some little refreshment indoors with Dawson while Marley saw to feeding, watering, and resting the horses. The stop could take some hours, he had told her. The sunshine had been unforgiveable, and the horses had worked themselves into quite a lather that morning.

The delay was causing her some anxiety, as was the conversation she owed her husband. No matter how many times she went over it in her head, the words never sounded right. Even to her, the practiced explanations felt empty and trite.

After nearly two hours, the travel party was finally moving in the right direction once again.

When the carriage pulled up in front of Rosings Park, Catherine did not wait for the footman to help her down. She leapt out of the conveyance, picking up her skirts while she took the stairs as quickly as possible.

When she entered the ornate front hall, the butler found her immediately.

"My lady, please pardon me. We were unaware of your arrival today."

"There is no need for apologies, only please tell me where I might find my husband."

"He rode out to the Pope farm not two hours ago. There was some concern about irrigation. The steward was summoned this morning and had not yet returned. Sir Lewis thought to follow him."

This changed her plans. Did she await her husband or go after him? She had not been on a horse in years. But she could not wait another minute after all the delays of the day.

"Please have a horse saddled for my use and send Dawson to my chambers."

Catherine had a general idea where the Pope property was, though she had never gone as far as viewing it. It mattered not, at this point, for her mind was made up.

Dawson was frantically pulling gowns out in the dressing room. "You only have the one riding habit, and it is blue, my lady. I apologise—"

Catherine blew out a breath of frustration. Nothing was going to plan.

"No need to apologise. I had no notion that I would go riding. I will ensure I am not seen."

She could not *ensure* that, and Dawson knew that as well. Wearing anything other than black would be entirely un-seemly, but she had little time to waste. Certainly not enough time to have one of the black gowns adjusted for riding—and she had no intention of sitting around and awaiting her hus-band's return. So, she would put herself on a horse in a blue gown, while in mourning, for she could do no less.

When Catherine approached the stables, a mare was being saddled in the paddock.

A stable boy helped her onto a block to allow her to climb onto the beast more easily, although immediately she was second guessing her choice. It had been many years since she had ridden, and she feared the horse could sense that, too. Animals had a way of understanding Catherine's distaste for them, and she knew horses comprehended more than most.

Catherine took the reins in one hand and brushed the cheeks of the horse with the other.

She whispered to the horse, "Let us make an agreement. You carry me safely to my husband, and I will promise that you shall never have to convey me anywhere again in your life. And I shall bring you some treats from the kitchens on the morrow."

The horse nickered a response, and Catherine unbelievably took it as acceptance.

Speaking to horses, she would have to address another day.

Giving the animal a little prod of her heel, they surged forward in the direction of the fields north of Rosings Park. Twice, she was forced to pull up to a gate, dismount, open the gate, guide the horse through, close the gate, and then climb into the saddle again using the fence for assistance. She must look ridiculous. Anne would have jumped the fences with great ease and enjoyed it, no less. Catherine, on the other hand, was caution's dearest friend.

When she heard the sound of hoof beats approaching her in the wood, she prayed that God would produce her husband and not any nefarious persons.

God did bless her in that moment, for coming around a bend was the person dearest to her heart. Sir Lewis looked more beautiful to her in that moment than ever before. His hair was tousled, his face slick with some perspiration, and his formidable arms in control of his much larger horse.

"Catherine!" he greeted her with no little surprise.

When he guided his horse to stand next to hers, his expression was indeed one of shock.

"Sir Lewis," she said, out of breath.

"What has happened? Why are you here?" Sir Lewis asked. He looked behind and around her, "Are you out here alone?"

"Why are *you* here?" Catherine asked stubbornly. "I left your bed and woke in mine to find you gone—departed from town without a word, not even a note. You must know how that felt after what we shared yesterday."

Sir Lewis grunted gruffly, pulling roughly on the reins, and his horse became agitated. He was usually more in control of himself.

Looking around, he nodded and said, "Follow me. I do not want to speak here."

Catherine agreed and guided her horse to the side of the rough path to allow her husband to pass and then turned her horse to follow him. He led her a different way than she had come, eventually arriving at a small cabin in the woods.

He dismounted his horse, tied the reins to a tree, and moved to assist Catherine with hers.

"This is the old steward's cabin. It is empty now, so we might speak in some privacy. I fear Don Pedro might have thrown me if we tried to have this conversation while riding."

Even making a little joke about his beloved horse tossing him did not bring about a smirk. He was all seriousness. It did not bode well for her.

She followed her husband onto a quaint porch where he guided her to a small wooden chair. Catherine carefully spread out her skirts and then took in Sir Lewis's face. Hardened as it was, it was dear to her.

He sat on another mismatched wooden chair next to her, careful to angle his boots away from her skirts. It felt a great distance from the intimacy of the prior day. His hands were in fists, and the sharp set of his jaw told her he would not make this easy on her.

"I did not mean to worry you," he began. "There was no need for you to rush to Kent. You should have remained with your family."

"My family? Why would I want to remain with them. *This* is my home."

"And so it is, by law, but I will not hold you here," Sir Lewis said sharply. His tone was laden with emotion.

"And what if I said that I wished to be here?" Catherine replied firmly.

"We both know that is a lie."

She drew her finger down her own forehead. "I am certain you do not find evidence here—for I know it in my heart, in my very bones, that there is nowhere else I would rather be . . . than with you."

His gaze hardened. He was a stubborn man, and her words did not sway him.

"Last night in the library—"

He stood at once. "Please, I beg you—I do not need an explanation—"

"I was bitter," she explained. "I was angry. I was finally able to tell Mr Darcy how much pain he caused."

"Lady Catherine, I warn you—"

"Warn me all you want, but I will not stop." She, too, stood. She pushed a finger at his chest and continued. "I intended to hurt him. I wanted him to feel the anguish he had caused me. I desired that he understand how little he had considered my future when compared to his own desires. But where I found the strength to put him in his place was entirely because of you."

His eyebrows rose.

"You helped me find confidence I never knew I had. You helped me find a way to speak my truth. But I did lie to Mr Darcy."

"Did you?" Sir Lewis asked.

"Yes. I did not tell him that his rejection was the best thing that ever happened to me. If Mr Darcy had proposed in January, I would never have had the opportunity to meet you. I might have never known what it is to be married to such as singularly wonderful man. It would have been the greatest failing in my life—for I would never have experienced the act of being loved."

His breathing was deep and full of feeling.

She reached out and grabbed one of his fisted hands and spread his fingers out gently, weaving hers with his. "I love you, Lewis."

There. She had dropped the title and dropped her inhibitions with it.

He turned his face away, not seeming to believe her.

"I was still distressed about how Mr Darcy had treated me. He *was* selfish. He hurt me—and my sister with him. And I finally found the strength to tell them both. But I should never have brought your name into our dispute. You were undeserving of that abuse. You have shown me nothing but compassion and kindness—and I thanked you by tarnishing your name to another."

Finally, he looked her in the eye.

She continued, "Hear me now. For I speak only the truth. I love you and want only you. If I had to experience it all again to have you, I would—even sending you round to the servants' entrance in the rain!"

The side of his mouth quirked up, a sign that her little provocation was helping to break down his defences.

She stepped closer to her husband, gentling her voice. "You are my truest friend and the only person I would ever choose to rely upon."

Finally, his eyes softened, and the tightness of his jaw slackened.

"I know why you ran," Catherine said. "I would have too. If I had heard you speak of my only being *tolerable*, it would have broken my heart. I owe you the most sincere apology. I am sorry. Please, I beg of you to forgive me."

Eyes locked on Catherine's, he took a step forward, followed by another, until Lewis backed her up against the rough wooden slats of the cabin. His divine, familiar scent enveloped her. Her eyes dropped to the pulse at the base of his throat, then travelled to the tense cords of his neck before snapping back up to his.

He pinned her to the spot and heated her skin with only a look. Lewis had Catherine cornered, like a predator, and she wanted to abandon her defences and hand over her whole heart.

She could not draw her attention away from him, for Catherine was a victim of his commanding presence.

"I awoke alone last night—cold without your presence," he said slowly and quietly. "I feared you might have regretted what had occurred between us, and so I sought you out to ensure all was well. When you were not in your bed chamber, I dressed and walked throughout the house looking for you. When I heard you in the library—I—I cannot describe the pain I felt, Catherine. I was out of my mind with jealousy! I wanted to tear into that room and beg you on my knees to love me in return."

Her heart jolted at that.

"To have you in my bed merely hours before and then to hear you speak to *him*, of all people, about how you regretted me."

"I do not—I never could." Catherine reached up to touch Lewis's face, and he allowed it.

"But you did—you spoke of being *forced* to marry me. I never meant to impose myself upon you. I never sought to cage you in. I thought I was giving you freedom, but I see now that in my selfishness to have you—to make you mine—" His voice was laden with regret.

"I am sincerely happy you were selfish that day. And I *am* yours. I will never be another's."

He was swimming in regret and defeat, and she had caused it.

Catherine closed the space between them, and she took his face in her hands and turned it towards her. "He means nothing to me, and you are everything. I will spend the remainder of my days ensuring you know this."

She pulled at his hand and ran his finger down her forehead. "See? I am speaking the truth."

He closed his eyes and rested his forehead against hers.

She lifted her chin and softly pressed her lips to his. When his lips did not shift against hers, she moved her mouth against him, trying to *show* him that she cared even if he would not believe her words.

"Lewis," she whispered against his lips, and his defences fell.

His mouth began moving against hers, and in unison they clung to one another. A wild pulse of want surged through Catherine's body while Lewis laid a trail of frenzied kisses down her neck. She could feel his muscled thigh pushing at the weight of her heavy petticoat, trying to get closer. So many emotions were pouring through her—desire, relief, affection—and all at once.

He stopped suddenly, out of breath and resting his head against hers. "I cannot believe you rode a horse to find me."

311

"That should have been the first indication that my affection was true. For I would ride for little else." She laughed lightly.

"I know, my girl. I must say, though, you do have a fine seat." His smirk was back, along with a healthy dose of sarcasm.

She batted at his chest, "I condescended to ride all the way here and you have the gall to mock me for my poor skills! For shame."

She could not help joining his laughter.

She leaned back and took in his beautiful smile. "Can we go home now?"

"Please," Lewis whispered and kissed her forehead.

CHAPTER TWENTY-THREE

That summer would be fondly remembered by Lady Catherine as the happiest of her life. She and Lewis were in harmony, and together they laid plans for their future. Of their properties, of their wealth, and hopefully one day, their heir—for all, they made careful plans. Lewis respected and encouraged Catherine to provide input on all aspects of their life, and she was thrilled to experience a partnership she had never witnessed nor expected.

Sometime in late October, Dawson brought to Catherine's attention the fact that she may be carrying a child. It was many weeks before she confessed it to Lewis, and they rejoiced together in the promise of an heir.

They travelled together to Oakley in December to attend Lady Anne and Mr Darcy's wedding. It was a small, family affair. Anne had been a devoted correspondent, and Catherine was more amenable to mending their relationship. Their visit was a first step in the right direction. Their time in Derbyshire was more comfortable than expected, and they decided to stay for the entire festive season.

As she and her husband lay together in Catherine's childhood bed—Catherine on her back and Lewis caressing the round proof of their legacy carried within her—Lewis said, "Tell me about the night we met."

Catherine chuckled. "I was having a dreadful week and was aggrieved. My entire future felt bleak and uncertain. I was embarrassed and ashamed of myself and my performance. I had been trained my whole life in securing a husband and had failed at my first attempt. I rather worried it would be my only attempt. And then, Lady Rosamund entered Oakley with such sympathy and kindness. I felt as if she was the first person to acknowledge my sorrow and its considerable influence on my life. It felt so significant in that moment. No one else had recognized me in that way. Feeling unburdened by the pain I had been carrying alone, I desired a moment to myself—to rejoice in it, frankly. And so, I took myself out front onto the terrace."

"And you looked across the lawn and saw your future, did you not?" Sir Lewis chuckled.

She swatted him for his insolence. "That I did not. If I had known my husband stood before me, my life would have been infinitely easier in the coming months. Instead, what I saw was a man, covered in muck from head to toe—a handsome, smiling man—a formidable one too, for he pushed a carriage with brute strength!"

"Such a handsome fellow." Lewis smiled and kissed her growing belly.

"I attest, his smile was kind and warm. And I acknowledged the smile—I believe I smiled back. But that was before a strong wind pushed the rain at me and left me drenched. That was the first time I heard your nefarious laughter. As it happens, that insolent creature began to ascend the steps, and I was fearful for my life!"

"You were not." He ran his finger down the front of her forehead, in a gesture that told her that her fabrication had not found its purchase.

"Well, not fearful, but certainly concerned that the dirty, bold servant would attempt to enter through the front door!"

Lewis laughed against her stomach. "I thought you the most endearing creature. I watched you before you saw me. I stood, drenched in the rain, watching you stare up at the sky and thought you looked truly contented. I envied you."

"You were far from the truth of it," she answered quietly.

"But it was not that which drew me to you. It was your spirited address when you sent me around the back to the servants' quarters."

Catherine hid her face under her hands. "I shall never not be teased for this, shall I?"

"It was your mettle that drew me to you. The way you ordered me away, truth be told. I shall admit, I enjoyed the horror on your face when you realized who I was at dinner the next evening. I was holding back laughter throughout the entire meal. I wondered, in fact, if I should fear retribution from that bold girl I had seen on the terrace. I pictured a toad in my bed or a snake in my boot."

"If only I had thought of that. I was only concerned with being caught for my insolent greeting and being punished for it."

"I was so confused when I met you again in Kent. I saw such a different side of you. One where I was certain you were hiding your true nature. You did not smile with your eyes or fight or yell or tell the truth. I had been longing to see that girl from the terrace at Oakley for weeks. Slowly but surely, I had been trying to get you to open up—to show me that fearsome lady once again. And when you sent Dawson after me . . . I could not deny that I wanted you."

Catherine stilled under his heated gaze.

"After holding you at the ball, on that balcony, and knowing that my cousin might have you—I did not sleep a wink. I wanted to act, and yet I knew not how. I went to see my wretched cousin that morning and threatened him within an inch of his life if he did not leave Kent directly. But I was still uncertain whether he might impose himself upon you. And so, if I had had more sleep, I might have used more tact that morning when I interrupted your conversation with your brother. I might have requested a private audience with you and given you a choice. But I had felt so protective of you in that moment. I would have done anything to safeguard you from a future linked to my cousin."

As fate saw fit, it was in that moment that Catherine first felt the de Bourgh heir move within her womb. The quickening was a welcome blessing, and Catherine fell asleep safely in her husband's embrace.

The late winter months found the de Bourghs returned to Kent to attend Lord Metcalfe and Virginia Sedgwick's lavish wedding breakfast. After many months away from home, Catherine desperately wanted to spend time in Kent before her confinement. She wanted to be with Lady Rosamund and her friends, hosting and attending parties, before their lives changed for good.

The idea of motherhood continued to baffle Catherine. Would it come easily to her? Sir Lewis swore she would be the best of mothers, and she trusted him implicitly. So much so, that she was trying to see things his way. Perhaps she would find much to enjoy about being a mother. For she had certainly not imagined a happy marriage, and Catherine had never been more pleased to be wrong.

The month of May found the de Bourghs planning for Catherine's upcoming confinement. For the birth of their anticipated heir, they would travel back to town because of the reputation for skilled accoucheurs. Catherine was conscious of the risks of childbearing and wanted to take every precaution.

The Darcys had been in Kent visiting since Easter, and Lady Anne would remain with Catherine, accompanying her to London in one week's time. Catherine could not say why she had forgiven her sister and Mr Darcy. *Better the villain you know than the one you do not*, Lewis would say.

On this particular morning, both of the ladies were saying goodbye to their husbands. Mr Darcy was returning to Pemberley, and Lewis was travelling to London to see to some business and oversee the proper opening of their house.

As their child grew within Catherine, so did Lewis's deep concern and overprotective nature. He seemed reluctant to leave her, and she teased him for being a mother hen.

"Mother hen? I have heard you call me worse," he said while he stood beside his horse. Lewis did not like the restriction of a closed carriage and had thus decided that he would ride to town that day. Their barouche would follow him with his trunks and his trusted valet.

Lady Anne was standing beside her husband's carriage and four, speaking quietly while Pemberley's new steward stood nearby. One of the reasons for the Darcys' visit to this part of the country was to meet a prospective new steward for their estate, and Catherine had been more than happy to give them counsel by recommending Lady Metcalfe's steward's son, Ben Wickham. The man was young and hungry for purpose, and Catherine was happy her condescension had led to a fortunate position for Ben and a competent steward for the Darcys. Ben and his new bride would follow Mr Darcy to Pemberley on tomorrow's post.

Lewis forcibly turned Catherine's face away from her sister and held her cheeks in his hands, gazing into her eyes. "I love you, Catherine, my girl."

She smiled up at him. "And I you."

"Behave while I am in town."

She chuckled at that. "You are better to tell your son to behave, for he has been kicking me in the ribs all morning."

He smiled at her. "Are you very uncomfortable?"

She reached around and pressed his hands low on her back. "I have tightness just here that comes and goes. I need only some time to rest."

Lewis looked uncertain. "I should stay."

"No—no you shall not. You had many things you wanted to take care of before my arrival. You said as much. Lady Rosamund has commanded that our son may not make an appearance until she is returned from Ramsgate. And the midwife says I have six weeks at least."

"That midwife is a kook."

Catherine rolled her eyes. "She has overseen the birth of nearly all of the children in our neighbourhood. I am certain she is more attuned to such things than you or I."

He was hesitating again.

Lewis would not say what he was really thinking. His own mother had been delivered of three children already dead, and she succumbed to childbed fever after the third. The English were too proud and superstitious to speak of these things to women who would soon have their lying in, but Catherine knew the risks. No lady was unaware of the dangers.

She knew she must lighten the mood and ensure their goodbye was not shrouded by worry.

"You must not let my sister see you swoon," she taunted. "Now, leave so I can start missing you."

He laughed at that and kissed her. His warm lips covered hers in a tenderness she had come to know so well. She cherished him—fully.

She stood on the drive until she saw Mr Darcy's carriage and Lewis's horse turn down the lane towards Hunsford.

Once the ladies were settled back in the house, they immediately called for tea.

"I have something to tell you," Lady Anne said.

"Will you finally admit to what I have already known this entire visit?" Catherine grinned behind her teacup.

Anne gasped. "You have known and said nothing?"

"It is not my news to share. Have you felt the quickening?" Catherine asked.

"Yes—just. Since I have only just today dispensed with the news to Darcy before his departure, I felt it right to tell you as well."

"Had he not noticed any changes in you?"

"He is a lovely man, perfect for me in every way, and yet one of the least observant gentlemen I know," Lady Anne said with good humour.

The ladies enjoyed a laugh together at that. Catherine had found it in her heart to forgive how her sister and Mr Darcy had hurt her, even if she had at first been reluctant.

"To think—we shall both bear our heirs soon!" Catherine said. "Lewis and I had thought to call our son Fitzwilliam Lewis. Have you given it much thought?"

"I was thinking George, but I have not spoken to Darcy on the subject. What of a girl? I have many ideas for a young lady."

"If it is a girl, I should think we shall choose a family name. Lewis's mother was Hester, and his grandmother, Prudence."

"What of our mother?" Anne asked carefully.

"Theodosia would serve. I had not considered it." The dowager continued to be a subject the sisters rarely canvassed.

Catherine was yet to forgive her mother for all her interference, though she was no longer angry. Her current circumstances were too wonderful to lend her time to bitterness.

"I might go lie down," Catherine said, reaching behind her to the tightness in her back.

"Is there something I might do?" Anne asked, standing when Catherine did so.

"No, I am only uncomfortable. Our son is demonstrating his strength today and causing trouble for his mama," Catherine said lightly.

The pain appeared to disperse when she moved, and the action of climbing the stairs helped somewhat. Once she reached her chambers, she called for Dawson help her into something more comfortable.

Twice while she was undressing, she had to reach out for a nearby chair and grit her teeth against the pain.

"My lady, should I call the midwife?"

"No, Dawson. My son is only signifying his importance. He shall be a fine master of Rosings. Indeed, it is much too soon for that."

But there was no denying that assistance was needed when a slow trickle of fluids began running down Catherine's leg. She had been warned of this, but it was too soon, and she froze in fear. She had heard tales about ladies being brought to bed so early, and they did not end well.

Dawson began fidgeting, worrying her hands and unable to put together a sentence.

Catherine grabbed her by the shoulders, "Listen to me carefully," she said between deep breaths. "Find my sister. Call for the midwife. And send a rider for my husband. He cannot be far yet. I am sure he can be turned around. Then tell the scullery maids to build up the fire in here. Everything should be done as we have been directed."

Dawson nodded and excused herself.

Wearing only her chemise, Catherine went around her chambers preparing the room as she had been instructed. She closed the windows, pulled the draperies shut, lit more candles, and then closed the curtains around her bed before climbing in. She had not expected to do this without a trained accoucheur or the nurse they had hired for her in London—not to mention the two wet nurses they had awaiting them also in town. Above all, she had never imagined bearing this child without Lewis close at hand.

By the time Lady Anne arrived in her chambers, Lady Catherine's brow was already glistening from the heat of the room. The pains were growing worse each time they arrived, and they came and went more quickly each time.

Dawson brought Catherine a heated, spiced ale to sooth her nerves, which did nothing of the sort, but Catherine did imbibe obediently.

The midwife arrived within the hour, drenched from the rain that had begun to fall outside. She immediately added to Catherine's nerves by agreeing that the babe was coming after using her hands to measure upon Catherine's stomach.

"Does he come too early?" Catherine asked, agitated.

The midwife gave Lady Catherine a sympathetic smile. "All will be well, my lady. Babies come in their own time."

"But you indicated that I had six more weeks."

"It is an art, the prediction of childbirth, and not one that is always precise. I have been wrong. I have delivered many babes who we thought were early who arrived strong and hale."

The midwife's words felt empty, reminding her of the way Nanny Janet would soothe her at nighttime as a young child—saying anything to get her to stay calm and remain in her bed.

Catherine slept on and off throughout the remainder of the afternoon, interrupted by the sounds of thunder or when the pains became too strong and close, and she could no longer rest. Occasionally they would ebb, and she would close her eyes.

Lady Anne visited her room with great frequency, while Dawson remained at her side. Her sister reported that a rider had been dispatched to find their husbands, another carried word to Elinor in town, and a letter for Lady Rosamund was in the post.

By dusk, there was no denying the concern on the midwife's face. While allowing Catherine as much privacy as possible, she continued to check on the status of the baby and found no change.

Catherine knew, deep within, that her body was not performing as it should. The heat in the room was overwhelming and was increasing her anxiety. At times, she found it difficult to take a full breath. She could hardly contain her tears as they mingled with the sweat on her cheeks. Dawson kept a damp cloth nearby and used it to wipe her face and cool the back of her neck.

"Please bring my sister to me," Catherine panted.

Nothing was going to plan. She was supposed to be in London, in the guest room they had already furnished particularly for her lying-in. She wished her husband were permitted in the room, for she could only imagine finding solace in his embrace. Squeezing her eyes shut, she took herself to a place in her head where it was only her husband's smiling face that she could see.

When the clock turned to the small numbers of the night, Catherine asked Dawson to bring her sister to her again.

When Anne arrived, she sat carefully on the side of the bed. Her expression betrayed her concern.

Catherine reached for her hand and whispered to her, "I am pleased you are here," she said between deep breaths. "Thank you for writing to me over the last year. I am glad to have your friendship. And your presence here today. It is good to have family nearby."

"Of course, Kitty. I would be nowhere else," she brushed Catherine's damp hairs away from her face and kissed her cheek. "What can I do for you? Shall I plait your hair? Would you like some wine?"

"No, I need you to carry my words to my husband. Tell—" Catherine lowered her voice and took her sister's hand in hers. "Tell Lewis that I love him."

"He knows you do," Anne replied with a soft smile. "This is not the time for grandiose farewells. You are healthy and strong. You will bring this child into the world."

Catherine released her sister's hand and sunk back against her pillows.

Catherine's mind became a fog of confusion by the time the sun rose the next day. Exhaustion overwhelmed her senses, but each time she opened her eyes, she found Lady Anne or Dawson in the high wingback chair settled next to the bed with a ready cloth to cool her forehead.

Her heart ached for her husband. Lewis's calming presence would be a relief to her, and she knew, too, that he was likely pacing the floors of Rosings with his own anxieties.

At one point the pain became so great that Catherine swooned. When she came to, there were more maids around her, whispers that she could not decipher, and the midwife was speaking in low instructions to the servants around the bed.

"What are you saying?" she asked, but no one paid her any mind.

Lady Anne leaned over and blocked her view, smiling at her. "You are doing so well, sister. The midwife would like to try to keep you awake. Would you be able to take some coffee?"

Food and drink sounded repulsive. All Catherine could focus on was the pain in her back and legs, growing in intensity and frequency.

At some point she must have drifted off once again, because she awoke to the mid-wife waving smelling salts in front of her face. Leaning close to Catherine's left ear, she said something indecipherable, but Catherine was beyond caring at this point.

She was clearly terrible at birthing a child and only wanted to sleep.

She heard a noise on her right side. Lady Anne had pulled up a second chair, and said quite clearly and more loudly, "You must speak to my sister on her right side," to the midwife.

Hearing Lady Anne advocate for her was a relief. If Sir Lewis were here, he would have said it much earlier. How long had she slept? A heavy fuzziness was present and pushing her to *sleep, sleep, sleep.*

CHAPTER TWENTY-FOUR

Catherine opened her eyes to reveal bright sun shining around the closed curtains. It must be afternoon. She swallowed hard, her throat dry, and noticed she was lying on fresh linens. Knowing not when that feat had been performed, Catherine considered another nap. She would only shut her eyes for a moment—the pain had become a part of her, ongoing and without end.

Before she nodded off, she caught a glimpse of Lady Anne speaking quietly near to the midwife across the room, and she was weeping. It saddened Catherine to see her thus.

A pain greater than one Catherine had felt in her life narrowed her attention back to reality. Her sister was on her right, Dawson on her left, and the midwife at her feet. They were telling her to be strong. Comforting, bolstering words were spilling in all around her.

Catherine could smell the acrid scent of blood and nearly closed her eyes again.

Lady Anne grabbed Catherine's face and turned it towards her. Dark, puffy circles under her eyes revealed her sister's exhaustion. She spoke fiercely and with great volume and steadiness, "Catherine de Bourgh, I demand you pay attention to me. Do not close your eyes. The fate of the de Bourgh family rests in your hands. You are bringing the heir of Rosings Park into this world. Now."

Catherine flinched and took in the expressions of the other ladies in the room. They looked desperate. They looked worried.

Lady Anne squeezed Catherine's hand and continued. "Push now, Catherine. Bring this babe into the world. I command it."

The strength and fortitude roused Catherine and enticed her to listen and to follow her sister's instructions, but she was so tired. She was uncertain she could rise to the challenge.

"I just want to sleep, Anne," Catherine said weakly.

"But you must not. Not now. It is time."

Catherine stared into her sister's eyes, seeing her stubborn resolve, and held her gaze through a push that felt like the weight of the world was tearing her open.

"Push," Anne said again, and Catherine stared into her eyes, blowing out air in a heavy gasp.

"Again," Anne demanded.

"Now," Anne continued.

"Again," Anne commanded.

"Push," Anne decreed.

On and on it went, until a feeling of great relief washed over Catherine and sounds of life began erupting around the room. The midwife raised the child into the air and called for some fresh cloth to wipe the babe clean. A young woman from the village was called up to the bed to begin attempts to feed the baby.

Dawson and Lady Anne continued ministrations to keep Catherine comfortable and cool while Catherine's eyes followed her baby across the room. She held her breath until she heard its cries. And when she did, she too cried out.

"My son has arrived," she whispered and began weeping once again.

The midwife turned back to her and smiled, "It is a daughter, my lady."

"A daughter," Catherine replied, empty of feeling or emotion, only very tired.

"Go tell Lewis." She squeezed her sister's hand to gain her attention. "Go tell him about his daughter."

Anne reached out and brushed the hair from Catherine's face. "He will be so proud. Now rest, my dearest."

It was a relief to finally be told she could rest. Catherine nodded at her sister and closed her eyes.

The following days were a blur.

Catherine woke to sounds in her bed chamber and instinctively rolled over to reach for her husband, finding the bed empty. The curtains were drawn around her bed, but she could hear that she was not alone. She reached for her stomach, finding her womb empty, and the events of the past days rushed over her.

The house was too quiet.

"Excuse me," she called into the room.

The curtains around the bed were pulled open to reveal Dawson.

Catherine pried herself up to a sitting position, which took some effort. She was in a fresh chemise, and it was clear that the linens had also been changed. She brushed the hair off her face to find it had been plaited.

"Dawson, it is you," she said, her voice gravelly with under use. "Might I have something to drink?"

Her loyal maid made quick work of pouring a glass of barley water. The liquid eased the pain in her throat.

"Have I been sleeping long?" Catherine inquired.

"Yes, my lady. Some time."

"Is the baby well?"

Dawson looked nervously at another part of the room, and Catherine wondered if someone else were present. Her maid was fidgeting and not looking her in the eye. It was unlike her.

"Are we alone?" Catherine asked cautiously.

"Yes, my lady."

"Tell me then, what it is you mean to say."

"You have been unwell, my lady. You lost a lot of blood during the birth. I have been watching you to ensure you do not have a fever."

Childbed fever. No wonder Dawson was concerned. Catherine instinctively reached up to feel her own brow. It was clammy but not warm.

"Has a doctor been called?" Catherine asked, more assertively now.

"Yes and visited," Dawson replied.

Catherine pursed her lips in frustration. It was moments like this when she wished her lady's maid were more loose-lipped.

"And shall I be well?" Her voice was laden with irritation.

"Yes, my lady."

"And the baby?"

"She is well. Small and mighty."

That was a relief to hear. Still Dawson looked uneasy. And Catherine did not think she had the strength to pull the girl's inner thoughts from her.

"Send my husband to me, if you will." Lewis would tell her all.

Dawson nodded and quickly left the room.

It was a chore to find a comfortable position. Catherine was sore and fatigued. She drank the last of the liquid in her cup and kept still. She knew that strict rest was required for ladies after giving birth. It would be four to six weeks before she was churched, and before then, she would not even leave the house.

It was well worth it, she thought, since it had brought Lewis's heir into this world.

She smiled at the thought. He was likely already coddling the little girl—or dreaming of ways to spoil her.

Catherine had only ever thought of the baby as a son. Most ladies did. It was heirs that their husbands wanted. Often daughters were never of so much consequence to a father. But Lewis had said from the beginning that a daughter could inherit all, and so she had delivered that to him. A legacy of their love and a new family formed.

Some little jealousy arose in her that everyone had seen her baby except for her.

And that thought left her worried. Was Dawson hiding something? Was the girl unwell? Lewis would tell her the truth—it was their way. If there were ill tidings, he would tell her, and they would work together on a solution. Theirs was a true partnership.

Luckily, Catherine did not have to sit with her dark thoughts long, for Lady Anne arrived and opened the curtains further to better see her sister.

"I cannot like how dark they keep it in here. Would you not like me to open the windows and let in some fresh air for you?"

Catherine replied, "It is not advised, as you know."

Lady Anne seemed as uneasy as Dawson.

"Sit, Anne," Catherine demanded. "And tell me the truth. Am I well? Is my baby well?"

Anne responded, "You lost some blood, but the midwife and local doctor agreed that you are strong and should survive it. You did not have a fever in the night, so that bodes well. You are ordered to keep to bed for at least three weeks, and after that, only small visits to the sofa or a nearby room. The midwife suggests you do not take dinner downstairs for six weeks total. She thinks you may be well enough to be churched at eight weeks."

It was longer than expected. Catherine let out a sigh. She was not one to envy being out of doors, but neither did the idea of keeping to her bed for a month sound pleasing.

"I understand. And the baby?"

Anne smiled at that. "She is beautiful. Rather small, the midwife said. But hale. They did mention that her early birth could make her more susceptible to illness and recommended that she be kept at home as much as possible for the first year."

Catherine nodded. Even healthy babies often perished of an illness in their first year. It would be difficult to not be over-protective of her with this knowledge. Sir Lewis would probably keep his daughter locked up at Rosings until her come out with this news. Catherine closed her eyes as the weight of the responsibilities of motherhood nudged her mind.

"Should you like to sleep?" Anne asked.

"No, I should think I have done enough of that. Please send Lewis to me," Catherine said, pulling up the bedclothes to ensure some additional modesty.

Anne bit her lip and began twirling her hands.

"What is it?" Catherine questioned.

"I wonder if some sleep might be good for you now," Anne said gently.

"*I* wonder if you might stop neglecting to tell me what is amiss," Catherine said, her voice raised. "Sir Lewis will not thank you for keeping him from me. Send him at once."

"Perhaps you—"

Catherine cut her sister off. "Unless you would like me to crawl off of this bed and drag my sore body to his door myself, you will go find him. Now."

"I cannot," Anne said in a small voice.

"If he is away, just say so."

"He is not away. There was an accident."

That perked Catherine up rather more, and she began leaning around the bed curtains to better see further into the room. "Is he in his bed chamber? Is he very hurt? If you help me, I shall go to him."

"You cannot." Anne put her hand upon her sister's. "He is not there."

"Heaven and earth! Will you not tell me where he is?"

"He is dead, Catherine."

The world must have turned on its side, shaking her from her place in existence and pouring her back down into a pile of rubble, for she did not feel whole. The shock of it rattled through her, pain unlike she had ever felt, and still she sat. The sob in her chest was waiting—praying she had heard wrongly.

She asked very quietly in a voice she did not recognize, "Where is he?"

"His body is laid out in the drawing room in the west wing. Callers have been visiting to pay their respects. But we did not want to bury him until you were well enough to say goodbye. Lady Rosamund will be here soon. She wants to see you, if you would welcome her visit."

Catherine stared past her sister at a nearby wall. She was not looking at anything in particular but could not tear her gaze away.

Her entire world had come crumbling in around her.

She felt dead inside.

And cold.

And unfeeling.

And lost.

And so, all she said to her sister that day was, "Leave me."

In the small, dark hours of the night, Lady Catherine de Bourgh called for a footman to carry her to her husband. He placed her in a chair next to her husband's body, laid out upon a table, and she felt exceedingly small and alone in the world.

A woollen shroud was wrapped around the strong, capable body that had sheltered her and celebrated her and brought her to life. Only to abandon her merely a year later. He had built a world for her that she had never thought possible, and now she found herself returned to reality. A life without Sir Lewis de Bourgh was indeed not one Catherine particularly wanted to enjoy.

But this—this felt closer to the existence her mother had promised her. Marriages were alliances, and love was an evil blight ruining perfectly suitable matches. More fool her. She had allowed herself to fall victim to the first lesson her mother had taught her about such alliances. Reaching her majority and marrying well was supposed to be about duty and decorum—about following a strict diet of perfection.

Instead, she had succumbed to love—an emotion she had pitied other ladies for feeling.

Catherine sat next to Lewis for a long time, willing it all to be a dream—a nightmare more like. She wanted to shake him awake. She wanted to shake herself out of this truth entirely.

And for a while, it was only silence in her head—a deafening silence, worming its way into her soul.

In parallel to the stillness of her mind, she found herself screaming into the empty, dark room in defeat, loudly and fervently mourning the loss of the greatest man she had ever known.

She sat, her mind as empty as her heart. The sobs that racked her body poured out of her in long, unfamiliar moans. Physical laments emanated from her like a mournful knell, signalling the end of an existence she had come to cherish. She laid her head down upon the table and made two promises to Lewis—to ensure his legacy and keep his daughter safe—at whatever cost. She could do no less for the man who taught her to love.

She said a silent prayer over his body and stood. When the footman came to carry her, she simply raised her hand in defiance and told him she would walk on her own.

As she stood in the front hall of Rosings Park and took in the enormity of the house and its responsibilities and remembered that her baby girl slept somewhere within, she promised herself she would never succumb to emotion or passion ever again. She was empty of love, a heart once again orphaned, right at its infancy.

After climbing the stairs, she walked down the corridor to the nursery and found her baby sleeping within. She excused the wet nurse and placed her daughter into her arms.

It was hard not to resent the child resting in her arms—to not want to barter her for Lewis. But she knew better. Lewis would not want that. He wanted his legacy secured.

She sent another silent prayer up to the heavens, asking Lewis to watch over her sister, Eloise. And then she thanked God that Elinor's advice had led her to Kent, and that Anne's strong conviction had pulled Catherine from the daze of labouring and allowed her to be delivered of her daughter.

She looked down at the unknown girl, and said quietly, "Since you shall never have sisters of your own, I shall loan you mine and call you Anne Eloise Elinor de Bourgh."

Chapter Twenty-Five

October 1783

"That will be all," Catherine told the wet nurse and nanny after their daily meeting in her study. After a long recovery from birthing her daughter, Catherine still found herself often out of breath by mid-afternoon. She seldom sat to receive callers and even more rarely went out of doors, with the exception of attending church on Sundays.

She ate without savouring, listened without concern, and commanded without deliberation. She was a shell of her former self, moving like a general who has gone to battle many times, directing with an emotionless precision.

Lady Anne remained in Kent, and in a strange twist of fate that Lady Catherine would never have guessed, Anne was brought to bed and delivered of the heir to Pemberley at Rosings Park. Master Fitzwilliam George Darcy was born plump and red-faced, with exceedingly large lungs that carried his cries throughout the manor house. Born on a beautiful afternoon in October, his mother remarked that he was strong and handsome at her first viewing of the child. And while his father said very little, Catherine saw a small tear drop from George Darcy's eye. His parents were attached to him from the start, adoration pouring out of them and love abounding.

Catherine found it hard to watch her sister and brother by marriage coo over their son. She wondered how differently these past months would have been if Lewis had been by her side when their own child was born.

No matter. Catherine felt stronger for standing on her own. She was the mistress of one of the largest properties in England, and her daughter the heiress to a great fortune.

She often found herself speaking to Lewis. His wisdom and guidance had made her the confident woman she was, and she would carry that conviction throughout the remainder of her life. The black fabrics she wore not only honoured his life but the future she lost when he died—rushing home to Rosings in a storm that washed away bridges and lanes as surely as it carried away the father of her child and the love of her life.

But she knew better than to look back. It hurt her too greatly. If her late husband had taught her anything, it was to look to the present and the future. And in doing so, she was more certain than ever that the future was not promised. She had the knowledge and wherewithal to endure whatever came their way, and she would shield her daughter the best she was able.

When Catherine's recovery had taken far longer than the expected six weeks, Lady Anne had refused to leave her sister's side. She oversaw the care of her namesake, Anne de Bourgh, making promises to Catherine that she was not alone. But now, in four weeks' time, she too would be gone. And Catherine would be as she had long ago feared—alone.

But now the thought of being lonely was not such a frightening condition. Her mother, the dowager, had warned her of becoming a spinster, but she was something entirely different now—she was a wealthy widow. The kind Lady Ashby had envied. A lady of her own property and a woman who could move in the world without answering to anyone. *Fitzwilliams never bow to anyone*, her mother would say, and yet, this was truer for Catherine than any of the ladies of her family.

The dowager countess wrote infrequently, but her words of wisdom from Catherine's upbringing were a constant companion. While one year of her life had been full of love, the other twenty had been shaped by a cold knowledge of the way of society—an existence that had shown its truth to Catherine boldly and without apology.

Catherine's relationship with her mother was much as it had always been—never ending instruction and guidance. Living in the dower house at Oakley had not been much to her mother's liking, and so the new earl had opened one of the family's lesser townhouses in London for the dowager countess's use. There she could reign over society and bend other mothers to her will on all manner of subjects.

Lady Rosamund visited Rosings often, but Catherine found her romantic notion of marrying again one day dreadful. Having her aunt nearby was a blessing, though, especially when she was in low spirits.

Virginia, Diana, and Emilia were regular visitors, but their pitying countenances and concerns for her well-being were exhausting. Nothing escaped her observation. Friendly, they tried to be, but none knew quite what to say. And Catherine would not know how to direct them if she could. It would likely require much time to feel at ease in their company again. Until then, her movements were long practiced, and no one but her husband would comprehend how often she told untruths to appease her company.

Her sister often tried to slip some furtive optimism into their conversations, but Catherine was well settled in her frank melancholy by the time little Fitzwilliam joined them. It was like a cloak protecting her wounded heart.

Lewis would have no need to worry over his legacy or his properties, for Catherine had been trained and educated in these matters. She would not succumb to sadness. She would take the reins and ensure Anne de Bourgh's future was settled. She would give Anne every advantage in life, but she could not allow her heart to be touched.

It was better, she decided, to protect herself from ever feeling such pain again. And the only manner by which she could think to do so was to keep herself at a distance from emotional connections. With anyone.

Control, she could endeavour to keep. Her heart—it was long gone.

It was better to be strong and shrewd and cautious—better to be forthright and meticulous—better to protect her heart and keep only that particular joy she felt with Lewis in her mind and memory. Locked away for only her to visit in her dreams.

Reality was not the happy endings one finds in frivolous novels. Nay—the world was just as her mother had cautioned. The same mother whose place in society was usurped when her husband died. The same that required her daughter-in-law to stand down and obey until a great power shift had allowed her a first taste of control. Her mother had been right, and Catherine would not take her position for granted.

Thoughts such as these kept Catherine in control, and maintaining that strained façade of strength would be her life's work.

But she had seen that type of strength in the dowager countess her entire life. It was the mask her mother pulled over any expression of emotion—that quick flip from kindness to coldness that had kept any affection at bay throughout her life. It was an appearance that she could feel moving through her like a physical change as she donned it day in and day out, telling anyone who asked that she was well—sometimes convincing even herself—and smothering all but the icy bitterness that cooled her features.

The formidable mother, the redoubtable mistress of her domain. That was who she would become.

The burden of all her good intentions and past mistakes began to dissipate. No longer would she stand by and watch her life swept under the flood of another human being. Standing on her own and seeing to Anne's future—that was the objective.

One day in early November, Anne suggested that the children be introduced and demanded Catherine join her. She and her husband would be leaving for Derbyshire soon, and Anne had become quite sentimental about leaving her elder sister on her own. The little master of Pemberley was carried gently in his mother's arms as they walked the corridor to Anne's nursery.

It was rare indeed for Catherine to visit the nursery beyond the two fixed appointments per day.

Lady Catherine looked coldly upon her sleeping daughter. She could not pretend the tender, maternal emotion her sister evidently felt for her own child. Baby Anne was still so tiny. Even little Fitzwilliam seemed stronger—and Lady Anne had a week yet before she would be churched.

Seeing the two little cousins together was painful. The juxtaposition between the loving mother and her strong son to the fragile daughter and her broken mother was so clear to her. It nearly caused Catherine to weep. How could she ensure their safety? Was their security inevitable? How would Catherine guide her daughter when even the strongest among them—the Dowager Lady Barringer—had been unable to protect Catherine from surrendering to something so foolish as *love*?

Guilt wracked her, wrapping around her fully and threatening to undo all of the work she had done to maintain her façade of strength.

Not only would she have to protect Anne from herself, but also from men like Arthur de Bourgh, who could be lurking around corners trying to snatch up unsuspecting and hopeful heiresses! She knew better than most that young ladies should always be properly guarded according to their station in life.

And guard her, she would. Anne would never go traipsing about the countryside looking for a husband—she would rather not even take her to town for a Season. Not when Catherine could settle it herself.

A lady could only hope to secure a safe place in the world. And Catherine could help ensure that now—she need not even wait, for the answer lay in her sister's arms.

Lady Anne was sitting next to her, staring at her beautiful baby boy in a way that Catherine could not fathom. Did not Anne see what had happened here at Rosings Park? Did not she see what free will and choice and temptation and passion had led to? Did not she see the risks she took in her deep devotion to Mr Darcy and their son?

"You have to promise me, Sister. Now. On your child's life. We must secure their futures, and we can today. We need not wait. And we will succeed where our mother did not. We shall see our children married—joining two of the grandest estates in all of England. They shall know an alliance was established while they were still in their cradles and shall never have to spend a day worrying over their prospects, for we have resolved to guard their fortunes. Do you not agree?"

Anne looked over her shoulder at Catherine with a pitying expression that made Catherine feel small. "Whatever you say, Catherine. It would be a joyful day indeed if they were to marry."

Catherine pulled a deep breath in through her nose and out through her mouth. It was a relief to find that they were in accord. She would not have to worry over her daughter's plight as she had worried over her own.

For it was settled and done.

The End

Author's Note

L ady Catherine de Bourgh claims in Jane Austen's *Pride and Prejudice* that she and her sister had planned a betrothal between their children, Fitzwilliam Darcy and Anne de Bourgh, from their infancy. Lady Catherine is relentless in canon, arguing that a marriage was her and her sister Anne's favourite wish. Readers have long speculated on the veracity of this commitment. This speculation led me to write this story—and for that, I will always be thankful.

The earldom that belongs to Darcy's aunt and uncle is never named in canon. Although many authors choose to use "Matlock." Because Matlock is a real location in England, I chose instead to design Oakley Manor, sitting at the foot of Kinder Scout, deep in the Peak District. The Barringer earldom and the Viscount's name, Ashby, are of my own imagination.

I styled Fitzwilliam's father as George, because his godson is named George and his daughter, Georgiana. It has long been speculated that his given name was likewise "George," but the text does not outright say so.

Many of the names and places used in this story came from canon. The lady's maid, Dawson; Lady Catherine's friend, Lady Metcalfe, who I enjoyed introducing to readers before her marriage; a Mr Webb, who I imagined as the father of the "Miss Webbs" who all play the pianoforte, though their father had not so good an income as Elizabeth Bennet's; the Bell in Bromley; the Pope family, which will one day provide a governess to Lady Metcalfe; and Lady Anne's maid, Reynolds, who I imagined being promoted to housekeeper at Pemberley by the time Elizabeth Bennet visited. Many of the names, also, are of my own imagination.

I enjoyed weaving in early views of some of our favourite characters from canon, including Charles Bingley's wealthy father, George Wickham's industrious and trustworthy father, and even the mention of a flirty girl in Hertfordshire pursuing a landed gentleman—the future Mr and Mrs Bennet. I took the liberty of imaging that at the time of this story, Mrs Bennet had begun to chase Mr Bennet but had not yet found success. You may have also noticed that I enjoyed writing about Lady Catherine's desire for a more submissive parson in her future. Alas, this still does not explain her choice in the exceedingly reverential Mr Collins.

It is unknown if Lady Catherine was friendly with her siblings or parents, so I enjoyed dreaming up the world that created one of the most beloved villains in literature.

And yes, St. Paul's Cathedral in London did, in fact, have to be raised four feet to accommodate the mode of hairstyling fashions in the mid-1700s.

Acknowledgements

I have to begin my acknowledgements by thanking my husband, John. His encouragement and consistent support helped me push past writer's block and a severe case of imposter syndrome while I wrote this book for two years. For believing in me and in this story—thank you. I love you.

And to Benjamin—for giving up your mom to writing, even on days when you would rather her play horse or mario kart.

Thank you to Diane, Emily, and Regan for being cheerleaders of my writing and phenomenal beta readers. Your feedback and insight helped shape this story.

Special thanks to Jennifer Altman—the best editor out there. For your friendship and for your razor-sharp editing talent—thank you. This story is stronger for your thoughtful feedback and care.

Thank you to my proofreader, Holly Kuck, who swooped in and ensured that this story would not be an exhibit of how thoughtless of a typer I can be.

To our neighbors—who brought food, shoveled snow, carpooled to soccer practices, and checked in regularly during a rough year—you have taught me what true community is. The last year would not have been doable without your kindness and support.

To Emily and Monica, for your friendship and for pushing me to read outside of my comfort zone. *My friends are with me, and I will not be afraid!*

Thank you to my dear friends and book club besties—Ali, Bailey, Becky, Diane, Lisa, Sarah, Rachel, Katie, Jenni, and Valerie. Thank you all for being an escape as well as an anchor during this crazy season of life.

To my Nani—who loves to introduce me to her friends as "my granddaughter, the author." I love you dearly. You are still the best storyteller I know.

Special thanks to Mom and Becky, for your unending support; and to Ali and Brittany—I love doing life with you.

And last, but certainly not least, I must thank the grand authoress herself, Jane Austen—for creating beloved characters that stand the test of time.

About the Author

Paige Badgett is a historical romance author of Austen-inspired fiction.

Paige lives in the Kansas City area with her husband and son. By day, she is a corporate communications professional. In her free time, she can often be found reading, drinking coffee from her favorite mug, gardening, or cheering from the sidelines of her son's soccer games.

Paige is a lifelong storyteller who credits her love of reading to her mother and her book club that has been reading together for seventeen years.

Her debut novel, *Against Every Expectation*, published in 2022. She was also a contributing author to the anthology, *An Inducement Into Matrimony*, which includes nine Pride and Prejudice inspired short stories. *The Making of Lady Catherine de Bourgh* is her second novel.

Learn more at www.paigebadgettwrites.com.

ALSO BY PAIGE BADGETT

Novel
Against Every Expectation

Anthology
An Inducement Into Matrimony

www.ingramcontent.com/pod-product-compliance
Lightning Source LLC
Chambersburg PA
CBHW020353260626
47156CB00007B/2088